The Founding Father

DIANA
PALMER

For Susan James

CHAPTER ONE

IT TOOK A LOT TO MAKE BIG John Jacobs nervous. He was tall, rawboned, with deep-set green eyes the color of bottle glass, and thick dark brown hair. His lean, rough face had scars left over from the War Between the States. He carried scars both inside and out. He was originally from Georgia, but he'd come to Texas just after the war. Now he lived in one of the wildest parts of southeast Texas on a ranch he'd inherited from his late uncle. He was building up the ranch frugally, heading cattle drives to Kansas and buying livestock with the proceeds. What he had was very little to show for fifteen years of hard work, but he was strong and had a good business head. He'd tripled his uncle's land holdings and bought new bulls from back East to breed with his mangy longhorns. His mother would have been proud.

He noted the deep cut on his left hand, a scar from a knife fight with one of a band of Comanches who'd raided his property for horses. John and his hired help had fought them to a standstill and put them on the run. His ranch was isolated and he had good breeding stock. Over the years he'd had to fight roaming Comanche raiders and renegades from over the Mexican border, as well as carpetbaggers. If it hadn't been for the military presence just after the war ended, courtesy of the Union Army, lawlessness would have been even worse.

John had more reason than most to hate Union officers. But in the part of Texas where his ranch was located, to the southeast of San Antonio, the peace had been kept during Reconstruction by a local commandant who was a gentleman. John had admired the Union officer, who'd caught and prosecuted a thief who stole two horses from the ranch. They were good horses, with excellent bloodlines, which John had purchased from a Kentucky thoroughbred farm. The officer, who rode a Kentucky thoroughbred of his own, understood the attachment a rancher felt to his blood stock. John had rarely been more grateful to another human being. Like John himself, the officer was fearless.

Fearless. John laughed at his own apprehension over what he was about to do. He didn't mind risking his life to save his ranch. But this was no fight with guns or knives. It was a much more civilized sort of warfare. In order to win this battle, John was going to have to venture into a world he'd never seen close up. He wasn't comfortable with high society folk. He hoped he wasn't going to embarrass himself.

He removed his dress hat and ran a big hand through his sweaty brown hair. He'd had Juana cut it before he'd left the 3J Ranch. He hoped it was conservative enough to impress old man Terrance Colby. The railroad magnate was vacationing in Sutherland Springs, not far from the 3J. The popular resort boasted over one hundred separate springs in a small area. John had ridden out there to speak to Colby, without a single idea of how he was going to go about it. He had figured the details would work themselves out if he made the trip.

He was uneasy in company. He'd had to pawn his grandfather's watch to buy the used suit and hat he was wearing. It was a gamble he was taking, a big one. Cattle were no good to anyone if they couldn't be gotten to market. Driving cattle to the railheads in Kansas was becoming ever more dangerous. In some areas, fear of Texas tick fever had caused armed blockades of farmers to deter Texas cattle from entry. If he was going to get his cattle to market, there had to be a more direct route. He needed a railroad spur close by.

Colby owned a railroad. He'd just announced his intentions of expanding it to connect with San Antonio. It would be no great burden to extend a line down through Wilson County to the Jacobs' ranch. There were other ranchers in the area who also wanted the spur.

Old man Colby had a daughter, Camellia Ellen, who was unmarried and apparently unmarriageable. Local gossip said that the old man had no use for his unattractive daughter and would be happy to be rid of her. She got in the way of his mistresses. So Big John Jacobs had come a courting, to get himself a railroad…

It started raining just as he got to town. He cursed his foul luck, his green eyes blazing as he noted the mud his horse's hooves was throwing up and splattering onto his boots and the hem of the one good pair of pants he owned. He'd be untidy, and he couldn't afford to be. Terrance Colby was a New York aristocrat who, from what John had heard, was always impeccably dressed. He was staying at the best hotel the little resort of Sutherland Springs could boast, which was none too luxurious. Rumor was that Colby had come here on a hunting trip and was taking the waters while he was in the area.

John swung down out of the saddle half a block from the hotel Colby was staying at, hoping to have a chance to brush the mud off himself. Just as he got onto the boardwalk, a carriage drew up nearby. A young woman of no particular note climbed down out of it, caught the hem of her dress under her laced shoe, and fell face-first into a mud puddle.

Unforgivably, John laughed. He couldn't help it. The woman's companion gave him a glare, but the look he gave the woman was much more expressive.

"For God's sake, woman, can't you take two steps without tripping over your own garments?" the man asked in a high-pitched British accented voice. "Do get up. Now that we've dropped you off in town, I must go. I've an engagement for which you've already made me late. I'll call on your father later. Driver, carry on!"

The driver gave the woman and Big John a speaking look, but he did as he was instructed. John took note of the stranger, and hoped to meet him again one day.

He moved to the woman's side, and offered her an arm.

"No, no," she protested, managing to get to her feet alone. "You're much too nicely dressed to let me splatter you. Do go on, sir. I'm simply clumsy, there's no cure to be had for it, I'm afraid." She adjusted her oversized hat atop the dark bun of her hair and looked at him with miserable blue eyes in a pleasant but not very attractive face. She was slight and thin, and not the sort of woman to whom he'd ever been attracted.

"Your companion has no manners," he remarked.

"Thank you for your concern."

He tipped his hat. "It was no trouble. I wouldn't have minded being splattered. As you can see, I've already sampled the local mud."

She laughed and her animated face took on a fey quality, of which she was unaware. "Good day."

"Good day."

She moved away and he started into the barbershop to put himself to rights.

"John!" a man called from nearby. "Thought that was you," a heavyset man with a badge panted as he came up to join him. It was Deputy Marshal James Graham, who often stopped by John's ranch when he was in the area looking for fugitives.

They shook hands. "What are you doing in Sutherland Springs?" John asked him.

"I'm looking for a couple of renegades," he said. "They were hiding in Indian Territory, but I heard from a cousin of one of them that they were headed this way, trying to outrun the army. You watch your back.''

''You watch yours,'' he retorted, opening his jacket to display the Colt .45 he always wore in a holster on a gunbelt slung across his narrow hips.

The marshal chuckled. ''I heard that. Noticed you were trying to help that poor young woman out of a fix.''

''Yes, poor little thing,'' he commented. ''Nothing to look at, and of little interest to a man. Two left feet into the bargain. But it was no trouble to be kind to her. Her companion gave her no more help than the rough edge of his tongue.''

''That was Sir Sydney Blythe, a hunting companion of the railroad magnate, Colby. They say the girl has a crush on him, but he has no use for her.''

''Hardly surprising. He might have ended in the mud puddle,'' he added on a chuckle. ''She's not the sort to inspire passion.''

''You might be surprised. My wife is no looker, but can she cook! Looks wear out. Cooking lasts forever. You remember that. See you around.''

''You, too.'' John went on into the barbershop unaware of a mud-covered female standing behind the corner, trying to deal with wiping some of the mud from her heavy skirt.

She glared at the barbershop with fierce blue eyes. So he was that sort of a man, was he, pitying the poor little scrawny hen with the clumsy feet. She'd thought he was different, but he was just the same as other men. None of them looked twice at a woman unless she had a beautiful face or body.

She walked past the barbershop toward her hotel, seething with fury. She hoped that she might one day have the chance to meet that gentleman again when she was properly dressed and in her own element. It would be a shock for him, she felt certain.

A short while later John walked toward the Sutherland Springs Hotel with a confidence he didn't really feel. He was grateful for the marshal's conversation, which helped calm him. He wondered if Colby's daughter was also enamoured of the atrocious Sir Sydney, as well as that poor scrawny hen who'd been out riding with him? He wasn't certain how he would have to go about wooing such a misfit, although he had it in mind.

At thirty-five, John was more learned than many of his contemporaries, having been brought up by an educated mother who taught him Latin while they worked in the fields. Since then, he'd been educated in other ways while trying to keep himself clothed and fed. His married sister, the only other survivor of his family, had tried to get him to come and work with her husband in North Carolina on their farm, but he hadn't wanted to settle in the East. He was a man with a dream. And if a man could make himself a fortune with nothing more than hard work and self-denial, he was ready to be that man.

It seemed vaguely dishonest to take a bride for monetary reasons, and it cut to the quick to pretend an affection he didn't feel to get a rich bride. If there was an honest way to do this, he was going to find it. His one certainty was that if he married a railroad tycoon's daughter, he had a far better chance of getting a railroad to lay tracks to his ranch than if he simply asked for help. These days, nobody rushed to help a penniless rancher. Least of all a rich Northerner.

John walked into the hotel bristling with assumed self-confidence and the same faint arrogance he'd seen rich men use to get their way.

"My name is John Jacobs," he told the clerk formally. "Mr. Colby is expecting me."

That was a bald lie, but a bold one. If it worked, he could cut through a lot of time-wasting protocol.

"Uh, he is? I mean, of course, sir," the young man faltered. "Mr. Colby is in the presidential suite. It's on the second floor, at the end of the hall. You may go right up. Mr. Colby and his daughter are receiving this morning."

Receiving. Go right up. John nodded, dazed. It was easier than he'd dreamed to see one of the country's richest men!

He nodded politely at the clerk and turned to the staircase.

The suite was easy to find. He knocked on the door confidently, inwardly gritting his teeth to gear himself up for the meeting. He had no idea what he was going to give as an excuse for coming here. He didn't know what Ellen Colby looked like. Could he perhaps say that he'd seen her from afar and had fallen madly in love with her at once? That would certainly ruin his chances with her father, who would be convinced that he only wanted Ellen's money.

While he was thinking up excuses, a maid opened the door and stood back to let him inside. Belatedly he swept off his hat, hoping his forehead wasn't sweating as profusely as it felt.

"Your name, sir?" the middle-aged woman asked politely.

"John Jacobs," he told her. "I'm a local landowner," he added.

She nodded. "Please wait here."

She disappeared into another room behind a closed door. Seconds passed, while John looked around him uncomfortably, reminded by the opulence of the suite how far removed he was from the upper class.

The door opened. "Please go in, sir," the maid said respectfully, and even smiled at him.

Elated, he went into the room and stared into a pair of the coldest pale blue eyes he'd ever seen, in a face that seemed unremarkable compared to the very expensive lacy white dress worn by its owner. She had a beautiful figure, regardless of her lack of beauty. Her hair was thick and a rich dark brown, swept up into a high bun that left a roll of it all around her head. She was very poised, very elegant and totally hostile. With a start, John recognized her. She was the mud puddle swimmer from the hotel entrance.

He must not laugh, he must not...! But a faint grin split his chiseled lips and his green eyes danced on her indignant features. Here was his excuse, so unexpected!

"I came to inquire about your health," he said, his voice deep and lazy. "The weather is cold, and the mud puddle was very large...."

"I am..." She was blushing, now apparently

flattered by his visit. "I am very well. Thank you!"

"What mud puddle?" came a crisp voice from the doorway. A man, shorter than John, with balding hair and dark blue eyes, dressed in an expensive suit, came into the room. "I'm Terrance Colby. Who are you?"

"John Jacobs," he introduced himself. He wasn't certain how to go on. "I own a ranch outside town..." he began.

"Oh, you're here about quail hunting," Colby said immediately. He smiled, to John's astonishment, and went forward to shake hands. "But I'm afraid you're a few minutes too late. I've already procured an invitation to the Four Aces Ranch to hunt antelope and quail. You know it, I expect?"

"Certainly I do, sir," John replied. And he did. That ranch was the sort John wanted desperately to own one day, a huge property with purebred cattle and horses, known all over the country—in fact, all over the world! "I'm sure you'll find the accommodations superior."

The older man eyed him curiously. "Thank you for the offer."

John nodded. "My pleasure, sir. But I had another purpose in coming. A passerby mentioned that the young lady here was staying at this hotel.

She, uh, had a bad fall on her way inside. I assisted her. I only wanted to assure myself that she was uninjured. Her companion was less than helpful,'' he added with honest irritation.

"Sir Sydney drove off and left me there," the woman said angrily with flashing eyes.

Colby gave her an unsympathetic glance. "If you will be clumsy and throw yourself into mud puddles, Ellen, you can expect to be ignored by any normal man."

Ellen! This unfortunate little hen was the very heiress John had come to town to woo, and he was having more good fortune than he'd dreamed! Lady Luck was tossing offerings into his path with every word he spoke.

He smiled at Ellen Colby with deliberate interest. "On the contrary, sir, I find her enchanting," he murmured.

Colby looked at him as if he expected men with nets to storm the room.

Ellen gave him a harsh glare. She might have been flattered by the visit, but she knew a line when she heard one. Too many men had sought access to her father through her. Here was another, when she'd hoped he might like her for herself. But when had that ever happened? Disappointed, she drew herself up to her full height. "Please excuse me. I am in the middle of important work.'' She lifted her chin and added deliberately, ''My father's dog is having her bath.''

She turned and stalked toward a door between rooms, while John threw back his head and laughed with genuine glee.

Colby had to chuckle, himself, at his daughter's audacity. She never raised her voice, as a rule, and he'd long since come to think of her as a doormat. But this man pricked her temper and made her eyes flash.

''An interesting reaction,'' he told John. ''She is never rude, and I cannot remember a time when she raised her voice.''

John grinned. ''A gentleman likes to think that he has made an impression, sir,'' he said respectfully. ''Your daughter is far more interesting with a temper than without one. To me, at least.''

''You have a ranch, you said?'' Colby asked.

John nodded. ''A small one, but growing. I have begun to cross breeds to good effect. I have a longhorn seed bull and a small herd of Hereford cattle. I hope to raise a better sort of beef to suit Eastern tastes and ship it to market in Chicago.''

The older man sized up his guest, from the worn, but still useful, shoes and suit and the well-worn gunbelt and pistol worn unobtrusively under the open jacket.

''You have a Southern accent,'' Colby said.

John nodded again. "I am a Georgian, by birth."

Colby actually winced.

John laughed without humor. "You know, then, what Sherman and his men did to my state."

"Slavery is against everything I believe in," Colby said. His face grew hard. "Sherman's conduct was justified."

John had to bite his tongue to keep back a sharp reply. He could feel the heat of the fire, hear his mother and sister screaming as they fell in the maelstrom of crackling flames....

"You owned slaves?" Colby persisted curtly.

John gritted his teeth. "Sir, my mother and sisters and I worked on a farm outside Atlanta," he said, almost choking on memories despite the years between himself and the memory. "Only rich planters could afford slaves. My people were Irish immigrants. You might recall the signs placed at the front gates of estates in the North, which read, No Colored Or Irish Need Apply."

Colby swallowed hard. He had, indeed, seen those signs.

John seemed to grow another inch. "To answer your question, had I been a rich planter, I would have hired my labor, not bought it, for I do not feel that one man of any color has the right to own another.'' His green eyes flashed. ''There were many other small landowners and sharecroppers like my family who paid the price for the greed and luxury of plantation owners. Sherman's army did not discriminate between the two.''

''Excuse me,'' Colby said at once. ''One of my laundresses back home had been a slave. Her arms were livid with scars from a mistress who cut her when she burned a dress she was told to iron.''

''I have seen similar scars,'' John replied, without adding that one of the co-owners of his ranch had such unsightly scars, as well as his wife and even their eldest daughter.

''Your mother and sisters live with you?'' Colby asked.

John didn't reply for a few seconds. ''No, sir. Except for a married sister in North Carolina, my people are all dead.''

Colby nodded, his eyes narrow and assessing. ''But, then, you have done well for yourself in Texas, have you not?'' He smiled.

John forced himself to return the smile and forget the insults. ''I will do better, sir,'' he said with unshakeable confidence. ''Far better.''

Colby chuckled. ''You remind me of myself, when I was a young man. I left home to make my fortune, and had the good sense to look toward trains as the means.''

John twirled his hat in his big hands. He wanted to approach Colby about his spur, which would give him the opportunity to ship his cattle without having to take the risk of driving them north to railheads in Kansas. But that would be pushing his luck. Colby might feel that John was overstepping his place in society and being ''uppity.'' He couldn't risk alienating Colby.

He shifted his weight. ''I should go,'' he said absently. ''I had no intention of taking up so much of your time, sir. I wanted only to offer you the freedom of my ranch for hunting, and to inquire about the health of your daughter after her unfortunate accident.''

''Unfortunate accident.'' Colby shook his head. ''She is the clumsiest woman I have ever known,'' he said coldly, ''and I have found not one single gentleman who lasted more than a day as a suitor.''

''But she is charming,'' John countered gallantly, his eyes dancing. ''She has a sense of humor, the ability to laugh at herself, and despite her companion's rudeness, she behaved with dignity.''

Colby was listening intently. ''You find her... attractive?''

"Sir, she is the most attractive woman I have ever met," John replied without choosing his words.

Colby laughed and shook his head. "You want something," he mused. "But I'm damned if I don't find you a breath of fresh air, sir. You have style and dash."

John grinned at him. "Thank you, sir."

"I may take you up on that invitation at a later date, young man. In the meantime, I have accepted the other offer. But you could do me a favor, if you're inclined."

"Anything within my power, sir," John assured him.

"Since you find my daughter so alluring, I would like you to keep an eye on her during my absence."

"Sir, there would not be adequate chaperones at my ranch," John began quickly, seeing disaster ahead if the old man or his daughter got a glimpse of the true state of affairs at the Jacobs' ranch.

"Oh, for heaven's sake, man, I'm not proposing having her live with you in sin!" Colby burst out. "She will stay here at the hotel, and I have told her not to venture out of town. I meant only that I would like you to check on her from time to time, to make sure that she is safe. She will be on her own, except for the maid we have retained here.''

''I see.'' John let out the breath he'd been holding. ''In that case, I would be delighted. But what of her companion, Sir Sydney?'' he added.

''Sir Sydney will be with me, to my cost,'' Colby groaned. ''The man is an utter pain, but he has a tract of land that I need very badly for a new roundhouse near Chicago,'' he confessed. ''So I must humor him, to some extent. I assure you, my daughter will not mourn his absence. She only went to drive with him at my request. She finds him repulsive.''

So did John, but he didn't want to rock the boat.

''I'm glad you came, young man.'' Colby offered his hand, and John shook it.

''So am I, sir,'' he replied. ''If you don't mind, I would like to take my leave of your daughter.''

''Be my guest.''

''Thank you.''

John walked toward the open door that contained a maid, Miss Ellen Colby and a very mad wet dog of uncertain age and pedigree. It was a shaggy dog, black and white, with very long ears. It was barking pitifully and shaking soapy water everywhere.

''Oh, Miss Colby, this doggy don't want no

bath,'' the maid wailed as she tried to right her cap.

''Never you mind, Lizzie, we're going to bathe her or die in the attempt.'' Ellen blew back a strand of loose hair, holding the dog down with both hands while the maid laved water on it with a cup.

''A watering trough might be a better proposition, Miss Colby,'' John drawled from the doorway.

His voice shocked her. She jerked her head in his direction and loosened the hold she had on the dog. In the few seconds that followed, the animal gave a yelp of pure joy, leaped out of the pan, off the table, and scattered the rugs as it clawed its way to the freedom of the parlor.

''Oh, my goodness!'' Ellen yelled. ''Catch her, Lizzie, before she gets to the bedroom! She'll go right up on Papa's bed, like she usually does!''

''Yes, ma'am!''

The maid ran for all she was worth. Ellen Colby put her soapy hands on her hips and glared daggers at the tall green-eyed man in the doorway.

''Now see what you've done!'' Ellen raged at John.

"Me?" John's eyebrows arched. "I assure you, I meant only to say goodbye."

"You diverted my attention at a critical moment!"

He smiled slowly, liking the way her blue eyes flashed in anger. He liked the thickness of her hair. It looked very long. He wondered if she let it down at bedtime.

That thought disturbed him. He straightened. "If your entire social life consists of bathing the dog, miss, you are missing out."

"I have a social life!"

"Falling into mud puddles?"

She grabbed up the soaking brush they'd used on the dog and considered heaving it.

John threw back his head and laughed uproariously.

"Do be quiet!" she muttered.

"You have hidden fires," he commented with delight. "Your father has asked me to keep an eye on you, Miss Colby, while he's off on his hunting trip. I find the prospect delightful."

"I can think of nothing I would enjoy less!"

"I'm quite a good companion," he assured her. "I know where birds' nests are and where flowers grow, and I can even sing and play the guitar if asked."

She hesitated, wet splotches all over her lacy

dress and soap in her upswept hair. She looked at him with open curiosity. "You are wearing a gun," she pointed out. "Do you shoot people with it?"

"Only the worst sort of people," he told her. "And I have yet to shoot a woman."

"I am reassured."

"I have a cattle ranch not too far a ride from here," he continued. "In the past, I have had infrequently to help defend my cattle from Comanche raiding parties."

"Indians!"

He laughed at her expression. "Yes. Indians. They have long since gone to live in the Indian Territory. But there are still rustlers and raiders from across the Mexican border, as well as deserting soldiers and layabouts from town hoping to steal my cattle and make a quick profit by selling them to the army."

"How do you stop them?"

"With vigilance," he said simply. "I have men who work for me on shares."

"Shares?" She frowned. "Not for wages?"

He could have bitten his tongue. He hadn't meant to let that slip out.

She knew that he'd let his guard down. She found him mysterious and charming and shrewd.

But he had attractions. He was the first man she'd met who made her want to know more about him.

"I might take you for a ride in my buggy," he mused.

"I might go," she replied.

He chuckled, liking her pert response. She wasn't much to look at, truly, but she had qualities he'd yet to find in other women.

He turned to go. "I won't take the dog along," he said.

"Papa's dog goes with me everywhere," she lied, wanting to be contrary.

He glanced at her over his shoulder. "You were alone in the mud puddle, as I recall."

She glared at him.

He gave her a long, curious scrutiny. He smiled slowly. "We can discuss it at a later date. I will see you again in a day or two." He lifted his hat respectfully. "Good day, Miss Colby."

"Good day, Mr....?" It only then occurred to her that she didn't even know his name.

"John," he replied. "John Jackson Jacobs. But most people just call me 'Big John.'"

"You are rather large," she had to agree.

He grinned. "And you are rather small. But I like your spirit, Miss Colby. I like it a lot."

She sighed and her eyes began to glow faintly as they met his green ones.

He winked at her and she blushed scarlet. But before he could say anything, the maid passed him with the struggling wet dog.

"Excuse me, sir, this parcel is quite maddeningly wet," the maid grumbled as she headed toward the bowl on the table.

"So I see. Good day, ladies." He tipped his hat again, and he was gone in a jingle of spurs.

Ellen Colby looked after him with curiosity and an odd feeling of loss. Strange that a man she'd only just met could be so familiar to her, and that she could feel such joy in his presence.

Her life had been a lonely one, a life of service, helping to act as a hostess for her father and care for her grandmother. But with her grandmother off traveling, Ellen was now more of a hindrance than a help to her family, and it was no secret that her father wanted badly to see her married and off his hands.

But chance would be a fine thing, she thought. She turned back to the dog with faint sadness, wishing she were prettier.

CHAPTER TWO

JOHN RODE BACK TO HIS RANCH, past the new-fangled barbed wire which contained his prize longhorn bull, past the second fence that held his Hereford bull and his small herd of Hereford cows with their spring calves, to the cabin where he and his foremen's families lived together. He had hundreds of head of beef steers, but they ranged widely, free of fences, identified only by his 3J brand, burned into their thick coats. The calves had been branded in the spring.

Mary Brown was at the door, watching him approach. It was early June, and hot in south Texas. Her sweaty black hair was contained under a kerchief, and her brown eyes smiled at him. "Me and Juana washed your old clothes, Mister John," she said. "Isaac and Luis went fishing with the boys down to the river for supper, and the girls are making bread."

"Good," he said. "Do I have anything dry and pressed to put on?" he added.

Mary nodded her head. "Such as it is, Mister

John. A few more holes, and no amount of sewing is gonna save you a red face in company."

"I'm working on that, Mary," he told her, chuckling. He bent to lift her youngest son, Joe, a toddler, up into his arms. "You get to growing fast, young feller, you got to help me herd cattle."

The little boy gurgled at him. John grinned at him and set him back down.

Isaac came in the back door just then, with a string of fish. "You back?" He grinned. "Any luck?"

"A lot, all of it unexpected," he told the tall, lithe black man. He glanced at Luis Rodriguez, his head vaquero, who was short and stout and also carrying a string of fish. He took Isaac's and handed both to the young boys. "You boys go clean these fish for Mary, you hear?"

"Yes, Papa," the taller black boy said. His shorter Latino companion grinned and followed him out the door.

"We have another calf missing, señor," Luis said irritably. "Isaac and I only came to bring the boys and the fish to the house." He pulled out his pistol and checked it. "We will go and track the calf."

"I'll go with you," John said. "Give me a minute to change."

He carried his clothing to the single room that

had a makeshift door and got out of his best clothes, leaving them hanging over a handmade chair he'd provided for Mary. He whipped his gunbelt back around his lean hips and checked his pistol. Rustlers were the bane of any rancher, but in these hard times, when a single calf meant the difference between keeping his land or losing it, he couldn't afford to let it slide.

He went back out to the men, grim-faced. "Let's do some tracking."

THEY FOUND THE CALF, butchered. Signs around it told them it wasn't rustlers, but a couple of Indians—Comanches, in fact, judging from the broken arrow shaft and footprints they found nearby.

"Damn the luck!" John growled. "What are Comanches doing this far south? And if they're hungry, why can't they hunt rabbits or quail?"

"They all prefer buffalo, *señor,* but the herds have long gone, and game is even scarce here. That is why we had to fish for supper."

"They could go the hell back to the Indian Territory, couldn't they, instead of riding around here, harassing us poor people!" John pursed his lips thoughtfully, remembering what he'd heard in Sutherland Springs. "I wonder," he mused aloud, "if these could be the two renegades from Indian Territory being chased by the army?"

"What?" Isaac asked.

"Nothing," John said, clapping him on the shoulder affectionately. "Just thinking to myself. Let's get back to work."

THE NEXT DAY, HE PUT ON his good suit and went back to the Springs to check on Ellen Colby. He expected to find her reclining in her suite, or playing with her father's dog. What he did find was vaguely shocking.

Far from being in her room, Ellen was on the sidewalk with one arm around a frightened young black boy who'd apparently been knocked down by an angry man.

"...he got in my way. He's got no business walking on the sidewalk anyway. He should be in the street. He should be dead. They should all be dead! We lost everything because of them, and then they got protected by the very army that burned down our homes! You get away from him, lady, he's not going anywhere until I teach him a lesson!"

She stuck out her chin. "I have no intention of moving, sir. If you strike him, you must strike me, also!"

John moved up onto the sidewalk. He didn't look at Ellen. His eyes were on the angry man, and they didn't waver. He didn't say a word. He simply flipped back the lapel of his jacket to disclose the holstered pistol he was carrying.

"Another one!" the angry man railed. "You damned Yankees should get the hell out of Texas and go back up north where you belong!"

"I'm from Georgia," John drawled. "But this is where I belong now."

The man was taken aback. He straightened and glared at John, his fists clenched. "You'd draw on a fellow Southerner?" he exclaimed.

"I'm partial to brown skin," John told him with a honeyed drawl. His tall, lithe figure bent just enough to make an older man nearby catch his breath. "But you do what you think you have to," he added deliberately.

"There," Ellen Colby said haughtily, helping the young man to his feet. "See what you get when you act out of ignoble motives?" she lashed at the threatening man. "A child is a child, regardless of his heritage, sir!"

"That is no child," the man said. "It is an abomination...."

"I beg to disagree." The voice came from a newcomer, wearing a star on his shirt, just making his way through the small crowd. It was Deputy Marshal James Graham, well known locally because he was impartially fair. "Is there a problem, madam?" he asked Ellen, tipping his hat to her.

"That man kicked this young man off the sidewalk and attacked him," Ellen said, glaring daggers at the antagonist. "I interfered and Mr. Jacobs came along in time to prevent any further violence."

"Are you all right, son?" the marshal asked the young boy, who was openmouthed at his unexpected defense.

"Uh, yes, sir. I ain't hurt," he stammered.

Ellen Colby took a coin from her purse and placed it in the young man's hand. "You go get yourself a stick of peppermint," she told him.

He looked at the coin and grinned. "Thank you kindly, miss, but I'll buy my mama a sack of flour instead. Thank you, too," he told the marshal and John Jacobs, before he cut his losses and rushed down the sidewalk.

Graham turned to the man who'd started the trouble. "I don't like troublemakers," he said in a voice curt with command. "If I see you again, in a similar situation, I'll lock you up. That's a promise."

The man spat onto the ground and gave all three of the boy's defenders a cold glare before he turned and stomped off in the opposite direction.

"I'm obliged to both of you," Ellen Colby told them.

John shrugged. "It was no bother."

The deputy marshal chuckled. "A Georgian defending a black boy." He shook his head. "I am astonished."

John laughed. "I have a former slave family working with me," he explained. His face tautened. "If you could see the scars they carry, even the children, you might understand my position even better."

The deputy nodded. "I do understand. If you have any further trouble," he told Ellen, "I am at your service." He tipped his hat and went back to his horse.

"You are a man of parts, Mr. Jacobs," Ellen told John, her blue eyes soft and approving. "Thank you for your help."

He shrugged. "I was thinking of Isaac's oldest boy who died in Georgia," he confessed, moving closer as the crowd melted away. "Isaac is my wrangler," he added. "His first son was beaten to death by an overseer just before the end of the war."

She stood staring up into his lean, hard face with utter curiosity. "I understood that all Southerners hated colored people."

"Most of us common Southerners were in the fields working right beside them," John said coldly. "We were little more than slaves ourselves, while the rich lived in luxury and turned a blind eye to the abuse."

"I had no idea," she said hesitantly.

"Very few northern people do," he said flatly. "Yet there was a county in Georgia that flew the Union flag all through the war, and every attempt by the confederacy to press-gang them into the army was met with open resistance. They ran away and the army got tired of going back to get them again and again." He chuckled at her surprise. "I will tell you all about it over tea, if you like."

She blushed. "I would like that very much, Mr. Jacobs."

He offered his arm. She placed her small hand in the crook of his elbow and let him escort her into the hotel's immaculate dining room. He wondered if he should have told Graham about the Comanche tracks he'd found on his place. He made a note to mention it to the man when he next saw him.

ELLEN LIKED THE LITHE, rawboned man who sat across from her sipping tea and eating tea cakes as if he were born to high society. But she knew that he wasn't. He still had rough edges, but even those were endearing. She couldn't forget the image she had of him, standing in front of the frightened boy, daring the attacker to try again. He was brave. She admired courage.

"Did you really come to see my father to inquire about my welfare?'' she asked after they'd discussed the war.

He looked up at her, surprised by her boldness. He put his teacup down. ''No,'' he said honestly.

She laughed self-consciously. ''Forgive me, but I knew that wasn't the real reason. I appreciate your honesty.''

He leaned back in his chair and studied her without pretense. His green gaze slid over her plain face, down to the faint thrust of her breasts under the green and white striped bodice of her dress and up to the wealth of dark hair piled atop her head. ''Lies come hard to me,'' he told her. ''Shall I be completely honest about my motives and risk alienating you?''

She smiled. ''Please do. I have lost count of the men who pretended to admire me only as a means to my father's wealth. I much prefer an open approach.''

''I inherited a very small holding from my uncle, who died some time ago.'' He toyed with the teacup. ''I have worked for wages in the past, to buy more land and cattle. But just recently I've started to experiment with crossing breeds. I am raising a new sort of beef steer with which I hope to tempt the eastern population's hunger for range-fed beef.'' His eyes lifted to hers. ''It's a long, slow process to drive cattle to a railhead up in Kansas, fraught with danger and risk, more now than ever since the fear of Texas fever in cattle has caused so much resistance to be placed in the path of the cattle drives. My finances are so tight now that the loss of a single calf is a major setback to me.''

She was interested. ''You have a plan.''

He smiled. ''I have a plan. I want to bring a railroad to this area of south Texas. More precisely, I want a spur to run to my ranch, so that I can ship cattle to Chicago without having to drive them to Kansas first.''

Her eyes brightened. ''Then you had no real purpose of inviting my father to hunt quail on your ranch.''

''Miss Colby,'' he said heavily, ''my two foremen and their families live with me in a one-room cabin. It looks all right at a distance, but close up, it's very primitive. It is a pretend mansion. As I am a pretend aristocrat.'' He gestured at his suit coat. ''I used the last of my ready cash to disguise myself and I came into town because I had heard that your father was here, and that he had a marriageable daughter.'' His expression became self-mocking when she blinked. ''But I'm not enough of a scoundrel to pretend an affection I do not feel.'' He studied her quietly, toying with a spoon beside his cup and saucer. ''So let me make you a business proposition.

Marry me and let your father give us a railroad spur as a wedding present.''

She gulped, swallowed a mouthful of hot tea, sat back and expelled a shocked breath. ''Sir, you are blunt!''

''Ma'am, I am honest,'' he replied. He leaned forward quickly and fixed her with his green eyes. ''Listen to me. I have little more than land and prospects. But I have a good head for business, and I know cattle. Given the opportunity, I will build an empire such as Texas has never seen. I have good help, and I've learned much about raising cattle from them. Marry me.''

''And...what would I obtain from such a liaison?'' she stammered.

''Freedom.''

''Excuse me?''

''Your father cares for you, I think, but he treats you as a liability. That gentleman,'' he spat the word, ''who was escorting you stood idly by when you fell in a mud puddle and didn't even offer a hand. You are undervalued.''

She laughed nervously. ''And I would not be, if I married a poor stranger and went to live in the wilds where rustlers raid?''

He grinned. ''You could wear pants and learn to ride a horse and herd cattle,'' he said, tempting her. ''I would even teach you to brand cattle and shoot a gun.''

Her whole demeanor changed. She just stared at him for a minute. "I have spent my entire life under the care of my mother's mother, having lost my own mother when I was only a child. My grandmother Greene believes that a lady should never soil her hands in any way. She insists on absolute decorum in all situations. She would not hear of my learning to ride a horse or shoot a gun because such things are only for men. I have lived in a cage all my life." Her blue eyes began to gleam. "I should love to be a tomboy!"

He laughed. "Then marry me."

She hesitated once again. "Sir, I know very little of men. Having been sheltered in all ways, I am uneasy with the thought of…with having a stranger…with being…"

He held up a hand. "I offer you a marriage of friends. In truth, anything more would require a miracle, as there is no privacy where I live. We are all under the single roof. And," he added, "my foremen and their families are black and Mexican, not white." He watched for her reactions. "So, as you can see, there is a further difficulty in regard to public opinion hereabouts."

She clasped her hands before her on the table. "I would like to think about it a little. Not because of any prejudice," she added quickly, and smiled. "But because I would like to know you a little better. I have a friend who married in haste at the age of fifteen. She is now twenty-four, as I am. She has seven living children and her husband treats her like property. It is not a condition which I envy her.''

''I understand,'' he said.

The oddest thing, was that she thought he really did understand. He was a complex man. She had a sudden vision of him years down the road, in an elegant suit, in an elegant setting. He had potential. She'd never met anyone like him.

She sighed. ''But my father must not know the entire truth,'' she cautioned. ''He has prejudices, and he would not willingly let me go to a man he considered a social inferior.''

His thin lips pursed amusedly. ''Then I'll do my utmost to convince him that I am actually the illegitimate grandson of an Irish earl.''

She leaned forward. ''Are there Irish earls?''

He shrugged. ''I have no idea. But, then, he probably has no idea, either.'' His eyes twinkled.

She laughed delightedly. It changed her face, her eyes, her whole look. She was pretty when she laughed.

''There is one more complication,'' he said in a half-serious tone.

''Which is?''

His smile was outrageous. ''We have lots of mud puddles at the ranch.''

"Oh, you!" she exclaimed, reaching for the teapot.

"If you throw it, the morning papers will have a more interesting front page."

"Will it? And what would you do?" she challenged brightly.

"I am uncivilized," he informed her. "I would put you across my knee and paddle your backside, after which I would toss you over my shoulder and carry you home with me."

"How very exciting!" she exclaimed. "I have never done anything especially outrageous. I think I might like being the object of a scandal!"

He beamed. "Tempting," he proclaimed. "But I have great plans and no desire to start tongues wagging. Yet."

"Very well. I'll restrain my less civilized impulses for the time being."

He lifted his teacup and toasted her. "To unholy alliances," he teased.

She lifted hers as well. "And madcap plots!"

They clicked teacups together and drank deeply.

IT WAS UNSEEMLY FOR THEM TO be seen going out of town alone, so Ellen was prevented from visiting John's ranch. But he took her to church on Sunday—a new habit that he felt obliged to acquire—and promenading along the sidewalk after a leisurely lunch in the hotel.

The following week, John was a frequent visitor. He and Ellen became friends with an elegant Scottish gentleman and his wife who were staying at the hotel and taking the waters, while they toured the American West.

"It is a grand country," the Scotsman, Robert Maxwell, told Ellen and John. "Edith and I have been longing to ride out into the country, but we are told that it is dangerous."

"It is," John assured him grimly. "My partners and I have been tracking rustlers all week," he added, to Ellen's surprise, because he hadn't told her. "There are dangerous men in these parts, and we have rustlers from across the border, also."

"Do you have Red Indians?" Maxwell exclaimed. His eyes twinkled. "I would like to meet one."

"They're all in the Indian Territory now, and no, you wouldn't like to meet one," John said. "The Comanches who used to live hereabouts didn't encourage foreign visitors, and they had a well-deserved reputation for opposing any people who tried to invade their land."

"Their land?" the Scotsman queried, curiously.

"Their land," John said firmly. "They roamed

this country long before the first white man set
foot here. They intermarried with the Mexican
population...."

Maxwell seemed very confused, as he interrupted, "Surely there were no people here at all
when you arrived," he said.

"Perhaps they don't know it back East, but
Texas was part of Mexico just a few decades
back," John informed him. "That's why we
went to war with Mexico, because Texas wanted
independence from it. Our brave boys died in the
Alamo in San Antonio, and at Goliad and San
Jacinto, to bring Texas into the union. But the
Mexican boys fought to keep from losing their
territory, is how they saw it. They considered us
invaders."

Ellen was watching John covertly, with quiet
admiration.

"Ah, now I understand," the Scot chuckled.
"It's like us and England. We've been fighting
centuries to govern ourselves, like the Irish. But
the British are stubborn folk."

"So are Texans," John chuckled.

"I don't suppose you'd go riding with us,
young man?" Maxwell asked him wistfully.
"We should love to see a little of the area, and
I see that you wear a great pistol at your hip. I
assume you can shoot any two-legged threats to
our safety."

John glanced at Ellen and saw such appreciation in her blue eyes that he lost his train of thought for a few seconds.

Finally he blinked and darted his green gaze back to the foreigners, hoping his heartbeat wasn't audible.

"I think I'd like that," John replied, "as long as Ellen comes with us."

"Your young lady," the Scotswoman, Nell Maxwell, added with a gentle, indulgent smile.

"Yes," John said, his eyes going back to Ellen's involuntarily. "My young lady."

Ellen blushed red and lowered her eyes, which caused the foreign couple to laugh charmingly. She was so excited that she forgot her father's admonition that she was not to leave the hotel and go out of town. In fact, when she recalled it, she simply ignored it.

THEY RENTED A SURREY and John helped Ellen into the back seat before he climbed up nimbly beside her. He noted that it was the best surrey the stable had, with fringe hanging all the way around, and the horses' livery was silver and black leather.

"I suppose this is nothing special for you," John murmured to her, looking keenly at the horses' adornments, "but it's something of a treat for me."

Ellen smoothed the skirt of her nice blue suit with its black piping. "It's a treat for me, too," she confessed. "I had very much wanted to drive out in the country, but my father only thinks of hunting, not sightseeing, and he dislikes my company."

"I like your company very much," John said in a deep, soft tone.

She looked up at him, surprised by the warmth in his deep voice. She was lost in the sudden intensity of his green eyes under the wide brim of his dress hat. She felt her whole world shift in the slow delight it provoked.

He smiled, feeling as if he could fly all of a sudden. Impulsively his big, lean hand caught hers on the seat between them and curled her small fingers into it.

She caught her breath, entranced.

"Are you two young people comfortable?" Maxwell asked.

"Quite comfortable, thank you, sir," John replied, and he looked at Ellen with possession.

"So am I, thank you," Ellen managed through her tight throat.

"We'll away, then," Maxwell said with a grin at his wife, and he flicked the reins.

The surrey bounded forward, the horses obviously well chosen for their task, because the ride was as smooth as silk.

"Which way shall we go?" Maxwell asked.

"Just follow the road you're on," John told him. "I know this way best. It runs past my own land up to Quail Run, the next little town along the road. I can show you the ruins of a log cabin where a white woman and her Comanche husband held off a company of soldiers a few years back. He was a renegade. She was a widow with a young son, and expecting another when her husband was killed by a robber. Soon after, the Comanche was part of a war party that encountered a company of soldiers trailing them. He was wounded and she found him and nursed him back to health. It was winter. She couldn't hunt or fish, or chop wood, and she had no family at all. He undertook her support. They both ran from the soldiers, up into the Indian Territory. She's there now, people say. Nobody knows where he is."

"What a fascinating story!" Maxwell exclaimed. "Is it true?"

"From what I hear, it is," John replied.

"What a courageous young woman," Ellen murmured.

"To have contact with a Red Indian, she would have to be," Mrs. Maxwell replied. "I have heard many people speak of Indians. None of what they say is good."

"I think all people are good and bad," Ellen

ventured. "I have never thought heritage should decide which is which."

John chuckled and squeezed her hand. "We think alike."

The Maxwells exchanged a complicated look and laughed, too.

THE LOG CABIN WAS POINTED OUT. It was nothing much to look at. There was a well tucked into high grass and briar bushes, and a single tree in what must once have been the front yard.

"What sort of tree is that?" Mrs. Maxwell asked. "What an odd shape."

"It's a chinaberry tree," John recalled. "We have them in Georgia, where I'm from. My sisters and I used to throw the green berries that grow on them back and forth, playing." He became somber.

"You have family back in Georgia?" Ellen asked pointedly, softly.

He sighed. "I have a married sister in North Carolina. No one else."

Ellen knew there was more to it than just that, and she had a feeling the war had cost him more than his home. She stroked the back of his callused hand gently. "Mama died of typhoid when I was just five. So except for Papa and Grandmother, I have no one, either."

He caught his breath. He hadn't thought about

her circumstances, her family, her background. All he'd known was that she was rich. He began to see her with different eyes.

"I'm sorry, about your family," she said quietly.

He sighed. He didn't look at her. Memories tore at his heart. He looked out beyond the horses drawing the surrey at the yellow sand of the dirt road, leading to the slightly rolling land ahead. The familiar *clop-clop* of the horses' hooves and the faint creak of leather and wood and the swishing sound of the rolling wheels seemed very loud in the silence that followed. The dust came up into the carriage, but they were all used to it, since dirt roads were somewhat universal. The boards that made the seats of the surrey were hard on the backside during a long trip, but not less comfortable than the saddle of a horse, John supposed.

"Do you ride at all?" he asked Ellen.

"I was never allowed to," she confessed. "My grandmother thought it wasn't ladylike."

"I ride to the hounds," Mrs. Maxwell said, eavesdropping, and turned to face them with a grin. "My father himself put me on my first horse when I was no more than a girl. I rode sidesaddle, of course, but I could outdistance any man I met on a horse. Well, except for Robert," she conceded, with an affectionate look at her husband. "We raced and I lost. Then and there, I determined that I needed to marry him."

"And she did," he added with a chuckle, darting a look over his broad shoulder. "Her father told me I must keep her occupied to keep her happy, so I turned the stables over to her."

"Quite a revolution of sorts in our part of the country, I must add," Mrs. Maxwell confessed. "But the lads finally learned who had the whip hand, and now they do what I say."

"We have the finest stable around," Maxwell agreed. "We haven't lost a race yet."

"When I have more horses, you must come and teach my partners how to train them," John told Mrs. Maxwell.

"And didn't I tell you that people would not be stuffy and arrogant here in Texas?" she asked her husband.

"I must agree, they are not."

"Well, two of them, at least," John murmured dryly. "There," he said suddenly, pointing out across a grassy pasture. "That is my land."

All three heads turned. In the distance was the big cabin, surrounded by pecan and oak trees and not very visible. But around it were red-and-white-coated cattle, grazing in between barbed wire fences.

"It is fenced!" Maxwell exclaimed.

"Fencing is what keeps the outlaws out and

my cattle in,'' John said, used to defending his fences. ''Many people dislike this new barbed wire, but it is the most economical way to contain my herds. And I don't have a great deal of capital to work with.''

''You are an honest man,'' Maxwell said. ''You did not have to admit such a thing to a stranger.''

''It is because you are a stranger that I can do it,'' John said amusedly. ''I would never admit to being poor around my own countrymen. A man has his pride. However, I intend to be the richest landowner hereabouts in a few years. So you must plan to come back to Texas. I can promise you will be very welcome as house-guests.''

''If I am able, I will,'' Maxwell agreed. ''So we must keep in touch.''

''Indeed we must. We will trade addresses before you leave town. But for now,'' John added, ''make a left turn at this next crossroads, and I will show you a mill, where we take our corn to be ground into meal.''

''We have mills at home, but I should like to see yours,'' Mrs. Maxwell enthused.

''And so you shall,'' John promised.

CHAPTER THREE

TWO HOURS LATER, TIRED AND thirsty, the tourists returned to the livery stable to return the horses and surrey.

"It has been a pleasure," John told the Maxwells, shaking hands.

"And for me, as well," Ellen added.

The older couple smiled indulgently. "We leave for New York in the morning," Maxwell said regretfully, "and then we sail to Scotland. It has been a pleasure to meet you both, although I wish we could have done so sooner."

"Yes," Mrs. Maxwell said solemnly. "How sad to make friends just as we must say goodbye to them."

"We will keep in touch," John said.

"Indeed we will. You must leave your address for us at the desk, and we will leave ours for you," Maxwell told John. "When you have made your fortune, I hope very much to return with my wife to visit you both."

Ellen flushed, because she had a sudden vivid

picture of herself with John and several children on a grand estate. John was seeing the same picture. He grinned broadly. "We will look forward to it," he said to them both.

The Maxwells went up to their rooms and John stopped with Ellen at the foot of the stairs, because it would have been unseemly for a gentleman to accompany a lady all the way to her bedroom.

He took her hand in his and held it firmly. "I enjoyed today," he said. "Even in company, you are unique."

"As you are." She smiled up at him from a radiant face surrounded by wisps of loose dark hair that had escaped her bun and the hatpins that held on her wide-brimmed hat.

"We must make sure that we build a proper empire," he teased, "so that the Maxwells can come back to visit."

"I shall do my utmost to assist you," she replied with teasing eyes.

He chuckled. "I have no doubt of that."

"I will see you tomorrow?" she fished.

"Indeed you will. It will be in the afternoon, though," he added regretfully. "I must help move cattle into a new pasture first. It is very dry and we must shift them closer to water."

"Good evening, then," she said gently.

"Good evening." He lifted her hand to his lips in a gesture he'd learned in polite company during his travels.

It had a giddy effect on Ellen. She blushed and laughed nervously and almost stumbled over her own feet going up the staircase.

"Oh, dear," she said, righting herself.

"Not to worry," John assured her, hat in hand, green eyes brimming with mirth. "See?" He looked around his feet and back up at her. "No mud puddles!"

She gave him an exasperated, but amused, look, and went quickly up the staircase. When she made the landing, he was still there, watching.

JOHN AND ELLEN SAW EACH other daily for a week, during which they grew closer. Ellen waited for John in the hotel dining room late the next Friday afternoon, but to her dismay, it was not John who walked directly to her table. It was her father, home unexpectedly early. Nor was he smiling.

He pulled out a chair and sat down, motioning imperiously to a waiter, from whom he ordered coffee and nothing else.

"You are home early," Ellen stammered.

"I am home to prevent a scandal!" he replied

curtly. "I've had word from an acquaintance of Sir Sydney's that you were seen flagrantly defying my instructions that you should stay in this hotel during my absence! You have been riding, in the country, alone, with Mr. Jacobs! How dare you create a scandal here!"

The Ellen of only a week ago would have bowed her head meekly and agreed never to disobey him again. But her association with John Jacobs had already stiffened her backbone. He had offered her a new life, a free life, away from the endless social conventions and rules of conduct that kept her father so occupied.

She lifted her eyebrows with hauteur. "And what business of Sir Sydney's friend is my behavior?" she wanted to know.

Her father's eyes widened in surprise. "I beg your pardon?"

"I have no intention of being coupled with Sir Sydney in any way whatsoever," she informed him. "In fact, the man is repulsive and ill-mannered."

It was a rare hint of rebellion, one of just a few he had ever seen in Ellen. He just stared at her, confused and amused, all at once.

"It would seem that your acquaintance with Mr. Jacobs is corrupting you."

"I intend to be further corrupted," she replied coolly. "He has asked me to marry him."

"Child, that is out of the question," he said sharply.

She held up a dainty hand. "I am no child," she informed him, blue eyes flashing. "I am a woman grown. Most of my friends are married with families of their own. I am a spinster, an encumbrance to hear you tell it, of a sort whom men do not rush to escort. I am neither pretty nor accomplished…"

"You are quite wealthy," he inserted bluntly. "Which is, no doubt, why Mr. Jacobs finds you so attractive."

In fact, it was a railroad spur, not money, that John wanted, but she wasn't ready to tell her father that. Let him think what he liked. She knew that John Jacobs found her attractive. It gave her confidence to stand up to her parent for the first time in memory.

"You may disinherit me whenever you like," she said easily, sipping coffee with a steady hand. Her eyes twinkled. "I promise you, it will make no difference to him. He is the sort of man who builds empires from nothing more than hard work and determination. In time, his fortune will rival yours, I daresay."

Terrance Colby was listening now, not blustering. "You are considering his proposal."

She nodded, smiling. "He has painted me a delightful picture of muddy roads, kitchen gardens, heavy labor, cooking over open fires and branding cattle." She chuckled. "In fact, he has offered to let me help him brand cattle in the fall when his second crop of calves drop."

Terrance caught his breath. He waited to speak until the waiter brought his coffee. He glowered after the retreating figure. "I should have asked for a teacup of whiskey instead," he muttered to himself. His eyes went back to his daughter's face. "Brand cattle?"

She nodded. "Ride horses, shoot a gun…he offered to teach me no end of disgusting and socially unacceptable forms of recreation."

He sat back with an expulsion of breath. "I could have him arrested."

"For what?" she replied.

He was disconcerted by the question. "I haven't decided yet. Corrupting a minor," he ventured.

"I am far beyond the age of consent, Father," she reminded him. She sipped coffee again. "You may disinherit me at will. I will not even need the elegant wardrobes you have purchased for me. I will wear dungarees and high-heeled boots.''

His look of horror was now all-consuming. ''You will not! Remember your place, Ellen!''

Her eyes narrowed. ''My place is what I say it is. I am not property, to be sold or bartered for material gain!''

He was formulating a reply when the sound of heavy footfalls disturbed him into looking up. John Jacobs was standing just to his side, wearing his working gear, including that sinister revolver slung low in a holster slanted across his lean hips.

''Ah,'' Colby said curtly. ''The villain of the piece!''

''I am no villain,'' John replied tersely. He glanced at Ellen with budding feelings of protectiveness. She looked flushed and angry. ''Certainly, I have never given Ellen such pain as that I see now on her face.'' He looked back at Colby with a cold glare.

Colby began to be impressed. This steely young man was not impressed by either his wealth or position when Ellen was distressed.

''Do you intend to call me out?'' he asked John.

The younger man glanced again at Ellen. ''It would be high folly to kill the father of my prospective bride,'' he said finally. ''Of course, I don't have to kill you,'' he added, pursing his lips and giving Colby's shoulder a quiet scrutiny. ''I could simply wing you.''

Colby's gaze went to that worn pistol butt. ''Do you know how to shoot that hog leg?''

''I could give you references,'' John drawled. ''Or a demonstration, if you prefer.''

Colby actually laughed. ''I imagine you could. Stop bristling like an angry dog and sit down, Mr. Jacobs. I have ridden hard to get here, thinking my daughter was about to be seduced by a bounder. And I find only an honest suitor who would fight even her own father to protect her. I am quite impressed. Do sit down,'' he emphasized. ''That gentleman by the window looks fit to jump through it. He has not taken his eyes off your gun since you approached me!''

John's hard face broke into a sheepish grin. He pulled out a chair and sat down close to Ellen, his green eyes soft now and possessive as they sketched her flushed, happy face. He smiled at her, tenderly.

Colby ordered coffee for John as well and then sat back to study the determined young man.

''She said you wish to teach her to shoot a gun and brand cattle,'' Colby began.

"If she wants to, yes," John replied. "I assume you would object...?"

Colby chuckled. "My grandmother shot a gun and once chased a would-be robber down the streets of a North Carolina town with it. She was a local legend."

"You never told me!" Ellen exclaimed.

He grimaced. "Your mother was very strait-laced, Ellen, like your grandmother Greene," he said. "She wanted no image of my unconventional mother to tempt you into indiscretion." He pursed his lips and chuckled. "Apparently blood will out, as they say." He looked at her with kind eyes. "You have been pampered all your life. Nothing that money could buy has ever been beyond your pocket. It will not be such a life with this man," he indicated John. "Not for a few years, at least," he added with a chuckle. "You remind me of myself, Mr. Jacobs. I did not inherit my wealth. I worked as a farm laborer in my youth," he added, shocking his daughter. "I mucked out stables and slopped hogs for a rich man in our small North Carolina town. There were eight of us children, and no money to be handed down. When I was twelve, I jumped on a freight train and was arrested in New York when I was found in a stock car. I was taken to the manager's office where the owner of the railroad had chanced to venture on a matter of business. I was rude and arrogant, but he must have seen something in me that impressed him. He had a wife, but no children. He took me home with him, had his wife clean me up and dress me properly, and I became his adoptive child. When he died, he left the business to me. By then, I was more than capable of running it.''

"Father!" Ellen exclaimed. "You never spoke of your parents. I had no idea…!"

"My parents died of typhoid soon after I left the farm," he confessed. "My brothers and sisters were taken in by cousins. When I made my own fortune, I made sure that they were provided for."

"You wanted a son," she said sorrowfully, "to inherit what you had. And all you got was me."

"Your mother died giving birth to a stillborn son," he confessed. "You were told that she died of a fever, which is partially correct. I felt that you were too young for the whole truth. And your maternal grandmother was horrified when I thought to tell you. Grandmother Greene is very correct and formal." He sighed. "When she knows what you have done, I expect she will be here on the next train to save you, along with however many grandsons she can convince to accompany her.''

She nodded slowly, feeling nervous. "She is formidable.''

"I wouldn't mind a son, but I do like little girls,'' John said with a warm smile. "I won't mind if we have daughters.''

She flushed, embarrassed.

"Let us speak first of marriage, if you please,'' Colby said with a wry smile. "What would you like for a wedding present, Mr. Jacobs?''

John was overwhelmed. He hesitated.

"*We* would like a spur line run down to *our* ranch,'' Ellen said for him, with a wicked grin. "So that we don't have to drive our cattle all the way to Kansas to get them shipped to Chicago. We are going to raise extraordinary beef.''

John sighed. "Indeed we are,'' he nodded, watching her with delight.

"That may take some little time,'' Colby mused. "What would you like in the meantime?''

"A sidesaddle rig for Ellen, so that she can be comfortable in the saddle,'' John said surprisingly.

"I do not want a sidesaddle,'' she informed him curtly. "I intend to ride astride, as I have seen other women do since I came here.''

"I have never seen a woman ride in such a manner!" Colby exploded.

"She's thinking of Tess Wallace," John confessed. "She's the wife of old man Tick Wallace, who owns the stagecoach line here. She drives the team and even rides shotgun sometimes. He's twenty years older than she is, but nobody doubts what they feel for each other. She's crazy for him."

"An unconventional woman," Colby muttered.

"As I intend to become. You may give me away at the wedding, and it must be a small, intimate one, and very soon," she added. "I do not wish my husband embarrassed by a gathering of snobby aristocrats."

Her father's jaw dropped. "But the suddenness of the wedding...!"

"I am sorry, Father, but it will be my wedding, and I feel I have a right to ask for what I wish," Ellen said stubbornly. "I have done nothing wrong, so I have nothing to fear. Besides," she added logically, "none of our friends live here, or are in attendance here at the Springs."

Her father sighed. "As you wish, my dear," he said finally, and his real affection for her was evident in the smile he gave her.

John was tremendously impressed, not only by

her show of spirit, but by her consideration for him. He was getting quite a bargain, he thought. Then he stopped to ask himself what she was getting, save for a hard life that would age her prematurely, maybe even kill her. He began to frown.

"It will be a harder life than you realize now," John said abruptly, and with a scowl. "We have no conveniences at all…."

"I am not afraid of hard work," Ellen interrupted.

John and Colby exchanged concerned glances. They both knew deprivation intimately. Ellen had never been without a maid or the most luxurious accommodations in her entire life.

"I'll spare you as much as I can," John said after a minute. "But most empires operate sparsely at first."

"I will learn to cook," Ellen said with a chuckle.

"Can you clean a game hen?" her father wanted to know.

She didn't waver. "I can learn."

"Can you haul water from the river and hoe in a garden?" her father persisted. "Because I have no doubt that you will have to do it."

"There will be men to do the lifting," John

promised him. "And we will take excellent care of her, sir."

Her father hesitated, but Ellen's face was stiff with determination. She wasn't backing down an inch.

"Very well," he said on a heavy breath. "But if it becomes too much for you, I want to know," he added firmly. "You must promise that, or I cannot sanction your wedding."

"I promise," she said at once, knowing that she would never go to him for help.

He relaxed a little. "Then I will give you a wedding present that will not make your prospective bridegroom chafe too much," he continued. "I'll open an account for you both at the mercantile store. You will need dry goods to furnish your home."

"Oh, Father, thank you!" Ellen exclaimed.

John chuckled. "Thank you, indeed. Ellen will be grateful, but I'll consider it a loan."

"Of course, my boy," Colby replied complacently.

John knew the man didn't believe him. But he was capable of building an empire, even if he was the only one at the table who knew it at that moment. He reached over to shake hands with the older man.

"Within ten years," he told Colby, "we will

entertain you in the style to which you are accustomed.''

Colby nodded, but he still had reservations. He only hoped he wasn't doing Ellen a disservice. And he still had to explain this to her maternal grandmother, who was going to have a heart attack when she knew what he'd let Ellen do.

But all he said to the couple was, "We shall see."

THEY WERE MARRIED by a justice of the peace, with Terrance Colby and the minister's wife as witnesses. Colby had found a logical reason for the haste of the wedding, pleading his forthcoming trip home and Ellen's refusal to leave Sutherland Springs. The minister, an easygoing, romantic man, was willing to defy convention for a good cause. Colby congratulated John, kissed Ellen, and led them to a buckboard which he'd already had filled with enough provisions to last a month. He'd even included a treadle sewing machine, cloth for dresses and the sewing notions that went with them. Nor had he forgotten Ellen's precious knitting needles and wool yarn, with which she whiled away quiet evenings.

"Father, thank you very much!" Ellen exclaimed when she saw the rig.

"Thank you very much, indeed," John added

with a handshake. "I shall take excellent care of her," he promised.

"I'm sure you'll do your best," Colby replied, but he was worried, and it showed.

Ellen kissed him. "You must not be concerned for me," she said firmly, her blue eyes full of censure. "You think I am a lily, but I mean to prove to you that I am like a cactus flower, able to bloom in the most unlikely places."

He kissed her cheek. "If you ever need me…"

"I do know where to send a telegram," she interrupted, and chuckled. "Have a safe trip home."

"I will have your trunks sent out before I leave town," he added.

John helped Ellen into the buckboard in the lacy white dress and veil she'd worn for her wedding, and he climbed up beside her in the only good suit he owned. They were an odd couple, he thought. And considering the shock she was likely to get when she saw where she must live, it would only get worse. He felt guilty for what he was doing. He prayed that the ends would justify the means. He had promised little, and she had asked for nothing. But many couples had started with even less and made a go of their marriages. He meant to keep Ellen happy, whatever it took.

ELLEN JACOBS'S FIRST glimpse of her future home would have been enough to discourage many a young woman from getting out of the buckboard. The shade trees shaded a large, rough log cabin with only one door and a single window and a chimney. Nearby were cactus plants and brush. But there were tiny pink climbing roses in full bloom, and John confessed that he'd brought the bushes here from Georgia planted in a syrup can. The roses delighted her, and made the wilderness look less wild.

Outside the cabin stood a Mexican couple and a black couple, surrounded by children of all ages. They stared and looked very nervous as John helped Ellen down out of the buckboard.

She had rarely interacted with people of color, except as servants in the homes she had visited most of her life. It was new, and rather exciting, to live among them.

"I am Ellen Colby," she introduced herself, and then colored. "I do beg your pardon! I am Ellen Jacobs!"

She laughed, and then they laughed as well.

"We're pleased to meet you, *señora*," the Mexican man said, holding his broad sombrero in front of him. He grinned as he introduced himself and his small family. "I am Luis Rodriguez.

This is my family—my wife Juana, my son Alvaro and my daughters Juanita, Elena and Lupita.'' They all nodded and smiled.

"And I am Mary Brown," the black woman said gently. "My husband is Isaac. These are my boys, Ben, the oldest, and Joe, the youngest, and my little girl Libby, who is the middle child. We are glad to have you here."

"I am glad to be here," Ellen said.

"But right now, you need to get into some comfortable clothing, Mrs. Jacobs," Mary said. "Come along in. You men go to work and leave us to our own chores," she said, shooing them off.

"Mary, I can't work in these!" John exclaimed defensively.

She reached into a box and pulled out a freshly ironed shirt and patched pants. "You go off behind a tree and put those on, and I'll do my best to chase the moths out of this box so's I can put your suit in it. And mind you don't get red mud in this shirt!"

"Yes, ma'am," he said with a sheepish grin. "See you later, Ellen."

Mary shut the door on him, grinning widely at Ellen. "He is a good man," she told Ellen in all seriousness as she produced the best dress she had and offered it to Ellen.

"No," Ellen said gently, smiling. "I thank you very much for the offer of your dress, but I not only brought a cotton dress of my own—I have brought bolts of fabric and a sewing machine."

There were looks of unadulterated pleasure on all the feminine faces. "New...fabric?" Mary asked haltingly.

"Sewing machine?" her daughter exclaimed.

"In the buckboard," Ellen assured them with a grin.

They vanished like summer mist, out the door. Ellen followed behind them, still laughing at their delight. She'd done the right thing, it seemed— rather, her father had. She might have thought of it first if she'd had the opportunity.

The women and girls went wild over the material, tearing it out of its brown paper wrapping without even bothering to cut the string that held it.

"Alvaro, you and Ben get this sewing machine and Mrs. Jacobs's suitcase into the house right this minute! Girls, bring the notions and the fabric! I'll get the coffee and sugar, but Ben will have to come back for the lard bucket and the flour sack."

"Yes, ma'am," they echoed, and burst out laughing.

THREE HOURS LATER, Ellen was wearing a simple navy skirt with an indigo blouse, fastened high at the neck. She had on lace-up shoes, but she could see that she was going to have to have boots if she was to be any help to John. The cabin was very small, and all of the families would sleep inside, because there were varmints out at night. And not just crawly ones or four-legged ones, she suspected. Mary had told her about the Comanches John and Luis and Isaac had been hunting when a calf was taken. She noted that a loaded shotgun was kept in a corner of the room, and she had no doubt that either of her companions could wield it if necessary. But she would ask John to teach her to shoot it, as well.

"You will have very pretty dresses from this material," Mary sighed as she touched the colored cottons of many prints and designs.

"*We* will have many pretty dresses," Ellen said, busily filling a bobbin for the sewing machine. She looked up at stunned expressions. "Surely you did not think I could use this much fabric by myself? There is enough here for all of us, I should imagine. And it will take less for the girls," she added, with a warm smile at them.

Mary actually turned away, and Ellen was horrified that she'd hurt the other woman's feelings.

She jumped up from the makeshift chair John had cobbled together from tree limbs. "Mary, I'm sorry, I…!"

Mary turned back to her, tears running down her cheeks. "It's just, I haven't had a dress of my own, a new dress, in my whole life. Only hand-me-downs from my mistress, and they had to be torn up or used up first."

Ellen didn't know what to say. Her face was shocked.

Mary wiped away the tears. She looked at the other woman curiously. "You don't know about slaves, do you, Mrs. Ellen?"

"I know enough to be very sorry that some people think they can own other people," she replied carefully. "My family never did."

Mary forced a smile. "Mr. John brought us out here after the war. We been lucky. Two of our kids are lost forever, you know," she added matter-of-factly. "They got sold just before the war. And one of them got beat to death."

Ellen's eyes closed. She shuddered. It was overwhelming. Tears ran down her cheeks.

"Oh, now, Mrs., don't you…don't you do that!" Mary gathered her close and rocked her. "Don't you cry. Wherever my babies gone, they free now, don't you see. Alive or dead, they free."

The tears ran even harder.

"It was just as bad for Juana," Mary said through her own tears. "Two of her little boys got shot. This man got drunk and thought they was Indians. He just killed them right there in the road where they was playing, and he didn't even look back. He rode off laughing. Luis told the *federales,* but they couldn't find the man. That was years ago, before Mr. John's uncle hired Luis to work here, but Juana never forgot them little boys."

Ellen drew back and pulled a handkerchief out of her sleeve. She wiped Mary's eyes and smiled sadly. "We live in a bad world."

Mary smiled. "It's gonna get better," she said. "You wait and see."

"Better," Juana echoed, nodding, smiling. *"Mas bueno."*

"Mas...bueno?" Ellen repeated.

Juana chuckled. *"¡!Vaya! Muy bien!* Very good!"

Mary smiled. "You just spoke your first words of Spanish!"

"Perhaps you can teach me to speak Spanish," Ellen said to Juana.

"Señora, it will be my pleasure!" the woman answered, and smiled beautifully.

"I expect to learn a great deal, and very soon," Ellen replied.

THAT WAS AN UNDERSTATEMENT. During her first week of residence, she became an integral part of John's extended family. She learned quite a few words of Spanish, including some range language that shocked John when she repeated it to him with a wicked grin.

"You stop that," he chastised. "Your father will have me shot if he hears you!"

She only chuckled, helping Mary put bread on the table. She was learning to make bread that didn't bounce, but it was early days yet. "My father thinks I will be begging him to come and get me within two weeks. He is in for a surprise!"

"I got the surprise," John had to admit, smiling at her. "You fit right in that first day." He looked from her to the other women, all wearing new dresses that they'd pieced on Ellen's sewing machine. He shook his head. "You three ought to open a dress shop in town."

Ellen glanced at Mary and Juana with pursed lips and twinkling eyes. "You know, that's not really such a bad idea, John," she said after a minute. "It would make us a little extra money. We could buy more barbed wire and we might even be able to afford a milk cow!"

John started to speak, but Mary and Juana jumped right in, and before he ate the first piece of bread, the women were already making plans.

CHAPTER FOUR

ELLEN HAD JOHN DRIVE HER into town the following Saturday, to the dry goods store. She spoke with Mr. Alton, the owner.

"I know there must be a market for inexpensive dresses in town, Mr. Alton," she said, bright-eyed. "You order them and keep them in stock, but the ones you buy are very expensive, and most ranch women can't afford them. Suppose I could supply you with simple cotton dresses, ready-made, at half the price of the ones you special order for customers?"

He lifted both eyebrows. "But, Mrs. Jacobs, your father is a wealthy man…!"

"My husband is not," she replied simply. "I must help him as I can." She smiled. "I have a knack for sewing, Mr. Alton, and I think I do quite good work. I also have two helpers who are learning how to use the machine. Would you let me try?"

He hesitated, adding up figures in his head. "All right," he said finally. "You bring me about six dresses, two each of small, medium and large ones, and we will see how they sell.''

She grinned. ''Done!'' She went to the bolts of fabric he kept. ''You must allow me credit, so that I can buy the material to make them with, and I will pay you back from my first orders.''

He hesitated again. Then he laughed. She was very shrewd. But, he noticed that the dress she was wearing was quite well-made. His women customers had complained about the lack of variety and simplicity in his ready-made dresses, which were mostly for evening and not everyday.

''I will give you credit,'' he said after a minute. He shook his head as he went to cut the cloth she wanted. ''You are a shrewd businesswoman, Mrs. Jacobs,'' he said. ''I'll have to watch myself, or I may end up working for you!''

Which amused her no end.

JOHN WAS DUBIOUS ABOUT HIS wife's enterprise, but Ellen knew what she was doing. Within three weeks, she and the women had earned enough money with their dressmaking to buy not one, but two Jersey milk cows with nursing calves. These John was careful to keep separate from his Hereford bull. But besides the milk, they made butter and buttermilk, which they took into town with their dresses and sold to the local restaurant.

"I told you it would work," Ellen said to John one afternoon when she'd walked out to the makeshift corral where he and the men were branding new calves.

He smiled down at her, wiping sweat from his face with the sleeve of his shirt. "You are a wonder," he murmured with pride. "We're almost finished here. Want to learn to ride?"

"Yes!" she exclaimed. But she looked down at her cotton dress with a sigh. "But not in this, I fear."

John's eyes twinkled. "Come with me."

He led her to the back of the cabin, where he pulled out a sack he'd hidden there. He offered it to her.

She opened it and looked inside. There was a man's cotton shirt, a pair of boots, and a pair of dungarees in it. She unfolded the dungarees and held them up to herself. "They'll just fit!" she exclaimed.

"I had Mr. Alton at the dry goods store measure one of your dresses for the size. He said they should fit even after shrinkage when you wash them."

"Oh, John, thank you!" she exclaimed. She stood on tiptoe and kissed him on the cheek.

He chuckled. "Get them on, then, and I'll

teach you to mount a horse. I've got a nice old one that Luis brought with him. He's gentle.''

''I won't be a minute!'' she promised, darting back into the cabin.

John was at the corral when she came back out. She'd borrowed one of John's old hats and it covered most of her face as well as her bundled-up hair. She looked like a young boy in the rig, and he chuckled.

''Do I look ridiculous?'' she worried.

''You look fine,'' he said diplomatically, his eyes twinkling. ''Come along and meet Jorge.''

He brought forward a gentle-looking old chestnut horse who lowered his head and nudged at her hand when she extended it. She stroked his forehead and smiled.

''Hello, old fellow,'' she said softly. ''We're going to be great friends, aren't we?''

John pulled the horse around by its bridle and taught Ellen how to mount like a cowboy. Then, holding the reins, he led her around the yard, scattering their new flock of chickens along the way.

''They won't lay if we frighten them,'' Ellen worried.

He looked up at her with a grin. ''How did you know that?''

''Mary taught me.''

"She and Juana are teaching you a lot of new skills," he mused. "I liked the biscuits this morning, by the way."

Her heart skipped. "How did you know that I made them?"

"Because you watched every bite I took."

"Oh, dear."

He only laughed. "I am constantly amazed by you," he confessed as they turned away from the cabin and went toward the path that led through the brush to a large oak tree. "Honestly, I never thought you'd be able to live in such deprivation. Especially after…Ellen?"

He'd heard a faint scraping sound, followed by a thud. When he turned around, Ellen was sitting up in the dirt, looking stunned.

He threw the reins over the horse's head and ran to where she was sitting, his heart in his throat. "Ellen, are you hurt?!"

She glared up at him. "Did you not notice the tree limb, John?" she asked with a meaningful glance in its direction.

"Obviously not," he murmured sheepishly. "Did you?" he added.

She burst out laughing. "Only when it hit me."

He chuckled as he reached down and lifted her up into his arms. It was the first time she'd been picked up in her adult life, and she gasped, locking her hands behind his neck so that she didn't fall.

His green eyes met her blue ones at point blank range. The laughter vanished as suddenly as it had come. He studied her pert little nose, her high cheekbones, her pretty bow of a mouth. She was looking, too, her gaze faintly possessive as she noted the hard, strong lines of his face and the faint scars she found there. His eyes were very green at the proximity, and his mouth looked hard and firm. He had high cheekbones, too, and a broad forehead. His hair was thick under the wide-brimmed hat he wore, and black. His ears were, like his nose, of imposing size. The hands supporting her were big, too, like his booted feet.

"I have never been carried since I was a child," she said in a hushed, fascinated tone.

"Well, I don't usually make a practice of carrying women, either," he confessed. His chiseled lips split in a smile. "You don't weigh much."

"I am far too busy becoming an entrepreneur to gain weight," she confessed.

"A what?"

She explained the word.

"You finished school, I reckon," he guessed. She nodded. "I wanted to go to college, but

Father does not think a woman should be over-educated.''

"Bull," John said inelegantly. "My mother educated herself and even learned Latin, which she taught me. If we have daughters, they'll go to college."

She beamed, thinking of children. "I should like to have children."

He pursed his lips and lifted an eyebrow. His smile was sheer wickedness.

She laughed and buried her face in his throat, embarrassed. But he didn't draw back. His arms contracted around her and she felt his breath catch as he enveloped her soft breasts against the hard wall of his chest.

She felt unsettled. Her arms tightened around his strong neck and she shivered. She had never been held so close to a man's body. It was disconcerting. It was…delightful.

His cheek slid against hers so that he could find her soft lips with his mouth. He kissed her slowly, gently, with aching respect. When he pulled back, her lips followed. With a rough groan, he kissed her again. This time, there was less respect and more blatant hunger in the mouth that ravished hers.

She moaned softly, which brought him to his senses immediately. He drew back, his green eyes glittering with feeling. He wasn't breathing steadily anymore. Neither was she.

"We would have to climb a tree to find much privacy, and even then, the boys would probably be sitting in the branches," he said in a hunted tone.

She understood what he meant and flushed. But she laughed, too, because it was very obvious that he found her as attractive as she found him. She smiled into his eyes.

"One day, we will have a house as big as a barn, with doors that lock!" she assured him.

He chuckled softly. "Yes. But for now, we must be patient." He put her back on her feet with a long sigh. "Not that I feel patient," he added rakishly.

She laughed. "Nor I." She looked up at him demurely. "I suppose you have kissed a great many girls."

"Not so many," he replied. "And none as unique as you." His eyes were intent on her flushed face. "I made the best bargain of my life when I enticed you into marriage, Ellen Colby."

"Thank you," she said, stumbling over the words.

He pushed back a lock of disheveled dark hair that had escaped from under her hat. "It never occurred to me that a city woman, an aristocrat, would be able to survive living like this. I have felt guilty any number of times when I watched you carry water to the house, and wash clothes as the other women do. I know that you had maids to do such hard labor when you lived at home."

"I am young and very strong," she pointed out. "Besides, I have never found a man whom I respected enough to marry, until now. I believe you will make an empire here, in these wilds. But even if I didn't believe it, I would still be proud to take your name. You are unique, also."

His eyes narrowed. He bent again and kissed her eyelids shut, with breathless tenderness. "I will work hard to be worthy of your trust, Ellen. I will try never to disappoint you."

She smiled. "And you will promise never to run me under oak limbs again?" she teased.

"You imp!" He laughed uproariously, hugging her to him like a big brother. "You scamp! What joy you bring to my days."

"And you to mine," she replied, hugging him back.

"Daddy! Mr. John and Mrs. Ellen are spooning right here in the middle of the road!" one of Isaac and Mary's boys yelled.

"Scatter, you varmints, I'm kissing my wife!" John called in mock-rage.

There was amused laughter and the sound of brush rustling.

"So much for the illusion of privacy," Ellen said, pulling back from him with a wistful sigh. "Shall we get back to the business at hand? Where's my horse?"

John spied him in the brush, munching on some small green growth of grass he had found there. "He's found something nice to eat, I'll wager," he said.

"I'll fetch him," Ellen laughed, and started into the brush.

"Ellen, stop!"

John's voice, full of authority and fear, halted her with one foot in the act of rising. She stopped and stood very still. He was cursing, using words Ellen had never heard in her life. "Isaac!" he tacked onto the end, "fetch my shotgun! Hurry!"

Ellen closed her eyes. She didn't have to look down to know why he was so upset. She could hear a rustling sound, like crackling leaves, like softly frying bacon. She had never seen a rattlesnake, but during her visit to Texas with her father, she had heard plenty about them from local people. Apparently they liked to lie in wait and strike out at unsuspecting people who came near them. They could cause death with a bite, or extreme pain and sickness. Ellen was mortally afraid of snakes, in any event. But John would save her. She knew he would.

There were running feet. Crashing brush. The sound of something being thrown and caught, and then the unmistakable sound of a hammer being pulled back.

"Stand very still, darling," John told her huskily. "Don't move...a muscle!"

She swallowed, her eyes still closed. She held her breath. There was a horrifying report, like the sound of thunder and lightning striking, near her feet. Flying dirt hit her dungarees. She heard furious thrashing and opened her eyes. For the first time, she looked down. A huge rattlesnake lay dismembered nearby, still writhing in the hot sun.

"Ellen, it didn't strike you?" John asked at once, wrapping her up in the arm that wasn't supporting the shotgun. "You're all right?"

"I am, thanks to you," she whispered, almost collapsing against him. "What a scare!"

"For both of us," he said curtly. He bent and kissed the breath out of her, still shaken from the experience. "Don't ever march into the brush without looking first!"

She smiled under his lips. "You could have caught the brush on fire with that language," she murmured reproachfully. "Indeed, I think the snake was shocked to death by it!"

He laughed, and kissed her harder. She kissed him back, only belatedly aware of running feet and exclamations when the snake was spotted.

He linked his big hand into her small one. "Luis, bring the horse, if you please. I think we've had enough riding practice for one day!"

"*Si, señor,*" Juan agreed with a chuckle.

THAT EVENING AROUND THE campfire all the talk was of the close call Ellen had with the snake.

"You're on your way to being a living legend," John told her as they roasted the victim of his shotgun over the darting orange and yellow tongues of flame. "Not to mention the provider of this delicious delicacy. Roasted rattler."

Ellen, game as ever, was soon nibbling on her own chunk of it. "It tastes surprisingly like chicken," she remarked.

John glowered at her. "It does not."

She grinned at him, and his heart soared. He grinned back.

"If you want another such treat, you will have to teach me how to shoot a gun," she proposed. "I am never walking into a rattler's mouth again, not even to provide you with supper!"

"Fair deal," he responded, while the others laughed uproariously.

IN THE DAYS THAT FOLLOWED, Ellen learned with hard work and sore muscles the rudiments of staying on a horse through the long days of watching over John's growing herd of cattle.

She also learned how not to shoot a shotgun. Her first acquaintance with the heavy double-barreled gun was a calamity. Having shouldered it too lightly, the report slammed the butt back into her shoulder and gave her a large, uncomfortable bruise. They had to wait until it healed before she could try again. The one good thing was that it made churning butter almost impossible, and she grinned as she watched Mary shoulder that chore.

"You hurt your shoulder on purpose," Mary chided with laughing dark eyes. "So you wouldn't have to push this dasher up and down in the churn."

"You can always get Isaac to teach you how to shoot, and use the same excuse," Ellen pointed out.

Mary grinned. "Not me. I am not going near a shotgun, not even to get out of such chores!"

Juana agreed wholeheartedly. "Too much bang!"

"I'll amen that," Mary agreed.

"I like it," Ellen mused. She liked even more knowing that John was afraid for her, that he cared about her. He'd even called her "darling" when he'd shot the snake. He wasn't a man to use endearments normally, which made the verbal slip even more pleasurable. She'd been walking around in a fog of pleasure ever since the rattler almost bit her. She was in love. She hoped that he was feeling something similar, but he'd been much too busy with work to hang around her, except at night. And then there was a very large audience. She sighed, thinking that privacy must be the most valuable commodity on earth. Although she was growing every day fonder of her companions, she often wished them a hundred miles away, so that she had even an hour alone with her husband. But patience was golden, she reminded herself. She must wait and hope for that to happen. Right now, survival itself was a struggle.

So was the shotgun. Her shoulder was well enough for a second try a week later. Two new complications, unbeknownst to Ellen, had just presented themselves. There were new mud puddles in the front yard, and her father had come to town and rented a buggy to ride out to visit his only child.

Ellen aimed the shotgun at a tree. The resulting kick made the barrel fly up. A wild turkey, which had been sitting on a limb, suddenly fell to the ground in a limp heap. And Ellen went backward right into the deepest mud puddle the saturated yard could boast.

At that particular moment, her father pulled up in front of the cabin.

Her father looked from Ellen to the turkey to the mud puddle to John. "I see that you are teaching my daughter to bathe and hunt at the same time," he remarked.

Ellen scrambled to her feet, wiping her hair back with a muddy hand. She was so disheveled, and so dirty, that it was hard for her immaculate father to find her face at all.

He grimaced. "Ellen, darling, I think it might not be a bad idea if you came home with me," he began uneasily.

She tossed her head, slinging mud onto John, who was standing next to her looking concerned. "I'm only just learning to shoot, Father," she remarked proudly. "No one is proficient at first. Isn't that so, John?"

"Uh, yes," John replied, but without his usual confidence.

Her father looked from one to the other and then to the turkey. "I suppose buying meat from the market in town is too expensive?" he asked.

"I like variety. We had rattlesnake last week, in fact," Ellen informed him. "It was delicious."

Her father shook his head. "Your grandmother is going to have heart failure if I tell her what I've seen here. And young man, this house of yours…!" He spread an expansive hand helplessly.

"The sooner we get *our* spur line," Ellen told her father, "the quicker we will have a real house instead of merely a cabin."

John nodded hopefully.

Terrance Colby sighed heavily. "I'll see what I can do," he promised.

They both smiled. "Will you stay for dinner?" Ellen invited, glancing behind her. She grinned. "We're having turkey!"

Her father declined, unwilling to share the sad surroundings that his daughter seemed to find so exciting. There were three families living in that one cabin, he noted, and he wasn't certain that he was democratic enough to appreciate such close quarters. It didn't take a mind reader to note that Ellen and John had no privacy. That might be an advantage, he mused, if Ellen decided to come home. There would be no complications. But she seemed happy as a lark, and unless he was badly mistaken, that young man John Jacobs was delighted with her company. His wife's mother was not going to be happy when he got up enough nerve to tell her what had happened to Ellen. She was just on her way home from a vacation in Italy. Perhaps the ship would be blown off course and she would not get home for several months, he mused. Otherwise, Ellen was going to have a very unhappy visitor in the near future.

He did make time to see John's growing herd of cattle, and he noticed that the young man had a fine lot of very healthy steers. He'd already seen how enterprising Ellen was with her dressmaking and dairy sales. Now he saw a way to help John become quickly self-sufficient.

WORD CAME THE FOLLOWING WEEK that Ellen's father was busy buying up right of way for the spur that would run to John's ranch. Not only that, he had become a customer for John's yearling steers, which he planned to feed to the laborers who were already hard at work on another stretch of his railroad. The only difficulty was that John was going to have to drive the steers north to San Antonio for Terrance Colby. Colby would be there waiting for him in a week. That wasn't a long cattle drive, certainly not as far as Kansas, but south Texas was still untamed and dangerous country. It would be risky. But John knew it would be worth the risk if he could deliver the beef.

So John and his men left, reluctantly on John's part, to drive the steers north. He and his fellow cowhands went around to all the other ranches, gathering up their steers, making sure they appropriated only the cattle that bore their 3J brand for the drive.

"I don't want to go," John told Ellen as they stood together, briefly alone, at the corral. "But I must protect our investment. There will be six of us to drive the herd, and we are all armed and well able to handle any trouble. Isaac and the older boys are going with me, but Luis will stay here to look after the livestock and all of you."

She sighed, smoothing her arms over the sleeves of his shirt, enjoying the feel of the smooth muscles under it. "I do not like the idea of you going away. But I know that it is necessary, so I'll be brave."

"I don't like leaving you, either," he said bluntly. He bent and kissed her hungrily. "When I return, perhaps we can afford a single night away from here," he whispered roughly. "I am going mad to have you in my arms without a potential audience!"

"As I am," she choked, kissing him back hungrily.

He lifted her clear of the ground in his embrace, flying as they kissed without restraint. Finally, he forced himself to put her back down and he stepped away. There was a ruddy flush on his high cheekbones, and his green eyes were fierce. Her face was equally flushed, but her eyes were soft and dreamy, and her mouth was swollen.

She smiled up at him bravely, despite her concern. "Don't get shot."

He grimaced. "I'll do my best. You stay within sight of the cabin and Luis, even when you're milking those infernal cows. And don't go to town without him."

She didn't mention that it would be suicide to take Luis away from guarding the cattle, even for that long. She and the women would have to work something out, so that they could sell their dresses and butter and milk in town. But she would spare him the worry.

"We'll be very careful," she promised.

He sighed, his hand resting on the worn butt of his .45 caliber pistol. "We'll be back as soon as humanly possible. Your father..."

"If he comes to town, I'll go there to wait for you," she promised, a lie, because she'd never leave Mary and Juana by themselves, even with Luis and a shotgun around.

"Possibly that's what you should do, anyway," he murmured thoughtfully.

"I can't leave here now," she replied. "There's too much at stake. I'll help take care of our ranch. You take care of our profit margin."

He chuckled, surprised out of his worries. "I'll be back before you miss me too much," he said, bending to kiss her again, briefly. "Stay close to the cabin."

"I will. Have a safe trip."

He swung into the saddle, shouting for Isaac and the boys. The women watched them ride away. The cattle had already been pooled in a nearby valley, and the drovers were ready to get underway. As Ellen watched her tall husband ride away, she realized why he'd wanted his railroad spur so badly. Not only was it dangerous to drive cattle a long way to a railhead, but the potential risk to the men and animals was great. Not only was there a constant threat from thieves, there were floods and thunderstorms that could decimate herds. She prayed that John and Isaac and the men going with them would be safe. It was just as well that Luis was staying at the ranch to help safeguard the breeding bulls and cows, and the calves that were too young for market. Not that she was going to shirk her own responsibilities, Ellen thought stubbornly.

Nobody was stealing anything around here while she could get her hands on a gun!

THE THREAT CAME UNEXPECTEDLY just two days after John and the others had left south Texas for San Antonio on the cattle drive.

Ellen had just carried a bucketful of milk to the kitchen when she peered out the open, glass-less window at two figures on horseback, watch-ing the cabin. She called softly to Juana and Mary.

Juana crossed herself. "It is Comanches!" she exclaimed. "They come to raid the cattle!"

"Well, they're not raiding them today," Ellen said angrily. "I'll have to ride out and get Luis and the boys," she said. "There's nothing else for it, and I'll have to go bareback. I'll never have time to saddle a horse with them sitting out there."

"It is too dangerous," Juana exclaimed. "You can hardly ride a saddled horse, and those men are Comanches. They are the finest riders of any men, even my Luis. You will never outrun them!"

Ellen muttered under her breath. They had so few cattle that even the loss of one or two could mean the difference between bankruptcy and sur-vival. Well, she decided, there was only one thing to do. She grabbed up the shotgun, loaded it, and started out the back door, still in her dress and apron.

"No!" Mary almost screamed. "Are you crazy? Do you know what they do to white women?!"

Ellen didn't say a word. She kept walking, her steps firm and sure.

She heard frantic calls behind her, but she didn't listen. She and John had a ranch. These were her cattle as much as his. She wasn't about to let any thieves come and carry off her precious livestock!

The two Comanches saw her coming and gaped. They didn't speak. They sat on their horses with their eyes fixed, wide, at the young woman lugging a shotgun toward them.

One of them said something to the other one, who laughed and nodded.

She stopped right in front of them, lifted the shotgun, sighted along it and cocked it.

"This is my ranch," she said in a firm, stubborn tone. "You aren't stealing my cattle!"

There was pure admiration in their eyes. They didn't reach for the rifles lying across their buckskinned laps. They didn't try to ride her down. They simply watched her.

The younger of the two Indians had long pigtails and a lean, handsome face. His eyes, she noted curiously, were light.

"We have not come to steal cattle," the young one said in passable English. "We have come to ask Big John for work."

"Work?" she stammered.

He nodded. "We felt guilty that we butchered one of his calves. We had come far and were very hungry. We will work to pay for the calf. We hear from the Mexican people that he is also fair," he added surprisingly. "We know that he looks only at a man's work. He does not consider himself better than men of other colors. This is very strange. We do not understand it. Your people have just fought a terrible war because you wanted to own other people who had dark skin. Yet Big John lives with these people. Even with the Mexicans. He treats them as family."

"Yes," she said. She slowly uncocked the shotgun and lowered it to her side. "That is true."

The younger one smiled at her. "We know more about horses than even his vaquero, who knows much," he said without conceit. "We will work hard. When we pay back the cost of the calf, he can pay us what he thinks is fair."

She chuckled. "It's not really a big cabin, and it has three families living in it," she began.

They laughed. "We can make a teepee," the older one said, his English only a little less accented than the younger one's.

"I say," she exclaimed, "can you teach me to shoot a bow?!"

The younger one threw back his head and laughed uproariously. "Even his woman is brave," he told the older one. "Now do you believe me? This man is not as others with white skin."

"I believe you."

"Come along, then," Ellen said, turning. "I'll introduce you to...Luis! Put that gun down!" she exclaimed angrily when she saw the smaller man coming toward them with two pistols leveled. "These are our two new horse wranglers," she began. She stopped. "What are your names?" she asked.

"I am called Thunder," the young one said. "He is Red Wing."

"I am Ellen Jacobs," she said, "and that is Luis. Say hello, Luis."

The Mexican lowered his pistols and reholstered them with a blank stare at Ellen.

"Say hello," she repeated.

"Hello," he obliged, and he nodded.

The Comanches nodded back. They rode up to

the cabin and dismounted. The women in the cabin peered out nervously.

"Luis will show you where to put your horses," Ellen told them. "We have a lean-to. Someday, we will have a barn!"

"Need bigger teepee first," Red Wing murmured, eyeing the cabin. "Bad place to live. Can't move house when floor get dirty."

"Yes, well, it's warm," Ellen said helplessly.

The young Comanche, Thunder, turned to look at her. "You are brave," he said with narrow light eyes. "Like my woman."

"She doesn't live with you?" she asked hesitantly.

He smiled gently. "She is stubborn, and wants to live in a cabin far away," he replied. "But I will bring her back here one day." He nodded and followed after Luis with his friend.

Juana and Mary came out of the cabin with worried expressions. "You going to let Indians live with us?" Juana exclaimed. "They kill us all!"

"No, they won't," Ellen assured them. "You'll see. They're going to be an asset!"

CHAPTER FIVE

THE COMANCHES DID KNOW more about horses than even Luis did, and they were handy around the place. They hunted game, taught Luis how to tan hides, and set about building a teepee out behind the cabin.

"Very nice," Ellen remarked when it was finished. "It's much roomier than the cabin."

"Easy to keep clean," Red Wing agreed. "Floor get dirty, move teepee."

She laughed. He smiled, going off to help Thunder with a new corral Juan was building.

JOHN RODE BACK IN WITH ISAAC and stopped short at the sight of a towering teepee next to the cabin he'd left two weeks earlier.

His hand went to his pistol as he thought of terrible possibilities that would explain its presence.

But Ellen came running out of the cabin, followed by Mary and Juana, laughing and waving.

John kicked his foot out of the stirrup of his

new saddle and held his arm down to welcome Ellen as she leaped up into his arms. He kissed her hungrily, feeling as if he'd come home for the first time in his life.

He didn't realize how long that kiss lasted until he felt eyes all around him. He lifted his head to find two tall Comanches standing shoulder to shoulder with Juan and the younger boys and girls of the group, along with Juana and Mary.

"Bad habit," Thunder remarked disapprovingly.

"Bound to upset horse," Red Wing agreed, nodding.

"What the hell…!" John exclaimed.

"They're our new horse wranglers," Ellen said quickly. "That's Thunder, and that's Red Wing."

"They taught us how to make parfleche bags," Juana's eldest daughter exclaimed, showing one with beautiful beadwork.

"And how to make bows and arrows!" the next youngest of Isaac's sons seconded, showing his.

"And quivers," Luis said, resigned to being fired for what John would surely consider bad judgment in letting two Comanches near the women. He stood with his sombrero against his chest. "You may fire me if you wish."

"If you fire me, I'm going with them," Isaac's second son replied, pointing toward the Indians.

John shook his head, laughing uproariously. "I expect there'll be a lynch mob out here any day now," he sighed.

Everybody grinned.

Ellen beamed up at him. "Well, they certainly do know how to train horses, John," she said.

"Your woman meet us with loaded shotgun," Red Wing informed him. "She has strong spirit."

"And great heart," Thunder added. "She says we can work for you. We stay?"

John sighed. "By all means. All we need now is an Eskimo," he murmured to Ellen under his breath.

She looped her arms around his neck and kissed him. "Babies would be nice," she whispered.

He went scarlet, and everyone laughed.

"I GOT ENOUGH FOR THE STEERS to buy a new bull," John told her. "Saddles for the horses we have, and four new horses," he added. "They're coming in with the rest of the drovers. I rode ahead to make sure you were all right."

She cuddled close to him as they stood out behind the cabin in a rare moment alone. "We had no trouble at all. Well, except for the Comanches, but they turned out to be friends anyway."

"You could have blown me over when I saw that teepee," he confessed. "We've had some hard battles with Comanches in the past, over stolen livestock. And I know for a fact that two Comanches ate one of my calves..."

"They explained that," she told him contentedly. "They were hungry, but they didn't want to steal. They came here to work out the cost of the calf, and then to stay on, if you'll keep them. I think they decided that it's better to join a strong foe than oppose him. That was the reason they gave me, at least."

"Well, I must admit, these two Comanches are unusual."

"The younger one has light eyes."

"I noticed." He didn't add what he was certain of—that these two Comanches were the fugitives that the deputy marshal in Sutherland Springs had been looking for. Fortunately for them, James Graham had headed up beyond San Antonio to pursue them, acting on what now seemed to be a very bad tip.

She lifted her head and looked up at him. "They rode up and just sat there. I loaded my shotgun and went out to see what they wanted."

"You could have been killed," he pointed out.

"It's what you would have done, in my place," she reminded him, smiling gently. "I'm not afraid of much. And I've learned from you that appearances can be deceptive."

"You take chances."

"So do you."

He sighed. "You're learning bad habits from me."

She smiled and snuggled close. "Red Wing is going to make us a teepee of our own very soon." She kissed him, and was kissed back hungrily.

"Yesterday not be soon enough for that teepee," came a droll accented voice from nearby.

Red Wing was on the receiving end of two pairs of glaring eyes. He shrugged and walked off noiselessly, chuckling to himself.

John laughed. "Amen," he murmured.

"John, there's just one other little thing," Ellen murmured as she stood close to him.

"What now? You hired a gunslinger to feed the chickens?"

"I don't know any gunslingers. Be serious."

"All right. What?"

"My grandmother sent me a telegram. She's coming out here to save me from a life of misery and poverty."

He lifted his head. "Really!"

She drew in a soft breath. "I suppose she'll faint dead away when she sees this place, but I'm not going to be dragged back East by her or an army. I belong here."

"Yes, you do," John replied. "Although you certainly deserve better than this, Ellen," he said softly. He touched her disheveled hair. "I promise you, it's only going to get better."

She smiled. "I know that. We're going to have an empire, all our own."

"You bet we are."

"Built with our own two hands," she murmured, reaching up to kiss him, "and the help of our friends. All we need is each other."

"Need teepee worse," came Red Wing's voice again.

"Listen here," John began.

"Your horse got colic," the elder of the Comanches stood his ground. "What you feed him?"

"He ate corn," John said belligerently. "I gave him a feed bucket full!"

The older man scoffed. "No wonder he got colic. I fix."

"Corn is good for horses, and I know what to do for colic!"

"Sure. Not feed horse corn. Feed him grass. We build teepee tomorrow."

John still had his mouth open when the older man stalked off again.

"Indian ponies only eat grass," Ellen informed him brightly. "They think grain is bad for horses."

"You've learned a lot," he remarked.

"More than you might realize," she said dryly. She reached up to John's ear. "These two Comanches are running from the army. But I don't think they did anything bad, and I told Mr. Alton that I saw two Comanches heading north at a dead run. He told the..."

"...deputy marshal," he finished for her, exasperated.

"When you get to know them, you'll think they're good people, too," she assured him. "Besides, they're teaching me things I can't learn anywhere else. I can track a deer," she counted off her new skills, "weave a mat, make a bed out of pine straw, do beadwork, shoot a bow and arrow, and tan a hide."

"Good Lord, woman!" he exclaimed, impressed.

She grinned. "And I'm going to learn to hunt just as soon as you take me out with my shotgun."

He sighed. This was going to become difficult if any of her people stopped by to check on her. He didn't want to alienate them, but this couldn't continue.

"Ellen, what do you think about schooling?" he asked gently.

She blinked. "Excuse me?"

"Well, do any of the children know how to read and write?"

She hadn't considered that. "I haven't asked, but I don't expect they can. It was not legal for slaves to be taught such things, and I know that Juana can't even read Spanish, although it is her native tongue."

"The world we build will need educated people," he said thoughtfully. "It must start with the children, with this new generation. Don't you agree?"

"Yes," she said, warming quickly to the idea. "Educated people will no longer have to work at menial jobs, where they are at the mercy of others."

"That is exactly what I think. So, why don't you start giving the children a little book learning, in the evenings, after supper?" he suggested.

She smiled brightly. "You know, that's a very good idea. But, I have no experience as a teacher."

"All you will need are some elementary books and determination," he said. "I believe there is a retired schoolteacher in Victoria, living near the blacksmith. Shall I take you to see him?"

She beamed. "Would you?"

"Indeed I would. We'll go up there tomorrow," he replied, watching her consider the idea. If nothing else, it would spare her the astonished surprise of her people if they ever came to visit and found Ellen in dungarees and muddy boots skinning out a deer.

He drove her to Victoria the next morning in the small, dilapidated buggy he'd managed to afford from his cattle sales, hitched to one of the good horses he'd also acquired. Fortunately it took to pulling a buggy right away. Some horses didn't, and people died in accidents when they panicked and ran away.

The schoolteacher was long retired, but he taught Ellen the fundamentals she would need to educate small children. He also had a basic reader, a grammar book and a spelling book, which he gave to Ellen with his blessing. She clutched them like priceless treasure all the way back down the dusty road to the 3J Ranch.

"Do you think the Brown and the Rodriguez families will let me teach the children?" she wondered, a little worried after the fact. "They might not believe in education."

"Luis and Isaac can't even sign a paper," he told her. "They have to make an 'x' on a piece of paper and have me witness it. If they ever leave the ranch, they need to know how to read and write so that nobody will take advantage of them."

She looked at him with even more admiration than usual. He was very handsome to her, very capable and strong. She counted her blessings every single day that he'd thought her marriageable.

"You really care for them, don't you?" she asked softly.

"When the Union Army came through Atlanta, they burned everything in sight," he recalled, his face hardening. "Not just the big plantations where slaves were kept. They burned poor white people's houses, because they thought we all had slaves down south." He laughed coldly. "Sharecroppers don't own anything. Even the house we lived in belonged to the plantation owner. They set it ablaze and my sister and mother were trapped inside. They burned to death while my other sister and I stood outside and watched." He touched his lean cheek, where the old scars were still noticeable. "I tried to kill the cavalry officer responsible, but his men saved him. They gave me these," he touched his cheek. "I never kept slaves. I hid Isaac and Mary in the root cellar when they ran away from the overseer. I couldn't save their oldest son, but Mary was pregnant. She and Isaac saved me from the Union Army," he said with a sigh. "They pleaded for my life. Shocked the cavalry into sparing me and my oldest sister. Isaac helped me bury my mother and my younger sister." He looked down at her soft, compassionate expression. "My sister went to North Carolina to live with a cousin, but I wanted to go to my uncle in Texas. Isaac and Mary had no place else to go, so they traveled with me. They said they wanted to start over, but they didn't fool me. They came with me to save me from the Union Army if I got in trouble. Those two never forget a debt. I owe them everything. My life. That's why they're partners with me."

"And how did you meet Luis and Juana?" she asked.

"Luis was the only cowboy my uncle had who wasn't robbing him blind. Luis told me what the others had done, and I fired the lot. I took care of my uncle, with their help, and rounded up stray calves to start my herd." He chuckled. "The cabin was the only structure on the place.

It got real crowded when Isaac and Mary moved in with me. Juana and Luis were going to live in the brush, but I insisted that we could all manage. We have. But it hasn't been easy.''

"And now the Comanches are building tee-pees for us," she told him. "They've been hunting constantly to get enough skins. We're going to have privacy for the very first time. I mean…'' She flushed at her own forwardness.

He reached for her small hand and held it tight. His eyes burned into hers. "I want nothing more in the world than to be alone with you, Camellia Ellen Jacobs," he said huskily. "The finest thing I ever did in my life was have the good sense to marry you!"

"Do you really think so?" she asked happily. "I am no beauty…"

"You have a heart as big as all outdoors and the courage of a wolf. I wouldn't trade you for a debutante.''

She beamed, leaning against his broad shoulder. "And I would not trade you for the grandest gentleman who ever lived. Although I expect you will make a fine gentleman, when we have made our fortune."

He kissed her forehead tenderly. "You are my fortune," he said huskily.

"You mean, because my father is giving us a

railroad spur for a wedding present," she said, confused.

He shook his head. "Because you are my most prized treasure," he whispered, and bent to kiss her mouth tenderly.

She kissed him back, shyly. "I had never kissed anyone until you came along," she whispered.

He chuckled. "You improve with practice!"

"John!" she chided.

He only laughed, letting her go to pay attention to the road. "We must get on down the road. It looks like rain." He gave her a roguish glance. "We would not want you to tumble into a mud puddle, Mrs. Jacobs."

"Are you ever going to forget that?" she moaned.

"In twenty years or so, perhaps," he said. "But I cannot promise. That is one of my most delightful memories. You were so game, and Sir Sydney was such a boor!"

"Indeed he was. I hope he marries for money and discovers that she has none."

"Evil girl," he teased.

She laughed. "Well, you will never be able to accuse ME of marrying you for your money," she said contentedly. "In twenty years or so," she added, repeating his own phrase, "you will be exceedingly rich. I just know it."

"I hope to break even, at least, and be able to pay my debts," he said. "But I would love to have a ranch as big as a state, Ellen, and the money to breed fine cattle, and even fine horses." He glanced at her. "Now that we have two extra horse wranglers, we can start building up our herd."

She only smiled. She was glad that she'd stood up to the Comanches. She wondered if they'd ever have wanted to work for them if she'd run away and hid.

THE TEEPEE THE COMANCHES built for the couple was remarkably warm and clean. No sooner was it up than Ellen built a small cooking fire near its center and put on a black iron pot of stew to cook. Red Wing had already taught her how to turn the pole in the center to work the flap for letting smoke out while she cooked. She also learned that she was born to be a rancher's wife. Every chore came easily to her. She wasn't afraid of hard work, and she fell more in love with her roguish, unconventional husband every day. She did still worry about her grandmother coming down to rescue her. She had no intention of being carted off back East, where she would have to dress and act with decorum.

She sat the children down in the cabin one evening after she and the other women and older girls had cleared away the precious iron cookware and swished the tin plates and few utensils in a basin of soapy water and wiped them with a dishrag.

"What are we going to do?" one of Juana's daughters asked.

Ellen produced the books that the retired Victoria schoolteacher had given her, handling them like treasure.

"I'm going to teach you children to read and write," she told them.

Mary and Juana stood quietly by, so still that Ellen was made uneasy.

"Is it all right?" she asked the adults, concerned, because she'd worried that they might think education superfluous.

"Nobody ever taught me to write my name," Mary said. "Nor Isaac, either. We can only make an x. Could you teach me to write? And read?"

"Me, too!" Juana exclaimed.

Their husbands looked as if they might bite their tongues off trying not to ask if they could learn, too, but they managed.

"You can all gather around and we'll let the

older folk help show the young ones how to do it,'' she said, managing a way to spare the pride of the men in the process of teaching them as well.

''Yes, we can show them, *señora*,'' Luis said brightly.

''Sure we can,'' Isaac added with a big grin.

''Gather around, then.'' She opened the book with a huge smile and began the first lesson.

SHE LOOKED DOWN AT THE dungarees she was wearing with boots that John had bought her. She had on one of his big checked long-sleeved shirts, with the sleeves rolled up, and her hair was caught in a ponytail down her back. She checked the stew in her black cooking pot and wiped sweat from her brow with a weary hand. The Comanches had gathered pine straw from under the short-leafed pines in the thicket to make beds, which Ellen covered with quilts she and the other women had made in their precious free time. It wasn't a mansion, but she and John would have privacy for the first time that night. She thought of the prospect with joy and a certain amount of trepidation. Like most young women of her generation, her upbringing had been very strict and moral. She knew almost nothing of what happened between married people in the dark. What she didn't know made her nervous.

The sudden noise outside penetrated her thoughts. She heard voices, one raised and strident, and she ran out of the teepee and to the cabin to discover a well-dressed, elderly woman with two young men in immaculate suits exchanging heated words with Juana, who couldn't follow a thing they were saying. Mary was out with the others collecting more wood for the fireplace in the small cabin.

"Do you understand me?" the old woman was shouting. "I am looking for Ellen Colby!"

"Grandmother!" Ellen exclaimed when she recognized the woman.

Her grandmother Amelia Greene was standing beside the buggy beside two tall young men whom Ellen recognized as her cousins.

Amelia turned stiffly, her whole expression one of utter disapproval when she saw the way her granddaughter was dressed.

"Camellia Ellen Colby!" she exclaimed. "What has become of you!"

"Now, Grandmother," Ellen said gently, "you can't expect a pioneer wife to dress and act as a lady in a drawing room."

The older woman was not convinced. She was bristling with indignation. "You will get your things together and come home with me right away!'' she demanded. "I am not leaving you here in the dirt with these peasants!''

Ellen's demeanor changed at once from one of welcome and uneasiness to one of pure outrage. She stuck both hands on her slender hips and glared at her grandmother.

"How dare you call my friends peasants!'' she exclaimed furiously. She went to stand beside Juana. "Juana's husband Luis, and Mary's husband Isaac, are our partners in this ranching enterprise. They are no one's servants!''

Mary came to stand beside her as well, and the children gathered around them. While the old woman and her companions were getting over that shock, John came striding up, with his gunbelt on, accompanied by Luis and Isaac and the two Comanche men.

Amelia Greene screeched loudly and jumped behind the tallest of her grandchildren.

"How much you want for old woman?'' Red Wing asked deliberately, pointing at Amelia.

Amelia looked near to fainting.

Ellen laughed helplessly. "He's not serious,'' she assured her grandmother.

"I should hope not!'' the tallest of her cousins muttered, glaring at him. "The very idea! Why do you allow Indians here?''

"These are our horse wranglers," Ellen said pointedly. "Red Wing and Thunder. And those are our partners, Luis Rodriguez and Isaac Brown. Gentlemen, my grandmother, Amelia Greene of New York City."

Nobody spoke.

John came forward to slide his arm around Ellen's waist. He was furious at the way her relatives were treating the people nearby.

"Hospitality is almost a religion to us out here in Texas," John drawled, although his green eyes were flashing like green diamonds. "But as you may notice, we have no facilities to accommodate visitors yet."

"You cannot expect that we would want to stay?" the shorter cousin asked indignantly. "Come, Grandmother, let us go back to town. Ellen is lost to us. Surely you can see that?"

Ellen glared at him. "Five years from now, cousin, you will not recognize this place. A lot of hard work is going to turn it into a show-place...."

"Of mongrels!" her grandmother said haughtily.

"I'm sorry you feel that way, but I find your company equally taxing," Ellen shot back. "Now will you all please leave? I have chores, as do the others. Unlike you, I do not sit in the parlor waiting for other people to fetch and carry at my instructions.''

The old woman glowered. ''Very well, then, live out here in the wilds with savages! I only came to try and save you from a life of drudgery!''

''Pickles and bread,'' Ellen retorted haughtily. ''You came hoping to entice me back into household slavery. Until I escaped you and came west with my father, I was your unpaid maidservant for most of my life.''

''What else are you fit for?'' her grandmother demanded. ''You have no looks, no talent, no…!''

''She is lovely,'' John interrupted. ''Gentle and kind and brave. She is no one's servant here, and she has freedom of a sort you will never know.''

The old woman's eyes were poisonously intent. ''She will die of hard work here, for certain!''

''On her own land, making her own empire,'' John replied tersely. ''The road is that way,'' he added, pointing.

She tossed her head and sashayed back to the buggy, to be helped in by her grandsons, one of whom gave Ellen a wicked grin before he climbed in and took the reins.

"Drive on," Amelia said curtly. "We have no kinfolk here!"

"Truer words were never spoken," Ellen said sweetly. "Do have a safe trip back to town. Except for cattle thieves from Mexico and the bordering counties of Texas, and bank robbers, there should be nothing dangerous in your path. But I would drive very fast, if I were you!"

There were muttered, excited exchanges of conversation in the buggy before the tallest grandson used the buggy whip and the small vehicle raced forward down the dusty dirt road in the general direction of town.

"You wicked girl!" John exclaimed on a burst of laughter, hugging her close.

"So much for my rescuers," she murmured contentedly, hugging him back. "Now we can get back to work!"

THAT NIGHT, ELLEN AND JOHN spent their first night alone, without prying eyes or ears, in the teepee the Comanches had provided for them.

"I am a little nervous," she confessed when John had put out the small fire and they were together in the darkness.

"That will not last," he promised, drawing her close. "We are both young, and we have all the years ahead to become more accustomed to each other. All you must remember is that I care more for you than for any woman I have ever known. You are my most prized treasure. I love you. I will spend my life trying to make you happy.''

"John!" She pressed close to him and raised her face. "I will do the same. I adore you!"

He bent and kissed her softly, and then not so softly. Tender caresses gave way to stormy, devouring kisses. They sank to the makeshift mattress and there, locked tight in each others' arms, they gave way to the smoldering passion that had grown between them for long weeks. At first she was inhibited, but he was skillful and slow and tender. Very soon, her passion rose to meet his. The sharpness of passion was new between them, and as it grew, they became playful together. They laughed, and then the laughing stopped as they tasted the first sweet sting of mutual delight in the soft, enveloping darkness.

When Ellen finally fell asleep in John's arms, she thought that there had never been a happier bride in the history of Texas.

CHAPTER SIX

ELLEN'S GRANDMOTHER AND cousins went back East. Her father came regularly to visit them in their teepee, finding it touching and amusing at once that they were happy with so little. He even offered to loan them enough to build a bigger cabin, but they refused politely. All they wanted, Ellen reminded him, was a spur of the railroad.

That, too, was finally finished. John loaded his beef cattle into the cattle cars bound for the stockyards of the Midwest. The residents of the ranch settled into hard work and camaraderie, and all their efforts eventually resulted in increasing prosperity.

The first thing they did with their newfound funds was to add to the cattle herd. The second was to build individual cabins for the Rodriguez and Brown clans, replacing the teepees the Comanches had built for them. The Comanches, offered a handsome log cabin of their own, declined abruptly, although politely. They could never understand the white man's interest in a stationary house that had to be cleaned constantly, when it was so much easier to move the teepee to a clean spot! However, John and Ellen continued to live in their own teepee for the time being, as well, to save money.

A barn was the next project. As in all young communities, a barbecue and a quilting bee were arranged along with a barnraising. All the strong young men of the area turned out and the resulting barn and corral were quick fruit of their efforts. Other ranches were springing up around the 3J Ranch, although not as large and certainly not with the number of cattle and horses that John's now boasted.

The railroad spur, when it came, brought instant prosperity to the area it served. It grew and prospered even as some smaller towns in the area became ghost towns. Local citizens decided that they needed a name for their small town, which had actually grown up around the ranch itself even before the railroad came. They decided to call it Jacobsville, for John Jacobs, despite his protests. His hard work and lack of prejudice had made him good friends and dangerous enemies in the surrounding area. But when cattle were rustled and houses robbed, his was never among them. Bandits from over the border made a wide route around the ranch.

As the cattle herd grew and its refinement continued, the demand for Jacobs's beef grew as well. John bought other properties to go along with his own, along with barbed wire to fence in his ranges. He hired on new men as well, black drovers as well as Mexican and white. There was even a Chinese drover who had heard of the Jacobs ranch far away in Arizona and had come to it looking for a job. Each new addition to the ranch workforce was placed under the orders of either Luis or Isaac, and the number of outbuildings and line camps grew steadily.

Ellen worked right alongside the other women, adding new women to her dressmaking enterprise, until she had enough workers and enough stock to open a dress shop in their new town of Jacobsville. Mary and Juana took turns as proprietors while Ellen confined herself to sewing chair and sofa covers for the furniture in the new white clapboard house John had built her. She and her handsome husband grew closer by the day, but one thing was still missing from her happiness. Their marriage was entering into its second year with no hope of a child.

John never spoke of it, but Ellen knew he wanted children. So did she. It was a curious thing that their passion for each other was ever growing, but bore no fruit. Still, they had a good marriage and Ellen was happier than she ever dreamed of being.

In the second year of their marriage, his sister Jeanette came west on the train with her husband and four children to visit. Only then did Ellen learn the extent of the tragedy that had sent John west in the first place. The attack by the Union troops had mistakenly been aimed at the sharecroppers' cabin John and his mother and sisters occupied, instead of the house where the owner's vicious overseer lived. The house had caught fire and John's mother and elder sister had burned to death. John had not been able to save them. The attack had been meant for the overseer who had beaten Isaac and Mary's son to death, along with many other slaves. John was told, afterward, but his grief was so sweeping that he hardly understood what was said to him. His sister made sure that he did know. The cavalry officer had apologized to her, and given her money for the trip to North Carolina, unbeknownst to John. His sister obviously adored him, and he was a doting uncle to her children.

She understood John's dark moods better after that, the times when he wanted to be alone, when he went hunting and never brought any wild game home with him. Ellen and Jeanette became close almost at once, and wrote to each other regularly even when Jeanette and her family went home to North Carolina.

Deputy Marshal James Graham had come by unexpectedly and mentioned to John that he hadn't been able to find the two Comanche fugitives who were supposed to have shot a white man over a horse. It turned out that the white man had cheated the Comanches and had later been accused of cheating several army officers in horse trading deals. He was arrested, tried and sent to prison. So, Graham told John, the Comanches weren't in trouble anymore. Just in case John ever came across them.

Thunder and Red Wing, told of the white man's arrest, worked a few months longer for John and then headed north with their wages. Ellen was sad to see them go, but Thunder had promised that they would meet again one day.

The Maxwells came to visit often from Scotland, staying in the beautiful white Victorian house John later built for his beloved wife. They gave the couple the benefit of their extensive experience of horses, and John branched out into raising thoroughbreds. Eventually a thoroughbred of the lineage from his ranch would win the Triple Crown.

YEARS PASSED WITH EACH YEAR bringing new

prosperity to the 3J Ranch. One May morning, Ellen unexpectedly fainted at a church social. John carried her to the office of their new doctor, who had moved in just down the boardwalk from the new restaurant and hotel.

The doctor examined her and, when John had been invited into the examination room, grinned at him. "You are to be a father, young man," he said. "Congratulations!"

John looked at Ellen as if she'd just solved the great mystery of life. He lifted her clear of the floor and kissed her with aching tenderness. His happiness was complete, now.

Almost immediately, he began to worry about labor. He remembered when Luis's and Isaac's wives had given birth, and he turned pale.

The doctor patted him on the back. "You'll survive the birth of your children, Mr. Jacobs, we all do. Yes, even me. I have had to deliver mine. Something, I daresay, you will be spared!"

John laughed with relief, thanked the doctor for his perception, and kissed Ellen again.

She bore him three sons and two daughters in the years that followed, although only two of their children, their son Bass and their daughter Rose Ellen, lived to adulthood. The family grew and prospered in Jacobsville. Later, the entire county, Jacobs, was named for John as well. He diversified his holdings into mining and real estate and banking. He was the first in south Texas to try new techniques in cattle ranching and to use mechanization to improve his land.

The Brown family produced six children in all. Their youngest, Caleb, would move to Chicago and become a famous trial lawyer. His son would be elected to the United States Senate.

The Rodriguez family produced ten children. One of their sons became a Texas Ranger, beginning a family tradition that lived on through subsequent generations.

John Jacobs founded the first bank in Jacobs County, along with the first dry goods store. He worked hard at breeding good cattle, but he made his fortune in the terrible blizzard of 1885-86 in which so many cattlemen lost their shirts. He endowed a college and an orphanage, and, always active in local politics, he was elected to the U.S. Senate at the age of fifty. He and Ellen never parted for fifty years.

His son, Bass Jacobs, married twice. By his young second wife, he had a son, Bass, Jr., and a daughter, Violet Ellen. Bass Jacobs, Jr., was the last of the Jacobs family to own land in Jacobs County. The 3J Ranch was sold after his death. His son, Ty, born in 1955, eventually moved to Arizona and married and settled there. His daughter, Shelby, born in 1961, stayed in Jacobsville and married a local man, Justin Ballenger. They produced three sons. One of them was named John Jackson Jacobs Ballenger, so that the founding father of Shelby's family name would live on in memory.

A bronze statue of Big John Jacobs, mounted on one of the Arabian stallions his ranch became famous for, was erected in the town square of Jacobsville just after the first world war.

Portraits of the Rodriguez family and the Brown family are prominently displayed in the Jacobs County Museum, alongside a portrait of Camellia Ellen Jacobs, dressed in an elegant blue gown, but with a shotgun in a fringed sheath at her feet and a twinkle in her blue eyes. All three portraits, which had belonged to Bass Jacobs, Jr., were donated to the museum by Shelby Jacobs Ballenger. In a glass case nearby are a bow and arrow in a beaded rawhide quiver, in which also resides a black-and-white photograph of a Comanche warrior with a blond woman and five children, two of whom are also blond. But that is another story...

Hawk's Way: The Substitute Groom

JOAN JOHNSTON

This book is dedicated to Aspen Lee.
May you grow in beauty, grace and charm.

Chapter 1

"*Watch your wingtip! You're too close. We're going to— Bail out, Huck! God, no, Huck!*"

Colt Whitelaw sat bolt upright in bed, his eyes wild with remembered terror. His heart was racing, his hands were clenched, and his sheet-draped body was drenched in sweat. It took him a moment to realize where he was. Home, at Hawk's Pride, his parents' ranch in northwest Texas. He'd been jet-lagged when he'd arrived late last night. That was the excuse he'd used, anyway, to go right to bed. To avoid doing what had to be done.

I have to see Jenny. I have to tell her there won't be any wedding next month, that Huck was killed six days ago in a midair collision over the Egyptian desert.

Colt felt the sting in his nose, the tickle at the back of his throat. He wasn't going to cry anymore. His best friend was gone, and nothing could bring him back.

"Colt, I heard some noise. Are you all right?"

"I'm fine, Mom," Colt said, blinking against the afternoon sun. He had locked the bedroom door, or he knew his mother would already have been inside. He was thirty-two, but he was her baby, the youngest of eight adopted kids and the only one who'd been an infant when Zach and Rebecca Whitelaw had made him a part of their family.

"Are you ready to get up?" his mother asked through the door. "Can I make you something to eat? Or do you need more sleep?"

He couldn't eat. He couldn't sleep anymore. He couldn't do anything until he'd spoken to Jenny. "I'm fine, Mom," he said. "I think I'll take a shower."

"Everything you need is in the bathroom. Make yourself at home."

Make yourself at home. He supposed he deserved that. Three of his sisters were married and lived nearby, while the rest of his siblings worked on the family ranch. He hadn't been back to Hawk's Pride except for a brief visit at Labor Day or Christmas for ten years. It wasn't his home anymore, although at one time his father had expected him to manage the ranch. Colt had wanted to fly jets.

His brother Jake had become ramrod instead. His brother Louis—who was calling himself Rabb these days, short for Rabbit, a nickname he'd acquired as a result of eating a lot of carrots as a kid—worked the cattle, while his sister Frannie trained cutting horses. His brother Avery did the bookkeeping and legal work.

There was no place for him at Hawk's Pride now.

Colt made himself get out of bed. He groaned as his bruised right knee protested, along with his left shoulder. He'd survived the crash between his and Huck's training jets with minor injuries. The Air Force had exonerated him of blame in the incident, but he was on leave until he was fully recuperated.

He walked gingerly across the hall to the bathroom wearing only a pair of Jockey shorts and caught his mother peeking around the corner at the end of the hall. She jumped back out of sight, and he felt himself grinning as he closed the bathroom door behind him. Even if he didn't plan to stay, it was good to be home.

A half hour later Colt looked himself over in the mirror above the dresser in his former bedroom. The doctor had said the six stitches across his chin wouldn't leave much of scar, but he'd decided not to try to shave around them. The day's growth of beard made him look disreputable but was countered by a military haircut that had left his black hair just long enough to part.

He rubbed his hands over the thighs of a pair of butter-soft jeans he'd found in a drawer and curled his toes in the scuffed leather cowboy boots he'd found in the closet. He wore a tucked-in white T-shirt but didn't have a Western belt, so the jeans rode low on his hips. He settled a battered Stetson on his head, completing his transformation into the Texas cowboy he once had been.

"Colt?"

Colt turned and found his mother standing in his open bedroom doorway, her heart in her eyes. There had always been a chance he'd be killed flying jets. This time he'd come damned close. He reached out and pulled her into his arms.

His birth mother had been a teenager, alone and

in trouble, when she'd given him up to the White-laws for adoption. He often wondered about her, but he didn't miss her. In Rebecca Whitelaw he had the best mother any kid could want.

"Are you all right?" she asked, leaning back to look into his eyes. "How about some break-fast? Is there anything I can do for you?"

"I'm fine, Mom. Really. I don't think I could eat anything. I need to see Jenny, to tell her about Huck."

His mother leaned back, her eyes wide with disbelief. "You mean the Air Force hasn't con-tacted her?"

Colt shook his head. "Huck named his father as next of kin for notification purposes. The way things are between her and the senator, you can bet Huck's dad hasn't said a word to her, and I didn't want to tell her over the phone."

"I can't believe what's happened. Jenny's been waiting years for her brothers to grow up, so she'd be free to marry. And now, with the youngest graduating in June and her wedding day set, Huck is killed. It's just not fair!"

Colt rocked his mother in his arms. "I know, Mom." Colt felt his throat swelling closed. *Oh, God, Jenny. I'm so sorry. For your sake, I wish it had been me.*

He let go of his mother and took a step back. "I may be gone awhile. If Jenny needs anything, I want to be there for her."

"I understand," his mother said. She brushed her fingertips across his chin, coming as near as she dared without touching his stitches. "I know how close the three of you were."

Inseparable, Colt thought. *We were inseparable.*

"I'm sure Jenny will appreciate having you there," his mother continued. "Tell her to call if there's anything we can do."

"I will, Mom."

Colt decided to ride horseback to Jenny's ranch, mostly because it postponed the moment when he would have to tell her about Huck's death. It also gave him a chance to see the changes that had been wrought in the eight months since he'd last been home. Hawk's Pride looked more successful than ever. Which, by contrast, made the poverty on Jenny's ranch, the Double D, even more evident.

Fields that should have been planted in hay lay barren, a windmill wobbled and squeaked, fence posts needed to be repaired or replaced, the stock needed fattening, and a sun-scorched barn needed paint. Nevertheless, with its deep canyons and myriad arroyos, the land possessed a certain rugged charm.

His first sight of the ranch house, which looked as though it belonged in a Depression-era movie, confirmed his growing suspicion. If Jenny wasn't flat broke, he'd eat his hat.

Colt was surprised when he rode around the side of the barn to find himself staring at another rider on horseback. "Jenny. Hi."

The instantaneous smile made her bluer-than-blue eyes crinkle at the corners. His gut clenched.

I thought with Huck dead I'd feel different. But, heaven help me, I'm still in love with my best friend's girl.

"Colt! What a wonderful surprise!" Jenny cried. "Where's Huck? Did he come home on leave with you?"

"I'm alone," he managed to say.

She wore frayed jeans and a faded Western plaid shirt and sat on a rawboned nag that looked like it was a week from the glue factory. She nudged the animal, and it took the few steps that put them knee to knee. He could see the spattering of freckles on her nose and the corn silk blond wisps at her temples that had escaped her ponytail.

"I'm so glad to see you!" she said, reaching

out to lay a hand on his thigh. "How long has it been?"

His flesh felt seared where she touched him. He reined his horse sideways to break the contact between them. "Since Labor Day."

"It seems like yesterday."

It seemed like forever. "How are you?" he asked.

Her smile broadened, creating an enchanting dimple in her left cheek. "Great! Counting down. After ten long years, just forty-two more days till I'm Mrs. Huckleberry Duncan."

Huck should have married her ten years ago, Colt thought. But Huck had followed where Colt led, and Colt had taken him off to fly jets. Jenny had stayed behind to raise her four younger brothers.

She was thirty-two now, Colt knew, because they were the same age. The freckles and the ponytail gave her a youthful appearance, but she wasn't a girl any longer. He loved the laugh crinkles that age had put at the corners of her eyes, but he hated the worry lines in her forehead, because he was at least partly responsible for putting them there.

Colt knew life hadn't been easy for Jenny. She'd been a nurse for her mother, who'd died of breast cancer when Jenny turned fifteen, and then mother to her four brothers. It was finally time for her chance at happily-ever-after. Only Huck was dead. "Jenny—"

"Come inside," she said, turning her horse toward the house. He kneed his horse and followed her.

There was no lush green lawn, no purple morning glories trailing up the porch rail, nothing to lessen the starkness of the faded, single-story, wood-frame ranch house that sat in the middle of the northwest Texas prairie. Jenny rode around back to the kitchen door, dismounted and tied the reins to a hitching post.

As she stepped up onto the sagging covered porch she said, "Let me get you something to drink. You must be thirsty after such a long, hot ride."

"A glass of iced tea would be nice," he said as he dismounted. "Are any of your brothers around?"

"I don't see much of Tyler or James or Sam, now that they're out on their own. Randy won't be home from school for another hour."

"Good," Colt said as he followed her into the

kitchen. "That'll give us some time alone to talk. How are things going?"

She shot him a mischievous grin as the screen door slammed behind him, then crossed to an old, round-cornered Coldspot refrigerator and pulled out a jar of iced tea. "It's a good thing Huck and I are finally getting hitched. If it weren't for the money he'll get from his trust fund when he marries, I'd have to turn the Double D over to the bank."

He hadn't expected her to be so honest. Maybe if she'd known about Huck, she wouldn't have been. "You're about to lose the Double D?"

"Not that I'd miss all the hard work, you understand, but this ranch has been in my family for so many generations, it'd be a shame to let it go."

"I didn't realize things had gotten so bad," he said.

"In forty-two days, all my troubles will be over. But enough about me. How'd you cut your chin? Fooling around with Huck, I'll bet. His last letter was full of—"

"Jenny, Huck is..." *Dead. Gone forever. Never coming back.* He swallowed hard.

"Huck is what?" she asked, her back to him as she reached for a glass from the cupboard above the sink.

"Huck died six days ago."

As she turned, her eyes wide, her mouth open in shocked surprise, the glass slipped from her hand and crashed to the floor. "No!" She pressed a clenched fist against her heart. "How?"

"I killed him."

All the blood left Jenny's head in a *whoosh*, and she swayed. She heard broken glass crunch under Colt's boots as he stepped close enough to catch her before her knees gave way and lifted her into his arms. She clung to his neck in a daze as he carried her into the bedroom and sat her on her four-poster bed.

He tried to stand up, to move away, but she clutched at him and wouldn't let go. "Stay here," she rasped past a throat that had swollen closed. "Explain."

She felt the tension in his shoulders. Felt the shudder that racked his frame as he settled down beside her. It took a long time for him to speak. She noticed the dust motes in the sunlight streaming through her bedroom window, the country tune about "friends in low places" on the radio that always played in the kitchen, the screech of a windmill that needed repair.

Everything was just as it had been a moment before. And nothing was the same.

Colt cleared his throat. "I knew Huck had been sick with some kind of flu bug the night before we were scheduled for a training flight. He said he was fine, but I should have known better and grounded him. Whatever illness he had affected his equilibrium."

She felt the slight shrug in Colt's shoulders before he said, "His wingtip brushed mine and..." He swallowed hard. "I bailed out. Huck didn't."

This isn't real. I'm dreaming. Colt isn't really sitting here beside me. He's with Huck, training jet pilots in Egypt.

She brushed a hand across the short dark hair at Colt's nape. *So soft.* She laid her cheek against his and felt the night's growth of beard. *So prickly.*

I can feel. So this must be real, she thought. As real as the tight band of pain that bound her chest and made it so hard to breathe.

Colt leaned back and looked into her face. She had never seen such agony in a human being's eyes. "I'm so sorry, Jenny. So very sorry. I should have done something. I should have—"

"I doubt you could've kept him on the

ground," she said in a shaky voice. "Huck was as crazy about flying as you are."

"I outranked him. I could've made it an order."

"You loved him too much to deny him anything he wanted," Jenny said simply. *Even me.*

Jenny didn't know where that last thought had come from, but she pushed it back into whatever dark hole it lived in. When they were kids, she'd known Colt Whitelaw had a crush on her. She'd even thought she might like to go out with him, if he asked. But Huck had liked her, too, and once Colt found out his best friend wanted her, he'd kept his distance. She had become—would always be—Huck's girl.

Only, now Huck was dead.

"Oh, God, Colt. I don't think I can bear it!" Jenny cried. "I don't think I can live without him!"

Many times over the past ten years she'd wondered what she would do if something happened to Huck, and he didn't come back to her. But he always did. Lately, like a combat veteran who counts the days until he can leave the battlefield, she'd counted the days until Huck would come home at last, and they'd be married and live happily ever after.

"It's not fair, Colt. It's not fair!" she wailed.

"I know," he said, rubbing her back soothingly. "I know."

The tears came then, spilling over in hot tracks down her face. And excruciating grief. She let out a howl of rage and pain. Throughout it all she clung to Colt, held tight to him, as though the mere presence of another human could keep her from hurting so much.

Jenny cried until her throat was raw, until she was too weak to lift a hand to wipe away the tears. It didn't take long for exhaustion to claim her. She was already worn-out from overwork and from too many sleepless nights spent worrying about how she was going to keep the ranch afloat on a sea of debt.

Jenny had pinned all her hopes for saving the ranch on the trust funds Huck would receive when they married. Now there would be no wedding. She hadn't merely lost the man she loved. She had also lost her home.

"What am I going to do, Colt?" she whispered. "How can I go on now?"

"I'm here, Jenny. I'll always be here for you," Colt murmured in her ear. "I love you, Jenny."

Jenny knew Colt hadn't meant it the way it sounded. Colt loved her the same way he loved

Huck. He'd been a good friend to her, always willing to pitch in to help with her brothers, something Huck never seemed to have the time to do. It had been easy to lean on Colt, to lay her troubles on his strong shoulders whenever Huck was too busy to lend a hand.

Jenny was suddenly aware of how tightly her arms were wrapped around Colt's neck. And in turn, how his hands were tangled in her hair.

"Colt, let go. Let me go!" She struggled to free herself from his embrace, from the illusion of safety, the awful, welcome comfort he offered.

He stared at her in confusion. "What's wrong, Jenny? Tell me what I can do to help."

"Nothing!" She took a deep, shuddering breath. "Get out, Colt. Go away. I don't want you here."

"Because I killed him?"

She should have let him believe that was why she wanted him gone. One look at his face, and she couldn't do it. "Oh, Colt, don't you see? It would be so easy to turn to you, to depend on you. That wouldn't be fair to you. No one can take Huck's place."

The color faded from his face, until there were only two blotches of red on his cheeks. "I feel responsible for what happened. The least I can do is make sure you don't lose the Double D. I've got money. Let me help you, Jenny.''

''You've always been there for me, and I love you for it. But money can't give me what I need most. Money can't bring Huck back.''

She saw him wince before he said, ''I miss him, too. He's going to leave a big hole in both our lives. But that doesn't change the fact this place needs a lot of work.''

The words stung. ''I've done the best I can.''

''I know that! But admit it, Jenny. You're going to need help holding on to this place.''

''I'm not admitting anything,'' she said stubbornly.

''You know Huck would want me to help you. Let me do this for him.''

She shook her head. ''I couldn't take your money, Colt. And I know how committed you are to flying jets. You'll be long gone before—''

''I've got up to sixty days' leave for recuperation. That's enough time to get some work done around here. I want to be here for you. Let me help you, Jenny. Please.''

She lifted her chin. ''I won't take charity, Colt. Even from you.''

''Don't be ridiculous. We're friends.''

"Friends. Not relations," Jenny said. "You have no obligation to help me, Colt."

His expression made it plain she'd offended him, but the only thing she had left was her pride. It was humiliating enough to be left at the altar— even if unwillingly—by Huck, without having to go begging for help to bail the Double D out of debt.

"You would have taken Huck's money," he said.

"He would have been my husband."

"Then marry me, Jenny, if that's what it takes. But damn it, let me help!"

The silence that followed his statement hung between them like temptation in the Garden of Eden. Jenny threaded her hands together to hide the fact they were trembling. "I know you must be hurting as badly as I am right now. But I won't take advantage of your grief—"

"Marry me, Jenny," he said, reaching out to separate her hands and hold them tightly in his. "On the day you would've married Huck. You should have a June wedding. You've waited long enough for it. You should walk down the aisle looking beautiful and knowing there's someone waiting who's willing to shoulder half the burden the rest of your life. We both know it's been your dream for a very long time. Let me make it come true. I owe you that much.''

She stared at Colt, unable to look away. He understood about lost dreams. He almost hadn't made good on his dream of becoming a jet pilot. She was the one who'd urged him to confront his parents and tell them he didn't want to be a rancher, that he wanted to fly jets. She'd also been the one who shared his joy when he realized his parents were happy for him, not disappointed as he'd expected them to be.

Colt knew better than anyone what it had meant to her to sacrifice her own dreams for the sake of her brothers. She looked down at Colt's hands— large and strong and capable—then up into his blue eyes, as red-rimmed as her own, and focused on her with such earnest entreaty that she found it hard to look away.

''Suppose we did marry, Colt. Then what? I can't follow you around the world the way Huck did. My home is here on the Double D. Are you willing to give up flying?''

She watched his Adam's apple bob as he swallowed. ''I can't.''

''Then I can't marry you.''

''Why not?''

"I won't trade one absentee partner for another," she said flatly. "I deserve better."

"Then take the damned money!"

"I don't need your charity."

"You sure as hell do!"

She yanked her hands free and said, "Get out, Colt. Leave. Go."

Colt stood his ground. "I owe Huck for not protecting him better. *I* stole your dream of happily ever after. Let me do this for you. For Huck. Marry me, Jenny."

Her chin quivered. She wanted so much to accept. It was the easy way out. But it was all wrong. "It wouldn't work, Colt."

"Why not?"

"For one thing, I don't love you."

"That doesn't matter."

She shook her head. "I can't believe you'd want to marry someone who—"

"Say yes, Jenny."

"What would people think—"

"To hell with what people think! At least you'd keep the Double D."

She stared at him, wanting to accept, but knowing such a marriage would be disastrous for both of them. "What happens when you fall in love with some other woman?"

"That isn't going to happen."

"How do you know?" she insisted.

He looked away, then turned back. "I gave my heart to someone a long time ago. There won't be anyone else."

"Oh." She was surprised by the jolt of jealousy she felt at his admission. Colt had often dated, but all the relationships had been brief. She'd never imagined him in love with some other woman. It had always been—only been— the three of them.

He reached for her hands again and held them tight. "If we don't get married, you're going to lose the only home you've ever known."

"Don't threaten me, Colt."

"It's the situation that's threatening."

"What about sex?" She lifted her eyes to his and saw the glint of humor there, despite everything. They'd always spoken freely to each other. She wasn't going to pull her punches now. "Or were you planning on a celibate marriage?"

"I wouldn't expect you to come to bed with me right away," he said, answering with as much care as the subject deserved. "But I'd expect our marriage to include physical relations eventually."

"I see." There had been a time—one time—

about six years ago when his hand had acciden-
tally brushed against her breast, and she'd felt her
insides draw up tight. They'd both been horribly
embarrassed, and it had never happened again.
But she'd been aware of him ever since in a way
she hadn't been before that day.

Still, it was unsettling to think of Colt having
the right to touch her as a man touched a woman.
It had always been forbidden, because she was
Huck's girl.

Huck is dead. Huck is never coming back.

"Say yes, Jenny."

She looked into Colt's eyes, searching for the
right answer. He looked so sure of himself. So
certain he was doing the right thing. She shuddered to think what people would say if she
showed up at church on the day she'd planned to
marry Huck with a substitute groom.

Then she imagined what it would be like if she
lost the ranch and had to go to work in town. Or
had to live as a maiden aunt in the home of one
of her brothers. And there were other considera-
tions, things Colt didn't know about and which
she could never tell him, that made her want to
cling to the only home she had ever known.

She needed time, but there wasn't much. Her
wedding date, June 20, was forty-two days away.

Ten days after that, another mortgage payment would come due. And she had no money to pay.

It was selfish to marry Colt under the circumstances. She was crazy even to consider the possibility. But it was the only solution she could see—at the moment—for her desperate situation.

"All right," she said at last. "I'll consider your proposal."

"When will I know your answer?"

Jenny managed a crooked smile. "As soon as I do."

Chapter 2

"Hey, Jenny, wake up!"

Jenny rolled over in bed and stared, bleary-eyed, at her eighteen-year-old brother, Randy. She'd spent most of the night crying and had only gotten to sleep as the sun was coming up. She groaned, rolled back over and mumbled, "Let me sleep."

"Colt's in the kitchen. He wants to know where he should start to work."

"Tell him..." She snuggled deeper into the covers, already drifting back to sleep.

"I've got to get moving, or I'm going to miss

the bus,'' Randy said. He gave her shoulder a shove and asked, ''What do you want me to tell Colt?''

''Tell him to go away,'' she said, covering her head with a pillow.

''Are you sure?''

''I'm sure.''

A persistent knock on her bedroom door drew her back to consciousness. She decided to ignore it. With any luck, Colt would take the hint and go away. She didn't want to see him. She didn't want to see anyone, looking and feeling like she did.

The door opened a crack and Colt said, ''Jenny? Are you awake?''

''How can I sleep with all these interruptions?'' she muttered irritably.

He took that as an invitation to come in, and a moment later she felt his presence by the bed. Which was when she realized she was wearing one of Randy's old football jerseys, and from what she could feel of the breeze from the open window on her bare thighs, it wasn't covering much.

She rolled onto her back, reaching for the sheet and blanket she must have kicked off and dragging them up to cover her. "What do you want, Colt?"

"I brought you a cup of coffee."

She squinted one eye open. "You expect me to drink that?"

"Why not?"

"It's likely to wake me up."

She saw the smile tilt his lips and the appearance of devastating twin dimples in his cheeks. "That's the general idea," he said. He seated himself beside her on the mattress and tousled her hair. "Come on, sleepyhead. Rise and shine."

She brushed his hand away. "I don't want to get up."

"Too bad," he said, sliding an arm under her shoulders to lift her up and sticking the coffee cup against her lips. "I need some marching orders, and you're the only one here to give them to me."

Against her better judgment, she took a sip of the scalding liquid. "Oh, Lord. That's strong enough that it might even work."

"I hope so," he said. "Because I'm planning to spend the day with you. I'll be glad to join you in bed, if that's what you'd prefer—"

She pushed the coffee away and scooted across the bed and out of it, tugging on the hem of the football jersey as she stood. "Give me a minute to get showered and dressed.'' She headed for her chest of drawers to retrieve clean underwear and socks.

''I'll leave the coffee here, in case you need another jolt,'' he said, setting the heavy ceramic mug on the end table beside her bed. ''Oh, and Jenny…''

She turned to look at him over her shoulder.

''If you're wearing Saturday on Wednesday, what happens when you get to the weekend?''

Jenny stared at him uncomprehendingly until she realized she was wearing panties her brother Randy had given her for Christmas that were labeled with the days of the week. ''So you'll only have to do laundry once every seven days,'' Randy had quipped.

She flushed with embarrassment at the thought of Colt glimpsing her underwear and snapped, ''Well, you could always barge into my bedroom again on Saturday to find out.''

''Touché,'' he said with a mock salute. ''I'll be waiting for you in the kitchen.''

The shower didn't help. Jenny's eyelids felt like they weighed a pound each, and they scratched her eyeballs every time she blinked. Her mouth was dry, her throat was sore, and her whole body ached. She was angry at being forced out of bed, but she didn't have the energy to fight.

"Your breakfast is on the table," Colt said when she arrived in the kitchen doorway.

She stared at the trestle table, where he'd put out a wrinkled cloth place mat and napkin—who had time to iron?—with a set of mix-matched silverware. He'd made scrambled eggs and toast and provided a cup of orange juice beside another cup of steaming coffee. She felt both grateful and resentful. "I could have made something for myself."

He pulled out the ladder-back chair at the head of the table and shoved her into it. "Sure you could. If you weren't dead on your feet. Eat."

"Are you going to join me?"

"I ate before I came over."

"Are you going to hover like that, watching every bite that goes into my mouth?"

He sat down in the chair to her right, then bounced up again. "Ouch!"

"Oh. Watch out for the nail in that chair."

"You've got nails sticking out of the kitchen chairs?"

She nodded, since her mouth was full of toast, then swallowed and answered, "My brothers' football buddies did a lot of leaning back in those chairs. Afraid they couldn't take the strain. Had to nail them back together."

"Why don't you fix them right?"

She shrugged. "No time. No money. No need." She gave him a beatific smile. "We know where the nails are."

"Any other sharp points I need to avoid—besides your barbed tongue?" he said. "If Huck were here—" Colt caught himself too late. The words were out, invoking Huck's presence.

Jenny felt the beginning of tears and blinked to fight them back. The fork fell from her hand and clattered onto her plate. She covered her face with her hands as an awful wave of grief rolled over her. "Why did this have to happen?"

She felt herself being lifted into Colt's arms, then felt him settling into the ladder-back chair in her stead. Her arms slid around his neck, and she hid her face against his throat. "I can't pretend this is just another day, Colt. Please, let me go back to bed. I want to sleep."

"When you wake up, he'll still be gone," Colt said soberly. "I know. I've had a week longer than you to deal with Huck's death. The only thing that helps is work."

"I'm so tired. I didn't sleep last night."

"If I let you sleep now, you'll be awake all

night tonight,'' Colt said. ''Then you'll be tired again tomorrow. Work now. Sleep later. Can you eat any more?''

She shook her head.

He forced her off his lap and onto her feet. ''Where do you suggest we start?'' he asked as he led her toward the back door.

''The cattle and horses need to be fed. I've got a few chickens that have probably laid eggs. The barn needs to be scraped and painted, the windmill in the west pasture isn't working, the back porch needs some new posts before it falls down, there's a leak in the roof that should be patched, I've got supplies to pick up in town—''

''Whoa!'' Colt said. ''We'll start with feeding the stock, then go pick up the supplies in town. Everything else can wait till we've both had a good night's sleep.''

Jenny looked at Colt—really looked at him. Judging by the dark circles under his eyes, he hadn't slept much, either. Perhaps he was right. Perhaps work was the best way to keep the demons at bay. But they both needed to rest, as well, and she'd just come up with a solution for the problem.

''The stock tank in the south pasture needs to be checked before the day is over,'' she said.

There happened to be a sprawling live oak near that tank. Once they got there, she'd tell Colt she needed to lie down for a little while in the shade and take a nap, and that she needed him to keep her company.

Even though Jenny was clearly exhausted, Colt had trouble keeping up with her throughout the day. The worst moments came when friends in town offered their condolences, along with memories of Huck that were so poignant they were painful.

At the feed store Mr. Brubaker said to Jenny, "Remember the time you and Huck and Colt climbed up and painted J.W. + H.D. = True Love on the town's water tower? If I ain't mistaken, it's still there."

Tom Tuttle at Tuttle's Hardware said to Colt, "Always knew one of you boys would get hisself killed flying them jets. Glad it weren't you, Colt. Sorry about Huck, Miss Jenny."

At the Stanton Hotel Café, Ida Mae Cooper said, "I recall the first time the three of you came in here together for a cherry soda. You were skinny as a beanpole in those days, Colt, and couldn't take your eyes off Huck's girl."

Colt shot a look at Jenny to see if she'd made

anything of Ida Mae's announcement, but she merely looked forlorn. She settled onto the red plastic seat of one of the several stools along the 1950s-era soda fountain and said, "No cherry soda for me, Ida Mae. Just strong black coffee."

Colt slid onto the stool next to her. "I'd like that cherry soda, Ida Mae."

Jenny glared at him as though he'd betrayed some trust, as though they couldn't have cherry sodas anymore because Huck wasn't there to have one with them.

He met her stare with sympathetic eyes. "Huck won't mind if we have a cherry soda, Jenny."

"Why does everybody keep talking about him?" she muttered. "Don't they understand it hurts?"

"They miss him, too," Colt said simply.

"Here's that soda, Colt," Ida Mae said. She eyed him speculatively and asked, "You planning to take care of Huck's girl, now that he's gone?"

The question was loud enough—and volatile enough—to bring conversation in the café to a halt. Colt felt everyone's eyes focus on him except Jenny's. She stared determinedly into her coffee cup. Ida Mae waited expectantly for an answer.

He took a deep breath and let it out. "Jenny

and I haven't made any plans beyond a memorial service a week from Friday. We'd like to invite everyone to come, if you'd be kind enough to pass along the word.''

''Sure, Colt,'' Ida Mae said, patting his hand. ''I can understand it wouldn't be a good idea to announce any more than that right now.''

Colt opened his mouth to tell her she was way off the mark and closed it again. A denial that anything was going on between him and Jenny would likely stir up more gossip than saying nothing.

It was late afternoon by the time they got back to the ranch. Jenny suggested they ride horseback to the stock tank. Apparently the spigot in the stock tank in her south pasture needed to be fixed. She was running on fumes by the time they got there. She dismounted and led her horse over to the aluminium tank for a drink, and Colt followed suit.

''Where's that faulty spigot?'' he asked, checking the spigot on the tank, which wasn't leaking as far as he could tell.

''I guess Randy must have fixed it. As long as we're here, we might as well take advantage of the shade.''

He eyed her suspiciously. "There never was anything wrong with that spigot, was there?"

"Nope."

There wasn't much grass growing in the shade of the sprawling live oak growing near the tank, but he watched Jenny find a patch of it and sit down. She patted the ground beside her and said, "Join me. It's time for a nap."

Colt sighed. "If we sleep now—"

"Sit down," she ordered, "and shut up."

That brought a snappy salute and a "Yes, ma'am." He dropped onto the ground beside her, suddenly feeling the results of too many haunted nights. He lay stretched out on his side, supporting his head with his palm. "Now what?"

She stretched out, facing him, and laid her cheek on her arm. "Lie down. I can't talk to you when your head's so far above mine."

Reluctantly, he came down off his elbow and laid his head on his arm, facing her. For a long time they stared at one another without speaking. He reached out to touch her cheek, to brush away a tear. "Don't cry, Jenny. I can't bear it when you cry."

"I can't help it. So many memories are shuffling around in my head."

"Mine, too," he admitted.

"Do you remember the last time we were here?"

He chuckled. "That isn't a day I'm likely to forget."

"I asked you if you'd teach me how to kiss," she said. "Do you remember what you said?"

"'No.' Or more precisely, 'Hell no!'"

Her eyes lit with laughter, and her lips curled up at the corners. "I begged until you relented, because I didn't want my first kiss with Huck to go awry."

"Craziest thing I've ever done in my life," he said. "Teaching my best friend's girl how to kiss."

"I wanted to know where my hands should go and where he'd put his hands."

"All over you," Colt muttered, "if he could get away with it."

He heard Jenny's laugh, a sound like a burbling brook, and realized it had been a very long time since he'd heard anything so pleasing. He smiled at her and let the memory of that long-ago day wash over him.

They'd ridden horseback to the stock tank, because she'd said she had something important to discuss with him in private. While their horses had taken a drink, she'd popped the question. After his refusal, she'd gone to work convincing him.

"You have to help me, Colt," she pleaded. "My first kiss with Huck has to be perfect, because I'll be remembering it the rest of my life. I don't want anything to go wrong."

"That's what makes the first kiss memorable," he argued. "Things go wrong."

She shook her head, her long blond hair shimmering like corn silk in the sunlight. "Please. Do this for me."

He'd been aware of his attraction to Jenny from the first moment he'd looked into her bluer-than-blue eyes, but Huck had been the first one to speak of her. Colt had felt honor-bound to wait and see if things developed between Jenny and Huck before he made his move. To his dismay, Jenny had said yes to Huck's overtures.

More than once Colt had thought of trying to steal Jenny away from Huck. But he knew in his heart that he couldn't live with himself if he betrayed his friend like that. It would taint what he felt for Jenny. So he went along and remained a good friend to both of them.

See how virtue had been rewarded? Jenny wanted him to kiss her first!

More than anything in the world he wanted to

hold Jenny Wright in his arms. But he had panicked when she came up with the harebrained notion that he should teach her to kiss. Would she be able to tell from his kiss how much he liked her? What if he got carried away and did something that scared her?

"I'll do this on one condition," he conceded at last.

"Anything," she promptly agreed.

"You never *ever* tell Huck."

"Why not?"

"Believe me, he wouldn't understand."

"Why not?"

"It's a guy thing," he said. "Promise," he insisted.

She crossed her heart with her forefinger. "Cross my heart and hope to die, stick a needle in my eye."

"I guess that'll do," he said.

"Okay, I'm ready," she said.

He rubbed his sweaty palms on the thighs of his jeans. "I'm not. I have no idea where to start."

"Why not put your arms around me?" she suggested.

He reached forward at the same time she

reached up, and their arms knocked into each other.

"Oops."

"Sorry."

"See what I mean?" she said, wrinkling her nose. "I guess I'll need to stand still while Huck puts his arms around me. You want to try again?"

"Sure." He slid his left arm around her waist and tugged her toward him. But she didn't move.

She looked up at him in confusion. "What?"

"You need to take a step to get closer," he instructed. He applied pressure to her back again, and this time she responded by closing the distance between them until her breasts were a hairsbreadth from his chest.

"Is this close enough?"

There was no spit left in his mouth, and he croaked, "Yeah. That's probably close enough."

She looked up expectantly. "Now what?"

"Huck will probably put his hand on your head to angle it in the right direction."

"Okay. I'm ready. Go ahead."

He'd only intended to palm her head with his hand, but somehow his fingers got tangled in her hair. "You've got really soft hair," he murmured.

He saw her cheeks pinken. "Thank you. Do you think Huck will do what you're doing? I mean, slide his fingers through my hair like that?''

''Why do you ask?''

She gave a negligent shrug. ''It feels good.''

Colt reminded himself he was holding Huck's girl. ''He might run his hands through your hair. But don't worry if he doesn't. Every guy is different.''

''Okay. Now what?''

''I'm a little taller than Huck, so some of what I'm saying might need to be adjusted for height,'' he said, trying to remain objective. He reminded himself to keep his hips apart from hers, so she wouldn't discover that his body was reacting as though this game of hers was the real thing. ''I can bend down to you, or you can come up on tiptoe to reach me,'' he explained.

''Or Huck and I could move toward each other—me up, him down.'' She frowned thoughtfully. ''It would be easier if I had my hands on Huck's shoulders. When should I do that?''

''Can you get your arms up between mine?'' he asked.

She slowly slid her hands up his chest and around his neck. ''How's that?''

His heart felt like a caged bird, racketing around inside his ribs. ''That's fine,'' he managed to rasp. "Now, you slide up on tiptoe, and I'll lower my head."

As she came up on tiptoe she lost her balance. She grabbed him around the neck, and his arm tightened around her, pressing her soft, warm breasts against his chest. He met her startled gaze and said, "Are you all right?"

"I think so. Whew! See why I need the practice? Who knew there were so many pitfalls to a simple kiss?"

He started to push her away, but she clung to his neck and said, "Let's keep going. What is Huck likely to do next?"

Kiss you till he can't see straight, Colt thought. But he said, "Let's see how good you are at hitting a target."

She grinned. "You mean, can I find his lips with mine?"

"Give it a shot."

Her fingertips at his nape urged his head down toward hers. He kept his eyes locked with hers until he couldn't bear the excitement anymore, then closed his eyes and waited for her lips to touch his. When they didn't, he opened his eyes to find her staring at him, her brow furrowed. "What's wrong?" he asked.

"I shouldn't be the one doing the kissing," she said. "Huck will want to be the aggressor."

"The *aggressor?*" Colt said.

"You know, the wolf stalking his prey, the Neanderthal dragging his woman back to his cave."

"Where do women get these ideas?" he said, shaking his head.

"From men," she said with a grin. "Admit it. Men like to make the first move. What would Huck think if *I* kissed *him* first?"

"That you liked him," Colt said flatly.

She looked thoughtful, then shook her head. "I'm an old-fashioned girl. Huck has to be the one to kiss first."

Which meant *he* had to kiss *her* first, Colt realized. "Let's get this over with." He leaned down, but before he could kiss her, she put her fingertips to his lips. "What's wrong now?" he asked in exasperation.

"Huck wouldn't do it like that."

"Like what?"

"In a big hurry."

"He might."

"He'll take his time. He'll make it count. He'll know how important this first kiss is. Do it right," she said.

"Do it right?" he muttered. "I'll do it right. Watch me *do it right.*"

He threaded his fingers through her hair again, then used his hold to angle her head back so her lips were aimed up at his. He lowered his head slowly, keeping his eyes on hers, *making it count.* This was the first time he was going to kiss the girl he loved. And he wanted her to know how important this moment was.

He felt a shock as their lips touched, and backed off to stare at her. She looked dazed. He lowered his mouth over hers a second time, feeling the firmness of her lips and then the supple give as she responded to him. He pressed a little harder and felt her hands slide into his hair.

He wanted to taste her, so he teased his tongue along the edge of her lips, waiting for her to open to him.

She broke the kiss abruptly and leaned back to stare at him, her pupils dilated, her lips wet, her body trembling. "What were you doing with your tongue?"

"I was tasting you."

"Will Huck want to do that?"

"I would if I were him," he said simply.

"Why?"

"Because it feels good."

"It makes me feel funny inside." She laughed nervously and said, "Look at me. I'm shaking."

"You want to quit?"

She hesitated, then shook her head. "I'd better practice if I'm going to get it right with Huck. I'm ready now, if you want to try again."

He leaned down and touched her mouth lightly with his once, and then again, teasing kisses that urged her to accept what was coming. He felt her lips become less rigid, felt them ease apart as his tongue slid along the crease, heard her moan as his tongue slid inside her mouth. Her hands clutched his hair as her hips arched instinctively into his.

Then she was jerking herself away and backing up, her hand rubbing at her mouth, her eyes wide, her body trembling. "Ohmigod. What am I doing? What are we doing?"

He stood without moving. He saw her eyes drop to the thick ridge along the zipper of his jeans and knew what had frightened her. But that was going to happen to Huck, too. She might as well know it now, as later.

"It's all right," he said in a matter-of-fact voice. "What happened to you—to us—is normal. It's what happens between a man and a woman when they kiss. I'm sorry if I scared you."

"Will Huck—? Of course he will," she said, thrusting an agitated hand through her hair. "I had no idea it would be like that. So...powerful. You stop thinking, you stop being a rational person, your body just sort of...explodes."

"Yeah," he said, huffing out a breath of air. "That pretty well describes it."

She looked up at him earnestly and said, "Thanks, Colt. I'm going to be forever in your debt. There aren't many friends who'd be willing to help out like this."

"Anytime," he said.

Colt became aware of a horse ripping up grass with his teeth near his head and opened his eyes, reluctantly letting go of the memory. He leaned up on his elbow and looked down at Jenny. She was sound asleep, her breathing quiet and even. He wondered if her first kiss with Huck had been everything she'd hoped. He'd never asked, and she'd never spoken about it.

"This is for you from Huck," he murmured as he leaned over and gently touched her lips with his. "A kiss good-bye."

Chapter 3

Too late, Jenny realized the trip to the stock tank in the south pasture had been a big mistake. It reminded her of something she'd chosen to forget: Her "first kiss" with Huck had come nowhere close to arousing in her the emotions of her "practice kiss" with Colt.

She had blamed the disturbing difference on the fact a girl could only get her "first kiss" once, and due to her own stupidity, she'd had her first kiss with the wrong man. It was only natural that her "second kiss" wasn't quite so exciting. Of course she'd loved Huck's kisses, because she'd loved Huck. But the spark she'd felt with Colt, that delicious electricity—that total loss of shame and scruples—had never occurred with Huck.

Since lying beside Colt yesterday in the shade of the live oak, those bewitching memories had made their insidious way back into her consciousness. Jenny's mind had begun replaying the moment when Colt's lips first touched hers, when his tongue first traced the seam of her mouth, when she first tasted him.

It was simple curiosity, she told herself, that made her wonder if that electricity had merely been the result of a "first kiss," or whether it would happen if they kissed again. She was ashamed of herself for what she was thinking, but she couldn't get the idea out of her head.

What if Colt could make her feel more than Huck ever had? What if she hadn't been kissed first by the wrong man? What if she'd been engaged to him?

That thought was too painful to face, since it would've meant she'd wasted ten years of her life—and Huck's. If she was going to have second thoughts, she should've had them a long time ago.

When? a voice asked. *After Huck was graduated from the Air Force Academy, he was never around for more than a few days at a time. You were busy with your brothers. You barely had time to make school lunches, let alone worry about your love life. It was convenient for both of you to be "in love." There was no time to stop and think. Until now.*

Jenny supposed everyone went through this sort of soul-searching at the time of such a significant loss. But she wasn't getting the answers she'd expected. She found her thoughts—and her eyes—focused more and more on Colt.

Sunday she went to church and surrounded herself protectively with her brothers. If anyone could keep Colt at a distance, it was Sam and Tyler and James and Randy. The idiot man simply shook each brother's hand as he moved past them into the pew and settled himself right beside her. It was a tight squeeze, because the pews weren't that large, and Sam wouldn't move over at first.

Colt finally speared Sam with a look that sent him scooting. "Hi, Jenny," he said. "I thought you might want company this first Sunday without Huck."

What were her brothers? Sliced baloney? With four brothers at her side, why did Colt think she needed him?

He shared a hymnal with her and sang the familiar refrains in a strong baritone voice that sent shivers down her spine. She found herself wondering how he would sound whispering love words in her ear.

It wasn't until after church, when everyone crowded around, that she conceded she was grateful for Colt's presence. Her brothers hovered, but they were clearly uncomfortable responding to the offers of condolence.

Colt slid an arm around her waist to hold her close enough that their hips occasionally bumped. He shook hands with the men and pulled several blue-haired old ladies close enough to kiss their cheeks. As though he coped with such emergencies every day, he enfolded Randy in a one-armed embrace when her brother unexpectedly broke into tears.

Colt didn't even let go when Sam and Tyler and James came one at a time to bid her goodbye. They were all big, tall men, like their father had been. Sam and Tyler were dark-haired and brown-eyed, while James had green eyes and chestnut hair. They were dressed in suits, but that didn't make them look particularly civilized. They might have been wolves from a free-roaming pack.

They would have intimidated a lesser man. Colt met them without backing off, staring down Sam when he eyed the way Colt's arm was wrapped around her.

"You look like hell," Sam said to her. "Get some sleep."

"Thanks a lot, Sam," she replied, making a face at him. "I'm trying."

"Try harder," Sam said, chucking her gently under the chin. It wasn't a large gesture of affection, but it was the equivalent of a bear hug from Sam. She met his gaze and saw the worry there and smiled to reassure him. "I'll be fine, Sam."

He turned to Colt and said, "I guess we won't be seeing as much of you, now that Huck's gone."

Jenny held her breath, waiting for Colt to tell Sam that he'd offered to marry her.

Colt shot her a quick look, but all he said was, "I'll be around for a while."

Sam was followed by Tyler, who brushed his knuckles against her cheek and said, "Take care of yourself, sis." He gave Colt a hard look and said, "You be careful now."

Jenny wasn't sure whether it was an admonition to be careful flying jets, or whether Tyler was warning Colt to watch his step around her.

Colt replied, "I'm always careful."

James kissed her brow and whispered, "God

works in mysterious ways. We can't know what he has planned for us.''

She felt a moment of panic, wondering if James had somehow surmised her unsettling daydreams about Colt. But when she met his gaze, he only looked sad and sympathetic.

''Where's Randy?'' Colt asked when her other brothers had all taken their leave.

Jenny looked around the church hall and saw Randy standing in a crowd of teenagers. ''He's over there by the Butler twins, Faith and Hope.''

''Let's go get him. My mom has invited the two of you to Sunday dinner at Hawk's Pride.''

She freed herself at last from Colt's embrace and turned to face him, her hands knotted to keep him from reaching for them. ''I can't go, Colt.''

''Why not?''

''I couldn't face your parents. Not when I haven't made up my mind yet whether I'm going to marry you.''

''They don't know about my proposal,'' Colt said.

''*I* know about it. I wouldn't feel comfortable. Please, Colt. Give them my regrets.''

''I'll tell them now and follow you home. We can pick up something to have for dinner on the way.''

Jenny stared after him as he stalked off, wondering how the situation had gotten so completely out of her control. Her attraction for Colt seemed to be growing stronger by the minute—along with her guilt over the rapidity with which she seemed to be transferring her affections from one man to another.

All I have to do is spend a little more time with Colt, and his faults will begin to show, Jenny thought as she waited for Colt to return.

She and Colt and Randy spent the afternoon sitting on the floor around the coffee table in the living room playing a game of Scrabble. She found herself fascinated by Colt's hands. Blue veins were prominent in the backs of his hands, and his knuckles bore tiny tufts of black hair. His nails were clean and cut bluntly, and his fingers were long and thick, with callused pads. She imagined what it might feel like if he slid one inside her. And blushed hotly.

"You look kinda warm, Jenny," Randy said. "You want me to open another window?"

She kept her eyes on the table. "That's a good idea. What's the score?" she asked,

"Colt's beating the pants off you," Randy said.

Jenny closed her eyes and bit her lip to stop the moan from escaping her throat. She'd had a flashing mental image of Colt tearing off her white cotton underwear—she was wearing Tuesday on Sunday. His hand lay on the table right beside hers, large and strong.

"You have such a big, strong...vocabulary," Jenny said, catching herself at the last moment.

"Thanks," Colt said. "I think it's my turn."

"'Xenophile'?" Randy questioned suspiciously as Colt laid down the *x* and *e* before Randy's two-letter word and then the *p-h-i-l-e*. "What's it mean?"

"Someone who's attracted to foreign things."

"Like eels and caviar?" Randy asked.

"Like veiled women," Colt quipped, leering at Jenny.

Jenny picked up a doilie that was covering a hole in the arm of the couch upholstery, held it across her nose and mouth and batted her eyelashes. "Take me away, O Sheikh of Araby!" she said melodramatically.

Randy laughed. "I give up. You win, Colt. Game's over."

"Not quite yet," Colt said. He rose and did a swami's bow toward Jenny. "Your wish is my command, O Maiden of the East."

"Is that East *Texas*, suh?" Jenny said with a

deep Southern accent, once again batting her
lashes.

Colt grabbed a patterned cotton blanket that
was draped across the couch—hiding another
worn bit of upholstery—and threw it over Jenny's
head as though he were really a sheikh come to
kidnap her. While she was laughing uncontrolla-
bly, he whisked her up over his shoulder, hauled
her into her bedroom and threw her onto the four-
poster.

Jenny was still giggling when Colt pulled the
blanket off her face. "I don't know when I've had
such a good time. Thanks, Colt. I—"

She stopped talking and stared at him. When
had he gotten so handsome? Had his cheekbones
always been so sharp? His lips so full and wide?
She wasn't aware of licking her lips until she
heard Colt's sharp intake of air.

She met his gaze and caught a glimpse of
something—what?—before his eyes were shut-
tered.

"Get some rest," he said as he backed his way
out of the room. "I'll see you tomorrow."

No faults, she thought with a groan. *Not one
damn fault.*

She dreamed of a woman in flowing, see-
through silks being carried across the desert by a

turbanned sheikh riding a magnificent Arabian stallion. They were running from something, but they couldn't escape because the horse kept getting bogged down in the sand. She looked up and realized a jet was falling out of the sky, about to crash right on top of their heads.

Jenny woke up before the jet hit the ground. She sat up in bed breathing hard and staring at the rising sun, wondering how she could have been laughing and playing such games last night when Huck was never coming back.

On Monday, Colt put new shingles on the leaky roof. Shirtless. His broad chest was covered in thick, dark curls. She couldn't help making the comparison to sandy-haired Huck, who'd had very little chest hair and not nearly so much muscle. Colt's shoulders bunched and relaxed as the hammer rose and fell.

She stood mesmerized as a single drop of sweat slid down the center of his back until it met his denim jeans. She found herself fascinated by the way the worn blue cloth molded his buttocks.

No faults there, either, she conceded.

Tuesday, Colt dug postholes to repair the rotten gate on the corral. "They used to punish cowboys with this job in the old days," he said, his eyes twinkling.

She found herself entranced by his gaze, unable to look away. His eyes reminded her of sapphires, except they weren't cold, like stone, but warm and welcoming. She noticed the spray of lines at the corners of his eyes where the sun had weathered his skin and realized he wasn't a boy anymore. He was a grown man. A very attractive grown man.

On Wednesday, she sat with Colt on the back porch after supper to drink a chocolate milkshake. She watched his Adam's apple bob as he leaned his head back and swallowed down the thick ice cream. Her body drew up tight as his tongue slipped out to lick the last of the milky chocolate off his upper lip.

"Are you going to drink the rest of that?" he asked, pointing to her half-finished shake.

She held out her frosty glass and said, "Help yourself."

He put his lips on the edge of the glass where hers had been and watched her as he took a sip. Tasting chocolate. Tasting her.

Her mouth went dry with desire.

She leaped up without excusing herself and ran inside, letting the screen door slam behind her, not stopping until she'd reached her bedroom. She closed the door and leaned back against it, aware of her pounding heart and the ache deep inside her.

She wanted him. It was sinful how much she wanted him. And they hadn't even had the memorial service for Huck.

What's wrong with me? How can I be having such thoughts about Colt when it's Huck I love…loved?

Several loud knocks on the door made her skitter away toward the center of the room. "Who's there?"

"It's me, Colt. Are you all right?"

"No, I'm not all right!" she said. *There's something terribly wrong with me. I can't help thinking of you. Wanting you.*

"Open the door, Jenny, and talk to me. I know something's been troubling you these past few days. I'd like to help."

"Go away, Colt." *Don't you understand? You're the problem!*

"Are you upset about that marriage proposal?"

Jenny grabbed at the excuse he'd offered. "It's been on my mind."

"Look, there's no need for you to decide about marriage right away. If you need money for the mortgage payment, I'll provide it, no matter what."

She yanked the door open. "I thought we agreed I can't take your money, Colt."

"It's no big deal, Jenny."

"It is to me."

He reached out and clasped her free hand in his. She felt the calluses on his fingertips, remembered what she'd been imagining his hands doing and jerked her hand out of his. "This isn't going to work!" she said desperately. "You can't keep coming here every day, Colt."

"Why not?"

"It's indecent!"

"Indecent? What the hell are you talking about?"

"I'm practically a widow—"

"You and Huck were never married. And in case you've forgotten, he was my friend, too."

Jenny stared at him, stricken. It wasn't Colt's fault she was attracted to him. *There's nothing wrong with him. I'm the one who's flawed.*

"I'm sorry," she said.

"If you really don't want me here, I'll stay away," he offered.

"No. Come tomorrow."

On Thursday, Jenny sent Colt out to repair a stall door in the barn while she stripped the beds, did the laundry and mopped the floors. She figured the distance would be good for both of them. If she wasn't forced to look at Colt all day, she was sure she wouldn't find herself thinking about him so much.

By noon she conceded that "absence makes the heart grow fonder." She went hunting for Colt to tell him lunch was ready, because that was the best excuse she'd been able to come up with to go after him.

"Colt? Are you out here?"

"Up here," Colt called down from the loft.

"Lunch is ready," Jenny said.

"Come on up here a minute. There's something I want to show you."

Jenny hesitated, then started up the ladder. When she reached the top, Colt grabbed her under the arms and lifted her the rest of the way up. She felt his touch all the way to her core. She was still standing where he'd left her when he turned and walked toward the corner of the loft.

"Over here," he said, going down on one knee.

Jenny told her feet to move, and they obediently headed in Colt's direction. She knelt beside him to look at what had been hidden in a bed of straw in the corner, then turned to share a smile with him. "They're adorable."

"Their eyes are still closed. They can't be more than a few days old."

"Six of them," Jenny said, counting the nursing kittens. "Jezebel, I didn't even know you'd been courting," she chided the mother cat.

Jezebel purred under Jenny's stroking.

Jenny looked at Colt and realized he was staring at her hand. His eyes locked with hers, his gaze heavy-lidded, his lips full and rigid. She stopped stroking the cat and rose abruptly.

"That stew is going to burn—"

Colt rose and grabbed her arm to keep her from fleeing. "You feel it, too."

She turned to him, her eyes wide with fright. "What are you talking about?"

"Don't bother pretending, Jenny. I've felt your eyes on me all week. I haven't been able to zip my damn jeans in the morning, thinking about you watching me."

She didn't know what to say, so she didn't say anything. A trickle of sweat tickled its way down her back. A fly buzzed, and one of the kittens mewed.

Colt let go of her and shoved his hand through his hair. "I'm afraid I don't know the proper etiquette for this situation. I suppose I should have kept on pretending right along with you, Jenny. But that wouldn't be fair to either of us."

"I can't help it," Jenny said quietly. She searched his face, saw the flare of heat in his eyes and responded to it.

"Neither can I," he replied in a hoarse voice.

"What are we going to do?"

"I could stay away."

"That wouldn't change how I feel," Jenny said. "I wonder if an experiment would help."

"What kind of experiment?" Colt said warily.

"I think maybe you should kiss me."

Colt stared at her. "What will that accomplish?"

She gave a shuddering sigh. "I'm not sure. Maybe nothing."

Colt shook his head and grinned wryly. "I feel like a fifteen-year-old kid again. How do you want to do this?"

She cocked a brow. "You're the expert, as I recall."

"All right. Come here."

As he slipped his arm around her waist, her hands slid up his chest and around his neck. He pulled the rubber band out of her ponytail and threaded his hand into her hair, angling her head for his kiss. She rose a little on tiptoe as his head lowered toward hers. She closed her eyes as his mouth covered hers.

Jenny waited with bated breath as Colt's lips pressed against hers, soft and a little damp. A frisson chased up her spine as his tongue teased the seam of her lips. She opened her mouth eagerly, and his tongue slipped inside. Without any warning, without any urging, her hips rocked into the cradle of his thighs, and she rode the hard ridge that promised so much pleasure.

So much feeling. So much heat. So much more than she had ever felt with Huck.

Jenny sobbed against Colt's mouth.

He put his hands on her shoulders and shoved her away. "Jenny?"

She sobbed again, unable to admit the horrible discovery she'd made. Her eyes blurred with tears until she could no longer see the stark look in his eyes.

He pulled her close, pressing her face against his chest and rubbing her scalp. "I guess your experiment didn't work," he said. "I'm sorry. What happens now?"

There were so many things Colt didn't know. So many things she couldn't tell him. A clock was ticking. She didn't have the luxury of waiting until the guilt was gone. They'd already lost so much time. She didn't want to lose any more. This physical thing between them wasn't love, but she was smart enough to know it was something very special. It didn't happen all the time. It hadn't happened between her and Huck.

Jenny didn't know how long they'd been standing in the loft before she became aware of Colt's heart thudding beneath her ear, of his hand stroking her hair, of his strength wrapped around her frailty. "I have—" She cleared the frog from her throat. "I have a favor to ask."

"Name it," Colt said.

She leaned back and laid her hand on his cheek. "Will you marry me?"

"Are you sure that's what you want?"

"It's the practical thing to do. Considering…everything."

Colt pulled her back into his arms. "It's been awful damned tough on you, hasn't it? All right, we'll do the practical thing and get married."

"In June," she said. "When I would have married Huck."

"Right. I'll just step up to the altar in place of my best friend and say 'I do.' Do you suppose anyone will notice?"

"I will," she said quietly.

Chapter 4

"I'm moving in with Jenny Wright tomorrow," Colt announced to his family at supper that evening.

The astonished faces of his brothers and sisters, the gasp from his mother and the frown on his father's face all demanded an explanation. "We're getting married in June," he said baldly, "on the day Jenny would have married Huck. I'm moving in so I'll be able to finish the repairs that need to be made at the Double D before my leave is over."

"I knew you wanted her for yourself," Jake

said in disgust. "But Huck isn't even cold in his grave!"

Colt was out of his seat and reaching for his brother before the last words were out of his mouth. Their father intervened, catching Colt around the chest and holding him back, while Rabb and Avery did the same with Jake.

Colt's hands were fisted at his sides, and his face was flushed with rage. "Take it back, Jake."

"It's the truth," Jake said.

"Did Jenny agree to this?" his mother asked.

Colt tried to answer, but when he couldn't get words past the knot in his throat, just nodded.

"You can't marry Jenny!" Frannie exclaimed. "She's Huck's girl."

Colt felt his stomach roll. They were only saying what everyone else in town would say when they heard what he and Jenny had decided. He'd hoped for more understanding from his family, but he didn't give a damn whether he got it or not. He was going to marry Jenny. "My mind is made up," he said.

"What's the rush?" Avery asked.

"Jenny's going to lose the Double D unless she gets some quick financial help. Marriage is the best security I can offer her."

"I knew she was having trouble making ends

meet,'' his father said. ''Are you sure marriage is
the best solution to the problem?''

Colt shook himself free. ''Huck was my best
friend. I owe Jenny whatever help I can give
her.''

''Everybody sit down, please,'' his mother
said. ''Let's discuss this calmly and rationally.''

Rabb and Avery let Jake go, and he sat down.
Colt was too agitated to rejoin his family at the
table. ''Look,'' he said. ''There's really nothing
to discuss. Jenny and I are getting married, and
nothing anybody says is going to stop us.''

''We're not trying—''

Colt interrupted his father. ''I'm sorry, Dad. I
think it'll be more comfortable for everybody if I
just move in with Jenny tonight.'' He turned and
headed for his bedroom to pack.

He heard a knock at the door a moment later.
He should have known they wouldn't let him go
without another lecture. When he opened the
door, he found Jenny standing there.

''What are you doing here?''

''I needed to talk to you.''

He looked out into the hall, which was surprisingly empty of his parents and siblings, then
dragged her inside and closed the door behind her.
''What's going on?''

"You tell me," she said. "I sneaked in through the patio door and heard a lot of yelling in the dining room."

His lips flattened. "My family isn't exactly thrilled at my upcoming nuptials."

"Neither is mine," she said. "I called my brothers and told them what we'd decided, and they all came over to try to talk me out of it. Sam was furious. He accused me of carrying on with you all these years. I couldn't believe the things he said. I..." She took a shuddering breath. "It was horrible."

He saw the anguish in her eyes and pulled her into his arms. "I know," he said. "Jake accused me of jumping the gun, too."

"We can't go through with this, Colt."

His heart lurched. He couldn't give her up now. Wouldn't give her up. Even if he was only going to have her for a matter of weeks before he left to return to Egypt.

"Do these second thoughts have anything to do with what happened in the loft? Because—"

She covered his mouth with her hand to silence him. "It's not that. It's the opposition from both our families. I don't want to be at war with my brothers, and I know you love your family as

much as I love mine. How can we do this to
them?"

"What other choice do we have?"

"I can give up the ranch and move into town."

"You don't want to do that."

She sighed. "No, I don't."

"Our families have been told, and we're both
still walking and talking. I'd say the worst is
over."

"Is it?" she asked, looking up at him.

"In fifty years, I guarantee you nobody will
remember how we ended up married."

She managed a wobbly smile, and Colt felt his
heart begin to thump a little harder. He was grateful he no longer had to hide his physical attraction
to her, but a larger problem remained. Colt was
in love with Jenny. It complicated everything; it
didn't change anything. The only way to help her
was to marry her. Unless she'd take money from
him without the connection.

"If you really think marriage is a bad idea, let
me make you a loan," he said. "I can work for
you at the Double D until my leave is up."

She shook her head. "I couldn't borrow as
much money from you as it would take to put the
ranch back on sound footing. I'd never be able to

pay it all back. And I'm going to need help on the Double D for a very long time. A lifetime.''

''Then marry me, Jenny. Huck wouldn't want you to lose the ranch. Huck would kill me if I let you lose the ranch.''

The attempt at humor brought a fleeting smile to her lips. She brushed her fingertips across the front of his shirt, pressing away a wrinkle and causing his body to tense beneath her hand. He held himself perfectly still, loving the touch, wanting it, yet aware of how precarious their relationship was precisely because of their fierce attraction to each other.

Her hand paused near his heart, and he wondered if she could feel it jumping in response to her touch. She looked deep into his eyes, searching, he supposed, for whatever reservations she might find there. There were none. At least none he was willing to let her see.

Finally she said, ''All right, Colt. If you're willing to go through with this marriage despite the opposition from our families, I'll go along.''

''There is one thing,'' he said.

''What?'' she asked.

''I told my family I was moving in with you tonight.''

She shook her head in disbelief. ''Colt—''

"I guess I can stay at a hotel in town."

"You can sleep in one of my brothers' rooms."

"Is Randy going to give you any trouble about this?"

"If he does, he can do his own cooking and laundry until he goes off to college." She laid her head on his chest. "I hope we're doing the right thing."

"As long as we're both convinced it's the right thing, then it is," he said with a certainty he wasn't feeling inside. He had plenty of fears.

What if she never learns to love me? What if I can't make her happy?

There were bound to be problems, especially since he would be away in the Air Force. And there was going to be talk. But together they could weather the storm. And Jenny would be his at last.

He'd imagined making love to her a thousand times over the years he'd known her. But that was all he'd ever done. Imagine. He'd never thought his dreams would come true. Soon he'd have the right to hold her naked in his arms. To put himself inside her. He wanted to make love to her. More important, he wanted her love.

There isn't enough time, a voice warned. *You've got less than sixty days before you have*

*to report back for duty in Egypt. Sixty days isn't
much time to woo a grieving woman.*

He had to find a way. He had to find the time.

Colt smoothed his hand over Jenny's hair with
a sense of wonder. He was going to be sleeping
in a room nearby her tonight. In a little more than
a month he'd have the right to lie beside her.

*I'm sorry, Huck, but she needs me. I know you
wouldn't want her to be alone. And I love her.*

"How did you get here tonight?" he asked.

"I drove Old Nellie."

Old Nellie was a rusted-out '56 Chevy pickup.
"If you'll give me a minute to finish packing, I'll
ride back with you," Colt said.

The door opened without anyone knocking, and
Colt found himself staring at his brother Jake over
Jenny's head. His arms were around her—in com-
fort—just as her arms held tight to him.

Jake took one look, and his eyes narrowed. "I
came here to apologize. Looks like I was right all
along."

Colt stared his brother down. He'd done nothing wrong. He'd loved Jenny for years, but he'd
never by word or deed done anything to suggest
to her how he felt. If Huck had come home and
married her, he would have lived his life without

her ever knowing he cared. He'd done nothing that required an apology. "Get out, Jake, and leave us alone."

"If alone is what you want, little brother, alone is what you'll get!" Jake backed out, slamming the door behind him.

Colt heaved a gusty sigh. "Damn it all to hell."

"Colt, if this marriage is going to cause problems—"

Colt laid his fingertips against Jenny's lips to silence her and felt himself quiver at that small touch. "Jake only sees things in black and white. He'll get over it—in fifty years or so."

He saw her try to smile…and fail.

"Cheer up," he said, tipping her chin up so he could look into her eyes. "The cavalry is riding to the rescue."

She stepped back, away from his touch. "Thanks, Colt. The least I can do is help you pack. Where do you want to start?"

It didn't take long to pack his things. He hadn't brought much with him from Egypt. He grabbed the small bag and headed down the hall.

His mother was waiting for him there.

"Hello, Jenny," she said, reaching out for Jenny's hand. "I'm very happy for you both."

"Thank you, Mrs. Whitelaw," Jenny replied.

The two women held hands for a moment before his mother turned to him. She didn't say anything, just stared, her heart back in her eyes.

"I'm sorry, Mom," he said at last. "I can't stay here."

She smiled bravely. "I know. I just wish..." She turned quickly back to Jenny and gave her a hug. "I wish you both the best." Then she reached up to touch his cheek. "Take care of yourself, Colt. Don't be a stranger."

She'd made no comment about whether they all planned to attend the wedding next month. He opened his mouth to ask and shut it again. It was better to let sleeping dogs lie.

Jenny slipped behind the wheel of the pickup as he threw his bag into the rusted-out truck bed. He settled onto the torn passenger seat, and she released the clutch and stepped on the gas.

The short drive from his home to hers had never seemed so long. He listened to the noisy rattle in the dash. The *clunk* as the carriage of the truck hit the frame when the worn-out shock absorbers failed. The sound of sand and gravel crunching under the bald tires. And, of course, every breath she took.

Colt searched for some safe subject to discuss. Everything seemed fraught with memories of

Huck. Maybe that wasn't so bad. The three of them had been best friends. It was fitting that Huck should be here on this journey with them.

"I miss him already," Colt said into the silence.

"I keep asking myself what he would think about what we're doing," she said.

"He'd understand," Colt said.

"Would he?" she asked, turning to look at him.

"He loved us both. He wouldn't want you to lose the ranch."

Jenny shot him an agonized glance. "I can't believe we're even thinking about—"

"Huck is dead, Jenny. We have to go on living."

"To marry you so soon… It seems… I feel like I'm betraying Huck. His memory, anyway. I'm attracted to you, Colt, but I don't love you. I loved Huck."

"We both loved him, Jenny. That's why getting married is the right thing to do."

"There's something wrong with the logic in that statement, but I'm too tired to figure it out right now." She pulled up to the kitchen door and shut off the engine. It ran for another couple of seconds before it died. "It looks like Randy's still up."

"Do you want me to talk to him?" Colt asked. "To explain?"

"Randy hasn't said a word against this marriage. I think he understands how bad things are."

And maybe how alone you'd be with Huck never coming back, Colt thought.

Jenny sighed, then pushed the truck door open and stepped down. "Come on in, and I'll show you where to sleep."

Colt grabbed his bag from the truck bed, then followed her up the back steps and into the kitchen. Randy was leaning back against the sink, a can of Pepsi in his hand.

"Hello, Randy. Long time no see," he said, extending his hand to the lanky teenager. Randy's hair was the same blond as Jenny's, but his eyes were hazel instead of blue and looked like they'd seen a great deal more of life than a boy his age should.

Randy hesitated, then took Colt's hand and shook it. "Hi, Colt. What's up?" He flushed as he realized the can of worms such a question might open up. "I mean…I thought you were moving in tomorrow."

"Change of plans," Colt replied. He turned to Jenny, whose face looked drawn. "Where do you want me?"

"Follow me," she said, hurrying from the kitchen.

"You gonna stay in Sam's room?" Randy asked, tagging along behind them.

"I'll stay wherever Jenny puts me."

"Sam's room is next to mine," Randy said. "Down the hall from Jenny's."

"Sounds like a good place to be," Colt said, meeting Jenny's glance over her shoulder. It seemed *down the hall* was as close to his sister as Randy wanted Colt.

Colt didn't know if Sam's old room was where she'd initially wanted to put him, but she took her cue from Randy's suggestion, and he found himself in the doorway to a small, feminine room a moment later.

"This is my sewing room now," she said. "I'll get my things out of here tomorrow."

The small room held a single, brass-railed bed and a bedside table with a delicate porcelain lamp. Her sewing machine sat on a table heaped with clothes that she was either making or mending. In the corner stood a clothing dummy wearing what looked like the beginning of a wedding gown.

The gingham curtains were trimmed in eyelet lace, and the bed was heaped with a bunch of frilly pillows and a pair of rag dolls. It might have been Sam's room once upon a time, but Jenny had made it hers.

This was a side of Jenny he'd rarely seen: the soft, feminine side. She'd done a man's work on the Double D for as long as he could remember, and he'd rarely seen her wearing anything but jeans. Everything in this room was soft, decorated in pastel pink and pale green. The dolls were a surprise. It smelled flowery, like maybe the drawers were filled with some kind of potpourri.

She flushed as he met her gaze. "I'll just take these with me," she said, scooping up the lacy pillows and the dolls, as though she were embarrassed for him to see them. "Randy can get you anything you need," she said as she backed out of the room.

"What bee got into her bonnet?" Randy asked, staring after her.

"I guess she wasn't expecting company tonight," Colt said.

"Why did you come tonight?" Randy asked.

Colt met Randy's troubled gaze and decided to tell the truth. "My family doesn't approve of this marriage any more than your brothers do. I thought it would make everybody more comfortable if I got this move over with.''

"If you hurt her, I'll take you out myself.''

Colt met the teenager's warning look with a steady gaze. "There isn't a man alive who cares more for your sister than I do, Randy. I only want to help her.''

The boy stared at him a moment longer before his shoulders sagged. "Jeez, Colt. We sure can use the help. Things have been pretty tight around here. Jenny hasn't let on to the others how bad things are, but it's a little hard to hide the truth from me, when all we ever have for supper is macaroni and cheese.''

Trust a youth to judge the state of things by what he put in his stomach, Colt thought wryly. "Things are going to get better, Randy. I'm here to make sure of it.''

"Thanks, Colt. Guess I'll get some sleep. The school bus comes early in the morning.''

"Good night, Randy. I'll see you at breakfast.''

Colt stripped to his shorts, which was what he'd worn to sleep in for the past ten years, when he might find himself jumping into a flight suit in the middle of the night, and slipped between the covers.

The sheets were printed with roses. The pillow

smelled like...Jenny. The springs squeaked and squealed as he turned over, trying to get comfortable. The mattress sagged in the middle, a reminder that everything in the house was old and worn-out and needed to be replaced. He turned out the delicate porcelain lamp and stared into the darkness. He could hear the crickets outside his window and the rustle of the wind through the grass.

It must have been hard to be the one female in a house full of men. With most of them gone, she'd created this feminine haven for herself. When he thought about it a little more, Colt realized it wasn't a woman's room, it was a girl's room. A place, perhaps, to recapture a lost childhood?

Colt remembered a time when he'd come to visit and had helped Jenny feed Randy. The kid loved squashed-up peas. Huck had decided he would rather go play than stay and help, so he'd had Jenny to himself for the whole afternoon— along with her four younger brothers. Her mother had been confined to her bed, watched over by Jenny's aunt.

Colt had enjoyed himself tremendously that day because it was all new to him—feeding Randy, changing Sam's diaper, then making sure Tyler and James took a bath. He'd been able to go home at the end of the day. Jenny had not.

The door opened almost before he heard the knock and was shut again after Jenny slipped inside.

"Colt?" she said.

He sat up and turned on the light. She was wearing an old chenille bathrobe and a pair of fluffy slippers. Her hair was down on her shoulders, and her face looked scrubbed. He felt his body tighten. "What are you doing in here, Jenny?"

"I can't do it, Colt."

He slid his legs over the side of the bed, but kept the sheet over his hips. "Do what?"

"I can't marry you."

He forgot about the sheet as he stood and crossed to take her by the arms. "What's going on, Jenny? I thought this was all settled."

Tears welled in her eyes and one plopped onto her cheek. He brushed it away with his thumb.

"Huck will always be there between us. Don't you see? Someday you're going to want a wife who can love you back, and I—"

"Let me worry about what I need," Colt said, pulling her into his arms. Her body was stiff and unyielding. He leaned back and separated her hands and put them around his waist, then pulled her close.

He was sorry as soon as he did. He could feel the soft warmth of her breasts against his naked chest. Feel her thighs through the wafer-thin robe. He angled his hips away, so she wouldn't become aware of his arousal. *I'm sorry, Huck. I can't help wanting her.*

He took Jenny's head between his hands and tilted her face up to his. "Listen to me, Jenny. I don't expect you to stop loving Huck. His memory will always be with us. I loved him, too, you know." He kissed a tear from her cheek and tasted the salt…and the sweetness of her. "Let me do this for him, for you, for both of you."

"I feel so guilty," she whispered.

"Why?"

"Because I'm glad you're here. Because I'm glad I don't have to face life alone anymore. And you're not even the man who was supposed to come home to me. What's wrong with me, Colt?"

He hugged her tight against him. "Nothing's wrong with you, Jenny. You're just human."

"I'm so tired of trying to hold everything together by myself. You can't imagine what it's been like, Colt. I've been counting the days until Huck got here to take some of the burden off my shoulders. I know it's not fair to lay so much on you. I just can't do it by myself anymore. I can't.''

She was weeping in earnest, and Colt lifted her into his arms and sat down on the sagging bed and let her cry. She kept her mouth against his neck to mute the sound, as aware as he was that her brother was in the next room. When the sobs became hiccups, he felt her fingertips move tentatively across his chest. Gooseflesh rose where she touched.

''You're cold,'' she said.

''It's the breeze from the window,'' he lied. ''I'll close it later.''

''I should go to bed. It's late.'' But she made no move to leave his lap. Her hand stole around his neck, and he quivered as she played with the short hair at his nape. ''I'm sorry I fell apart like that.''

''You're entitled. I don't know how you've managed to do so much with so little help. Why haven't you said something to Sam and Tyler and James?''

''They've got their own lives. The ranch is my problem.''

''And mine now.''

''Until your leave is up.''

"Yeah," he said, realizing for the first time how little help he was going to be if he left her behind and returned to Egypt.

At last she lifted her head. Her eyes were red-rimmed, and her lower lip was swollen where she'd chewed on it. "I'm so used to carrying all the responsibility on my shoulders, I'm not sure how I'll adjust to having someone around to help."

"I'm sure you'll manage. You always have."

She looked at him strangely. "Yes. I have."

It took Colt a moment to identify what he was feeling, what she'd heard in his voice. He was angry. Furious, really. At his friend. How could Huck have left her alone all these years and gone off to fly jets? Why hadn't Huck stayed home and married Jenny and run the ranch with her? Why hadn't Huck given her babies of her own, instead of leaving her alone to raise her brothers?

He was no better. He'd known for a long time how little time Huck spent with her, how little help Huck had provided, but he hadn't encouraged his friend to marry her. *Because as long as Huck never married Jenny there was always the chance she might be yours someday.*

Colt felt sick inside. It was hard to face such truths. He had a chance now to redress the wrongs of the past. He could be there for Jenny. Love her. Take care of her.

For Huck's sake? Or for your own? a voice asked.

For Jenny's sake, he answered. She deserved a better life, and he was going to make sure she got it.

"You'll feel better after a night's sleep," Colt said as he stood and set Jenny's feet on the floor. He had to unwrap her arms from around his neck. He held her hands for a moment, his thumbs moving across her work-worn knuckles. "I promise I'll always take care of you, Jenny. It's the least I can do for Huck." *And for the woman I love.*

Chapter 5

Jenny rose the next morning feeling—for the first time in a very long time—like anything was possible. She dressed in the same worn jeans, another faded Western shirt, and the same boots with the holes in the soles that were layered with newspaper. But she didn't feel the least forlorn. *Why do I feel so different?* she wondered. Hope. It was as simple as that.

"Good morning."

Jenny was surprised to find Colt in the kitchen ahead of her. His short black hair was still shiny wet from the shower. She must have been more exhausted than she'd thought, to sleep through the groaning water pipes.

He rubbed at the beard darkening his cheeks and chin and said, "Hope you don't mind. Figured I'd wait to shave again till these stitches come out."

Growing up in a houseful of men, she'd seen many an unshaven face at the breakfast table, but never one she found so appealing. "I'll make us some coffee," she said, suddenly aware that she'd been standing there admiring the way his chest filled out his white T-shirt and the way his jeans molded…everything.

He pointed to the percolator. "Coffee's made." He had a pan on the stove and was laying strips of bacon in it.

"I should be making your breakfast," she said.

He grinned. "Tell you what. You clean up the mess, and we'll call it even."

"Deal," she said, crossing to stand beside him and pour herself a cup of coffee.

The heat of his body reminded her that she was no longer alone. And revived the unwanted attraction that lay between them. She hadn't stopped loving Huck; she'd merely acknowledged this physical *thing* that existed between her and

Huck's best friend. She refused to feel guilty for taking the only road open to her.

Jenny took a sip of hot, black coffee, savoring the bitter taste of it, before she swallowed. According to Colt, there had been some delay in returning Huck's body to the States, but the senator had promised to contact Colt regarding the funeral arrangements. "Do you know yet when and where Huck's funeral is being held?" she asked. "I'll need to make arrangements to be there."

"Huck's being buried on the family farm in Virginia, where the senator makes his home when he's in Washington. Family and close friends only. I'm sorry, Jenny. I told the senator you should be there."

"Oh." Huck's father had never accepted her, but it hurt to be excluded from the funeral more than she'd thought it would. Her hands began to tremble, and she carefully set down the coffee cup. Huck wouldn't know she wasn't there. But it was hard to let him go when she'd never gotten the chance to say good-bye. She blinked furiously to fight back the tears. She was done with crying for what couldn't be changed.

Colt's arms closed tightly around her. "Huck will know you wanted to be there. And why you weren't."

"It hurts. Oh, God, I hurt inside."

"Me, too," he admitted hoarsely.

They stood wrapped in a comforting embrace until the smell of burning bacon forced them apart. Colt let go of her, grabbed a fork and turned the blackened bacon. "I hope you like your bacon crisp," he said.

"I like bacon any way I can get it." Jenny flushed as she realized Colt must have made an early morning trip to the convenience store. She and Randy hadn't eaten bacon at breakfast for quite a while, because it didn't fit into their meager budget.

She met Colt's eyes, which urged her not to make a big deal of it. It rankled to accept even this much charity. "Colt, I don't think you should be buying food—"

Randy arrived in the kitchen with his hair askew, teenage whiskers mottling his face, wearing a pair of pajama bottoms and scratching his bare stomach. "I smell bacon."

"Go get dressed," Jenny told him, wanting Randy out of the kitchen so she could finish making her point to Colt. "Breakfast will be ready by the time you are."

"Will you make me a lunch?" Randy asked.

"Sure," Jenny said. "Get moving." Randy

was supposed to make his own lunch, but she knew why he hadn't. He hated the monotonous menu of peanut butter and jelly sandwiches, but that was all they could afford. She opened the refrigerator to get out the jelly and gasped. "What did you do? Buy out the store?"

She shot a look at Colt, whose face had taken on a mulish cast. "If I'm going to be eating your food, I figured I ought to provide my share of it," he said.

"Oh, Colt, you shouldn't have done this."

"Don't push me," he said, throwing down the fork he was using to turn the bacon and putting his fisted hands on his hips. "I'm mad as hell about what I've found here. It wouldn't take much to send me over the edge."

"Mad? About what?"

"That you never told me—or Huck, who would've told me—just how bad things are around here. Damn it all, Jenny! Macaroni and cheese? Peanut butter and jelly? Huck was rich, and I've got a trust fund of my own. Why didn't you ask us for help?"

"I didn't want your help."

"Why the hell not?"

Jenny felt her stomach twist into a knot. *Because if I'd asked for help, you'd have found out*

the secret I've been keeping from both of you.
"Pride," she said, her own fisted hands landing
on her hips. "I didn't want to admit how badly
I'd failed. There. Are you satisfied?"

Colt huffed out a gust of air, then hooked his
thumbs in his back pockets. "I'm sorry. I guess
it's easy to criticize when you're not around to
see how difficult it is to shoulder the load. But
please let me help, now that I'm here."

"All right, Colt." She reached up to get plates
from the cupboard and noticed her hands were
shaking. Another bullet dodged. She didn't dare
tell Colt the truth. No one knew the truth. Not
even Randy, who lived with her.

"Where's breakfast?" Randy asked, setting his
book bag on the floor beside the empty table.
"The bus'll be here in a couple of minutes!"

Jenny set plates and silverware on the table,
then made Randy's lunch while Colt fried a couple of eggs for her brother "over easy," as he'd
requested. They were just sitting down with their
own eggs, toast and bacon, when Randy stuffed
down his third slice of toast and bolted for the
door. "See you after school!" he said as the
screen door slammed behind him.

"Whew!" Colt said with a grin. "I'd forgotten
how hectic school mornings can be."

Jenny managed a smile. "It's hard to believe there's less than a month left before he's done."

Jenny thought of all the years she'd made sure her brothers got off to school. She'd been looking forward to the day when Randy graduated, because it meant she could begin her life with Huck. That wasn't going to happen now. She looked across the table and met Colt's concerned gaze.

"I'm here, Jenny. It's going to be all right."

The comforting words did nothing to ease the tension in her shoulders. "I'm afraid you'll regret this later, Colt." *When you find out the truth about me.*

"Let's take it one day at a time, shall we?"

Jenny released a shuddering breath. "All right. Where do you want to start today?"

"Suppose you tell me."

"If I don't get some fence repaired, what few cattle I have are going to be long gone."

"Fence it is," Colt said as he rose to take his plate to the sink.

The fence was barbed wire stretched between mesquite posts. Some of the posts had rotted, and some of them had been pushed down by cattle rubbing against them. It was hard work digging new postholes and restretching the barbed wire. Jenny told herself the lack of supplies had discouraged her from tackling the job. The truth was, it was grueling work that required more brute strength than she had.

As she watched the corded sinews flex in Colt's arms, Jenny conceded there were simply some things a man could do better than a woman. "Thanks, Colt," she said as she stapled the barbed wire into place. "I couldn't have done this without you."

He grabbed the kerchief from his back pocket, lifted his hat and wiped the sweat from his face and neck. He retrieved his T-shirt from the post where he'd left it, hung his Stetson there while he slipped his shirt back on, then resettled the Stetson low enough to shade his eyes. "Digging postholes is a lot harder work than flying jets," he said with a crooked smile.

She pointed at the white contrail left by a jet flying overhead. "So you'd rather be up there than down here?"

He tipped up his Stetson and squinted at the plane overhead. "Flying is all I ever wanted to do." He looked back at her. "But right now, there's no place I'd rather be than here with you."

"Digging postholes?" she said with a teasing grin.

"Better me than you," he said, his voice turning serious.

She turned and headed for the truck, tools in hand. "I don't mind a little hard work."

He caught her by the elbow and swung her around. He held on to her arm while he took the posthole digger and the staple gun out of her hands one at a time and threw them into the rusted-out bed of the pickup. Then he grasped both arms and turned her to face him.

"A little hard work is one thing, Jenny. Running yourself into the ground trying to do too much by yourself is another thing entirely. I've been watching you this past week, and it's plain to me that you're worn-out."

"I can't sleep," she retorted.

"This is more than lost sleep," he said. "You're wrung out. And so skinny a hard wind could blow you over."

She pulled herself free and took a step back. Colt was so much more perceptive than Huck. Huck hadn't noticed how thin she was—and how tired she was—four months ago, when he'd come for the Christmas holidays. Colt was so close to discovering the truth. She wanted to blurt it out to him. But that would send him running for sure.

"I'll admit I'm overworked," she said, feeling

her way carefully. "It's been tough doing everything myself. I guarantee you I'll sleep better—
and eat better, especially with the way you're
shopping—now that you're here."

"I wish you'd said something sooner."

"Would you have stopped flying jets and come
home to help me?" she asked in a quiet voice.

He looked stunned at the suggestion. "I... You
know I would have..." He shrugged. "I don't
honestly know. I like to think I'd have come if
you'd said you needed me."

She shook her head. "You're only fooling
yourself, Colt. You're just like Huck. All you
have to do is sniff jet fuel, and you're off into the
wild blue yonder."

He laughed. "I'm not that bad."

"You've asked me to marry you knowing full
well you intend to return to Egypt to finish your
tour there. What if I said I needed you here? That
I wanted you to stay here with me? Would you
resign from the Air Force?"

A shuddery breath escaped before Colt said,
"Are you asking me to resign?"

Jenny made a face. "I don't know. It hardly
seems fair to ask you to stay here when we aren't
going to have a real marriage."

"Whoa, there, woman. Who said it wasn't going to be a real marriage?"

She flushed. "I suppose I meant a normal marriage. You know, where the two parties love each other and plan to spend their lives together."

Colt's brow furrowed, and his hands caressed her arms where he'd been tightly gripping her. "I wish I could give you that. I really do, but—"

"We don't love each other, and you plan to spend your life flying jets," she finished for him. She reached up to gently smooth the furrows from his brow with her thumb. "Don't worry, Colt. I'll be fine. I don't blame you for what happened to Huck. Truly I don't."

"I just wish—"

She put her fingertips over his lips. "No regrets. I'm grateful for whatever help you're able to give me during the next few weeks. I'm not going to ask for more."

He pulled her hand down, grasping it in his own. "That's the problem," he said. "You never ask for anything. What is it you want out of life, Jenny? I mean, besides scraping a meager living out of this place?"

"I want—wanted—to wake with my husband beside me and lie in bed listening to the morning sounds. I wanted us to work side by side, making the Double D as wonderful a place to live as it once was. And I wanted children of my own.'' She sighed wistfully. ''It's too late for a family now.''

''Why?'' Colt asked.

She realized what she'd almost revealed and smiled to distract him. ''I'm too old, for one thing. And the man I'm about to marry would rather fly jets.'' She stepped back and pulled her hand free, breaking all contact between them.

Colt cleared his throat and stuck his thumbs in his back pockets to keep from reaching for her again. ''So you're going to spend your life on this godforsaken ranch all alone?''

''I'm sure my brothers will come around on holidays.''

''Don't any of them want to live here with you? What's Randy going to do when he finishes college?'' Colt asked.

''He wants to go into business for himself and earn lots of money.''

''Fine. What about Sam and Tyler and James?''

''Sam's foreman for a nearby ranch,'' Jenny said. ''Tyler's headed to medical school in Houston. And James...''

''What about James?''

She gave him a wondering look. ''James is

studying to become a minister. So you see, I'm on my own.''

Colt saw a great deal. She'd given up her own hopes and dreams to make sure her brothers realized theirs. Every extra penny must have gone for tuition or books or clothes. That was why the ranch had suffered. She was obviously very proud of them, and their opposition to this marriage was proof of how much they cared for her.

He couldn't just marry her and leave her here to manage on her own. On the other hand, he didn't think he could give up flying, either.

''Have you ever thought about selling the Double D?'' he asked.

''I've thought about it,'' she admitted.

''And?''

Her eyes searched the horizon. He looked along with her and didn't see much, just a few scrub mesquite, some cactus and buffalo grass and bluebonnets, and in the distance, a few craggy bluffs that marked deep canyons similar to those that graced Hawk's Pride.

''I know it doesn't seem like much,'' she said. ''But I love it. I feel connected to everyone who came before me.'' She turned to look at him. ''I want—wanted—my children to grow up here and to love their heritage as much as I do.''

Colt imagined Jenny playing with a bunch of kids, tickling them and laughing with them and having fun...without him. Because he'd be off flying jets.

It wouldn't be fair to leave her alone and pregnant.

Is it any more fair to deprive her of the one thing she wants that you can give her?

Colt took two steps toward Jenny and brushed a stray wisp of hair from her brow. His hand lingered on her cheek. "It's not too late for children, if you really want them."

"I can't raise them alone, Colt. Or rather, I won't do that to them. My dad left us and...I just wouldn't do that to any child of mine. Not if I could help it."

"I see." Colt looked deep into Jenny's eyes, wondering how it had come to this—a choice between the woman he had always loved, and the thing he loved doing most.

It didn't make it any easier to know that she didn't love him. That her heart belonged—would always belong—to his best friend.

Chapter 6

Colt studied Jenny in the sleeveless black sheath she'd worn to the memorial service for Huck. She was surrounded by friends who'd come to the Double D to bring mountains of food and offer their condolences. Her hair was gathered in a shiny golden knot at her crown, leaving her neck and shoulders bare, so he could see her body curved in all the right places. But she left a frail shadow on the ground, and her face looked wan. It dawned on him suddenly that she might be sick.

Sick people sometimes die.

Colt forced back the feeling of panic. *Jenny*

isn't sick. She's just tired. The fear that she might be ill was like a living thing inside him, clawing at him, tearing at his insides. He knew his feelings were irrational, but his dread was born of first-hand experience.

When he was too young to know better, he'd made friends of the kids who attended Camp LittleHawk, the camp for kids with cancer started by his mother at Hawk's Pride. He was eight when he met Tom Hartwell. Like many of the kids at camp, Tom had leukemia, but it was in remission. He and Tom had become blood brothers. Tom wanted to fly jets someday. Colt said he'd never thought much about it, but it sounded like fun.

Colt felt his insides squeeze at the memory of the freckle-faced, blue-eyed boy. Tom had worn a baseball cap to cover his head, left bald by chemotherapy. "My hair's really, really red," Tom had said with a grin. "Wait till it grows back in. You won't believe it!"

But the leukemia had come back, and neither Colt's raging nor his prayers—nor the best doctors money could buy—had been able to save his blood brother. Tom had died before Colt ever got a chance to see his red hair.

Jenny's not sick. She's just tired, he repeated to himself.

Nevertheless, he moved hurriedly through the crowd of mourners, briefly greeting neighbors he hadn't seen in years, catching brief snatches of conversation.

"...Remember when Huck and Jenny and Colt..."

"Then Huck and Jenny and Colt went galloping across..."

"—going to take Huck's place at the altar. Can you believe..."

He stood at Jenny's shoulder and knew she was aware of him when she leaned back against him and reached for his hand. He interrupted old Mrs. Carmichael to say, "Jenny and I are going out onto the porch for some air. Please excuse us," and led her away without looking back.

It wasn't easy getting through the kitchen, which was also full of people, including most of his own siblings. He didn't allow anyone to stop them. "Jenny needs some air," he said as he headed inexorably for the back porch.

Even there they found no respite. His mother and father stood on the porch, along with two of Jenny's brothers.

"There they are now," Sam said when he spied

them. "I want to talk to you, Colt. I don't think—"

"Not now," Colt said without stopping. "Jenny and I are going for a walk." He put himself between her and everyone else and headed off down the rutted dirt road that led away from the ranch.

Jenny stumbled once in her black pumps, and he put his arm around her waist and kept on walking.

"Where's the fire?" Jenny asked.

Colt stopped abruptly and stared at her. "What?"

"Where are we going in such a hurry?"

Colt realized he'd been blindly running from his fear, which stabbed him anew when he looked down and saw the gauntness beneath her cheekbones and the shadows beneath her eyes. He had to work to keep his voice steady as he asked, "Are you all right?"

She gave him a quizzical look. "My fiancé is dead, and I've agreed to marry another man in a matter of weeks, but otherwise I suppose—"

He shook his head impatiently. "I mean, are you feeling all right? You look so thin, so exhausted. I thought you might be…sick."

She stiffened and looked away. "If I were, I wouldn't expect you to take care of me."

The air soughed slowly from Colt's lungs. Jenny knew better than anyone how assiduously he avoided sick people. When they were kids, he hadn't come near her house for a long time because her mother was dying of cancer, and he couldn't face seeing the ravages of the disease. He put a hand on her shoulder, and she jerked free and turned to face him.

"To answer your question, I'm fine, just very tired and very unhappy," she snapped. "We should go back now."

She'd already started back toward the house when he caught her elbow and turned her around again. "This way," he said, leading her along the twin dirt tracks that had been created by wagon wheels more than a century before.

She went along but asked, "Where are we going?"

"You need to rest."

She laughed. "Rest? You've practically got me jogging in high heels. I'm going to sprain an ankle—"

He scooped her up into his arms, making her cry out in surprise and grab his shoulders. He left the road, heading across country toward a single live oak that created a circle of shade.

She laughed at him uneasily. "Colt, where are you taking me?"

"Somewhere you can take a nap in peace and quiet."

"I've got company at the house."

"All of whom are perfectly capable of entertaining themselves with stories of 'Huck and Jenny and Colt,'" he said.

He set her down on the patchy grass, then sat with his back against the trunk of the live oak, his legs stretched out in front of him, and pulled her down beside him. "Lay your head on my lap and relax," he said.

"Colt—"

He tugged on her hand. "Humor me, Jenny."

When she was settled with her head on his thigh, she closed her eyes and heaved a great sigh. The wind rustled the leaves of the live oak, and cattle lowed in the distance. A jay complained on a branch above them. They might have been a thousand miles from another human being.

"Thank you, Colt," Jenny murmured. "I didn't realize how much I needed a little peace and quiet."

He reached down and pulled the pins from her

hair, then ran his fingers through the silky mass, massaging her scalp where the knot had been.

"That feels wonderful," she said.

Colt wanted to do a lot more, to hold her in his arms, to lie next to her, body to body. Instead he settled his hand on her nape, where he gently massaged the tense muscles.

"I'm not sure I could have heard one more story about Huck and me and you without breaking into tears," Jenny confessed in a quiet voice. "Thanks for rescuing me."

"That's too bad. I've got one I'd like to tell," Colt said.

Jenny's eyes opened, and she started to sit up. "Oh?"

He pressed her back down and said, "Relax. It's a good story, I promise."

"All right. Go ahead."

He could feel the rigidity in her body, the physical wariness. She'd taken so many blows lately, and he wanted to spare her any more pain. But avoiding the subject wasn't the answer. Neither of them was likely to forget the part Huck had played in their lives. They both had to accept his loss and move on.

Colt brushed a stray curl from Jenny's brow and said, "Huck and I were riding camels—"

Jenny's head popped up. "Camels? Really?"

"Lie down and listen," Colt said with a chuckle. When Jenny was settled again with her cheek on his thigh, he continued. "Huck and I were riding camels in Cairo, tourists traveling from one pyramid to the next, when he turned to me and said, 'I wish Jenny were here, because she'd have the nerve to see just how fast this beast can go. We'd be galloping across the desert instead of walking sedately behind some guide.'"

"Did Huck really say that?"

"He did," Colt confirmed. "And he was right. You're an amazing woman, Jenny."

She lifted her head and looked at him. "If I'm so amazing, why didn't he come back sooner? Why did he leave me alone so long?"

Colt hesitated. There was no excuse for Huck's behavior. There was an explanation. "He loved flying."

"More than he loved me," she said bitterly. She sat up abruptly, her back to Colt, her head bowed.

He saw her shoulders heave and knew she was crying again, though she made no sound. He sought words to comfort her. "He missed you terribly, Jenny. He ached for you. He admired you for taking care of your brothers." He had never heard Huck say any of those things out loud, but he had felt them himself, and he couldn't believe Huck hadn't felt them, as well.

"I hate those damned jets!" Jenny said vehemently. "I hate—" A sob cut her off.

Colt could resist no longer. He wrapped his arms tightly around her from behind, pressing his cheek against hers. "Huck's father had a great deal to do with keeping him away, Jenny. The senator didn't think his son should be saddled with the responsibility of raising someone else's family. It didn't help that Huck was rich, and you were poor."

"He thought Huck could do better," Jenny said. "He told me so to my face the one time I met him."

Colt bit back a gasp of disbelief. He'd known how Huck's father felt; he hadn't known Senator Duncan had been so blunt with Jenny. "Huck never let the senator sway him, Jenny. He always loved you."

"Just not enough," Jenny said.

Randy had been watching Faith Butler for almost an hour without going anywhere near her. Faith stuck pretty close to her twin sister, Hope, who'd gathered a crowd of admiring boys around her. Faith stood behind Hope like a shadow of her sister. It had been that way for as long as Randy could remember.

Hope Butler's behavior was *outrageous*. At least, that was the word Jenny used to describe her. Her face was usually slathered with makeup, and she wore her dresses cut low enough to cause problems with the fit of a guy's jeans. She smoked and drank and drove her car like a bat out of hell.

Randy figured she worked so hard to attract attention to herself so nobody would notice Faith. That is, so people would spend more time talking about the difference in their personalities rather than the other, more obvious difference between them.

They were both beautiful, with long, straight black hair they wore parted in the middle, and dark chocolate eyes and smooth, creamy skin. But something had gone wrong when they were in the womb, and Faith's left hand had stopped growing. Her arm ended shortly beyond the wrist, and she wore a plastic prosthetic device with a metal hook that substituted for her missing hand.

Like most of the guys, Randy had been attracted to Hope at first. Some guys said she "put out," and he'd been hoping he'd get lucky and score with her. Somewhere along the line, he'd gotten distracted by Faith.

He watched her now, standing serenely behind her sister, her left hand unobtrusively tucked behind her back. Faith smiled at Hope's anecdotes and seemed not to mind that her sister was the center of attention. Faith never made a big deal about the fact she didn't have a left hand.

Randy wondered if Faith ever minded all the guys paying attention to her sister instead of her, or if she ever felt angry or bitter about being the "imperfect" twin. He wondered what it would be like to date a girl like that. And shuddered involuntarily when he thought of that hook at the end of her arm anywhere near him.

He flushed with shame. It wasn't Faith's fault she was born like that. Remorse moved him in her direction. He walked right up to her and said, "Hi. I noticed your glass is almost empty. Can I get you something else to drink?"

She looked startled and frightened, like a deer he'd come upon suddenly in the brush when he was hunting. He was no more able to hurt her than he'd been able to kill that deer. "I noticed you from across the room," he said.

That only seemed to make her more self-conscious, so he quickly added, "I mean, I was noticing how pretty you look."

Her lashes lowered over her eyes, and two red spots appeared on her cheeks. "Thank you," she said in a barely audible voice.

The more shy she was, the more protective he felt. "I wondered if you might want to go to the movies with me sometime."

Her lashes lifted and she looked up at him and he felt his heart skip a beat. "Are you asking me out?" she asked.

With the full force of her gaze directed at him, he couldn't catch his breath to speak. His mind had turned to mush.

She smiled at his confusion and for the first time her left hand came out from behind her back. "You must have mistaken me for my sister."

He made himself look at the hooked hand she'd brought out to make sure he knew she was the imperfect twin. He shook his head, but was still unable to speak.

She smiled sweetly. "I'll tell Hope—"

"I meant you," he blurted. "I want to take you out on a date."

She looked surprised again. "Why?"

He was startled into a laugh. "That's a stupid question."

She lowered her lashes again. "I meant it seriously. And I'd like an answer."

He wished she would look up, but she didn't, and he didn't have the nerve to reach over and tip her chin up. He noticed they were starting to get attention from some friends of his, and he figured he'd better get this over with before they came over and started giving him a hard time. "I just thought it might be interesting to get to know you," he said.

When she looked up, she caught him glancing at two buddies of his who were whispering behind their hands. "Did someone dare you to go out with me?"

"Are you kidding?" He saw from her face that she wasn't.

"It's happened to me before," she said defensively.

He felt his insides clench and struggled to keep the pity—and anger—from his voice. "All I want to do is take you out on a date."

"So you say."

Frustrated, he'd already turned to leave when she reached out, touching him with the hook. He barely managed to keep himself from jerking away.

"Wait," she said. "If you want to see me, you can come over to my house tomorrow morning."

He raised a brow in question. "What's going on at your house?"

She smiled and his loins tightened. "I'm in charge of making favors for your sister's wedding. You can help. I'll provide lunch."

"All right. I'll see you then."

"Everything all right here?"

Randy was surprised by Hope's interruption. He wouldn't have thought she paid much attention to what her sister did. He caught the militant look in Hope's eyes and realized she was there to protect Faith. "We're done," he said. He opened his mouth to say "See you tomorrow" to Faith, but shut it again when he realized everybody's attention was now turned in their direction.

He walked away without looking back, because he didn't want to see what Faith thought of his hasty retreat. It wasn't that he was embarrassed about their date or anything, but he didn't want to put up with his friends teasing him about it. He knew he wouldn't be able to keep from getting upset, and the more upset he got, the more brutal their teasing would be. Better to keep the whole business to himself.

"Are you all right?" Hope whispered to her sister.

"I'm fine," Faith said.

"He didn't—"

"I'm fine," Faith said with a smile that Hope recognized. Faith used smiles the way a knight used a shield to ward off harmful blows.

Hope would have urged Faith to leave right then, except she hadn't yet found an opportunity to talk with Jake Whitelaw. Not that he wanted to talk to her. Or even knew she was alive. When she'd said hello to him earlier, he'd scowled and replied, "That's the wrong dress for a funeral."

She'd bitten back a sharp retort. Since she'd only worn the dress to get his attention, it had served its purpose. Hope sighed as she looked down at the long legs revealed by the short skirt. Why couldn't Jake have admired her legs instead of criticizing the dress?

Everything she did—smoking, driving fast, even wearing makeup so she'd look older—was calculated to make him notice her. But she might as well be eight years old instead of eighteen. All he saw was a kid. Someday she was going to figure out a way to convince Jake Whitelaw that Hope Butler was the woman of his dreams.

* * *

Colt kept Jenny away from the house as long as he dared, but brought her back in time to say good-bye to everyone. Her family and his were the last to leave, and they stood on the back porch together bidding them farewell.

"We're so glad you're going to be part of the family," his mother said as she hugged Jenny good-bye.

"Colt's a lucky man," his father said as he gave Jenny a kiss on the forehead.

"You'd better take damned good care of her," Jenny's brother Sam warned quietly as he shook Colt's hand.

Colt knew Sam was only worried about his sister, so he simply said, "I will." He wished he could tell Sam that he loved Jenny, but it was too soon after Huck's death to admit to such feelings. Besides, loving her wasn't enough. Huck had loved Jenny, yet he'd left her alone to raise her brothers.

Jake was last in line to say good-bye, and Colt met his elder brother's hard-eyed look without flinching.

"I hope you know what you're doing," Jake said. "I think you're asking for heartache."

"It's my heart," Colt said. "Let me worry about it."

Jake gave a grudging nod. "All right, little brother. Don't say I didn't warn you."

When Colt and Jenny were finally alone, they were completely alone, since Randy had escaped to the movies with some friends. Colt was surprised when he ushered Jenny inside to find the kitchen as clean as a whistle.

"I expected to spend the evening washing casserole dishes," he said. "What are we going to do with all this free time?"

"I've got books that need to be balanced," Jenny said.

Colt shook his head. "Not tonight. You're too tired."

"I'll decide whether I'm too tired," Jenny retorted irritably.

"There. See? You're so tired you're snapping at me."

"I'm not—" Jenny cut herself off and hissed out a breath of air. She gave him a plaintive look. "I don't know how to do nothing, Colt."

"Then we'll do something," he promised as he slid his arm around her waist and headed her into the living room.

"Like what?" she demanded as she plopped down onto the couch.

"Well, there's always necking," he teased as

he dropped down beside her. "Let's see if I remember how it's done. I sneak my arm along the
back of the couch, like so."

Jenny giggled as she watched his arm move
snakelike along the couch behind her.

"Then I take your hand in mine, to kind of
distract you from what my other hand is doing."
He suited word to deed and threaded the fingers
of her left hand with the fingers of his. He waggled his right hand, which now completely encircled her. "Then this hand comes to rest ever so
lightly on your shoulder. *Voilà! I yam readee for
zee zeduction,*" he said in a terrible French accent.

Jenny laughed. "Being the very good girl that
I am, I will, of course, pretend not to notice your
hand on my shoulder," she said, joining his game.

"Of course," he agreed, returning her grin with
one of his own.

"But secretly," she said, shooting him an impish look, "I'll be enticing you to do more."

His brows waggled. "You will?"

She nodded, grinning broadly.

"How?" he asked, intrigued.

"Oh, in little ways, like making sure that our
hands rest on *your* thigh, instead of mine."

Colt looked down and discovered that their

joined hands were indeed lying on his thigh instead of hers. He could suddenly feel the heat of her hand through his black suit trousers. A more intense physical response was not long in coming. He hoped to hell she didn't notice. "Then what?" he asked in a raspy voice.

"I'd lean a little closer and bat my eyelashes at you and look demure." She did so in a way that should have been funny, but which merely left him wondering what secrets she was hiding beneath her lowered lids.

He leaned close to her ear and whispered, "Then what?" and felt her body quiver.

"I'd wait to see if you took the bait," she murmured.

"Look at me, Jenny."

She lifted her lids, and their gazes caught and held. He lowered his head toward hers, drawn by her parted lips. He kept his eyes on her mouth, waiting for even the slightest indication that she didn't want this to happen. Sure enough, she backed away.

"I'd resist at first," she said, her eyes lambent but still full of mischief. "But when you least expected it, I'd turn to you and make all your adolescent male dreams come true." She reached out with her free hand, caught his nape and drew his head down to hers, their mouths meshing before she slipped her tongue between his lips to taste him.

An instant later she was on her feet, wiping her mouth and backing away from him. "Ohmigod. I shouldn't have done that."

He was on his feet and headed toward her, his hands outstretched in supplication. "It was just a game, Jenny."

"You're right. I'm tired. I need to rest. Good night, Colt."

An instant later she was gone.

Colt took a step after her and stopped himself. His body was rock hard with no hope of satisfaction, but he only had himself to blame. "What did you expect, Whitelaw?" he muttered. "When you play with fire, you'd better damn well expect to get burned."

Chapter 7

Jenny woke to the sound of a hammer against wood. The sun was high and a warm breeze billowed the lace curtains at the open window. She hadn't set her alarm because it was Saturday, and she didn't have to make sure Randy got off to school on time. But it was rare that she slept so late.

Then she remembered. *I kissed Colt last night. And not by accident. I wanted it to happen. I helped it to happen. And I could have done a lot more. He wouldn't have stopped me.*

She had fled, afraid of the powerful feelings

evoked by that brief meeting of lips. It wasn't like her to run away, but nothing about the past ten days had been the least bit normal. It was time to face facts. Time to stop pretending her life had even the remotest chance of turning out happily ever after.

She couldn't marry Colt. It wouldn't be fair. Not unless she told him the truth about herself. And she knew what would happen if she did that. She had to call the whole thing off. Now. Before it was too late.

Jenny yanked on a pair of jeans and slipped into a chambray shirt. She ran a brush through her hair but didn't even take time to put it up in a ponytail. The noise was coming from the back of the house, and as she hurried through the kitchen she saw the remnants of two blueberry pancake breakfasts in the sink. She stopped at the screen door and stared.

Colt and Randy were working side by side, both stripped to the waist. Colt's shoulder muscles flexed as he supported a portion of the back porch roof while Randy slipped a new post in place under it. Colt's bronzed skin glistened with sweat and beads of perspiration pearled in the dark hair on his chest. His jeans had slid down so she could see his navel and the line of black down leading into his jeans.

Her body tightened viscerally.

Jenny was shocked at how quickly she'd responded to the sight of Colt's half-naked body and clutched at the doorjamb to keep herself from bolting again. She would surely get over this aberrant attraction once Colt was gone. She started to push the screen door open but hesitated when he spoke.

"That's it, boy. Easy does it." Colt let go of the rotting post he'd been holding, and the weight of the roof settled onto the new post.

"Holy cow! We did it!" Randy exclaimed.

"We make a good team," Colt said, laying a hand across Randy's youthful shoulders. Her brother beamed with pride.

Jenny felt her throat swell closed. This was what her brothers had missed. A father to teach them to be men. She'd done her best, but there were some things a mother couldn't provide.

She swallowed down the ache in her throat that arose whenever she acknowledged what had been stolen from her...from all of them...when their father had run away rather than face their mother's illness. She'd been the eldest, the one who remembered him best, so his abandonment had hit her the hardest. She wasn't about to set herself up for that kind of heartache again.

"How long are you going to hang around?" Randy asked.

Jenny saw the startled look on Colt's face. She didn't usually eavesdrop, but she was curious to hear his answer.

Colt picked up a hammer to knock the post farther into place and said, "Long enough to help your sister put this place back together."

"How long is that?" Randy persisted.

"What does it matter to you?" Colt asked. "If I understood your sister right, you're headed off to college in the fall. Bring me one of those rails, will you?"

Randy brought him a porch rail and squatted beside him as he measured and began to saw. "I'm asking because I am going off to college. I hate the thought of leaving Jenny here all alone."

"Yeah," Colt agreed. "That's tough. You want to try nailing this in place?"

"Sure," Randy said.

Jenny watched as Colt showed Randy how to run a plumb line so the porch rail would be straight. She wondered for a moment how he could know so much about carpentry, until she remembered Colt had been trained his whole life to take over Hawk's Pride. There wasn't much he didn't know about running a ranch, and that included the kind of repairs he'd been doing for the past ten days.

Jenny had discovered it was easier to do the repairs herself than take the time to train her brothers. She realized now that she had cheated them of the pride in a job well-done and herself of the pleasure of teaching them that she saw on Colt's face.

"I'm real worried about Jenny living here all alone," Randy admitted as he began nailing the rail in place. "I mean, when you go back to flying jets."

"Maybe I can talk Jenny into selling this place and coming with me."

Randy turned to gape at Colt, and the hammer came down on his thumb. "Yow!" He leaped up and flung his hand around, trying to ease the pain. Eventually the thumb ended up in his mouth.

By then Jenny was out the door and standing on the porch beside her brother, reaching for his hand. "Are you all right?"

Randy yanked his hand away and said angrily, "Why are we bothering to fix this place up, if you're just going to sell it?"

"I never agreed—"

"This is our home," Randy interrupted. "You can't sell it!"

Jenny was furious with Colt for putting such an idea in Randy's head, but equally annoyed with her brother. "You know I'd never sell the Double D if I had a choice." She shot a quick glance at Colt, who looked chagrined. "It appears I may not have a choice."

Randy turned to Colt. "Is that true, Colt? Are you going to force Jenny to sell the Double D?"

Colt's lips pursed, and he shook his head. "I was only suggesting it might be better if she did."

"How would you feel if your parents sold Hawk's Pride?" Randy demanded. "What if it belonged to someone else and you could never go back? You'd hate it, wouldn't you?"

"I guess I would," Colt conceded. "But—"

"No buts," Randy said. "Look, I've got to get out of here. I promised I'd ride over and visit a friend this morning." He grabbed his shirt from the rail where he'd left it and turned to Jenny, his face anguished. "Just don't do anything without thinking it through, all right?"

"Shouldn't you wash up first?" Jenny suggested, knowing as soon as the words were out of her mouth how much Randy would resent them.

"I'll rinse off at the sink in the barn." He practically ran down the porch steps, headed for the barn.

Jenny whirled on Colt, determined to send him away. But the words caught in her throat. She met his gaze and remembered what had happened the previous night. She had to speak quickly, or she'd lose the will to speak at all.

"When did you intend to let me in on this little plan of yours to sell the Double D?" she asked pointedly.

"It's not a bad idea."

"Forget it! If you didn't want to marry me, all you had to do was say so. I can manage on my own. I always have."

"You shouldn't have had to carry the burden by yourself for so long," he retorted. "Huck should have been here."

She looked into Colt's eyes and drew a sharp breath. "Don't you dare pity me! I don't need your sympathy. I don't need anyone. I can manage on my—"

He grabbed her shoulders and shook her. "Damn it, Jenny. Why won't you let me help?"

"I don't want you here. I don't want you touching me or kissing me or...or touching me!"

She fought him, but his arms circled around her, pulling her close so she couldn't strike out at him. He was saying something, but the sound was drowned out by the pulse pounding in her ears. She kicked his shin and heard him yelp, but he held on. One of his hands tangled in her hair, and he yanked her head back. "Look at me, Jenny. Look at me!"

She stared into eyes that were filled with compassion. And regret. And something else she was afraid to name.

"I'm glad you kissed me last night," he said.

Jenny felt her heart begin to race. "It can't happen again, Colt. Huck's only been dead—"

"We're alive. We're going to be husband and wife. It's not as if we're strangers. We've been friends for a long time."

"*Friends.* Nothing more."

"Not yet," he said softly. His lips had a certain fullness and rigidity she recognized, and which made her heart pound all the harder.

"You're a beautiful woman, Jenny. Why are you so surprised that I find you desirable? Or that you might desire me? Why are you fighting so hard not to feel anything?"

She swallowed hard. *Because it can't last. Because it's entirely likely I'm not going to be here on this earth much longer than Huck.*

"You can grieve Huck and still go on living," Colt said in a gentle voice.

She was frightened by how persuasive he sounded. She groped for an explanation that he would accept—besides the truth. "I can't just forget Huck. He was—"

"Never here," Colt said implacably. "How often did you see him over the past ten years?"

"I saw him lots!" Jenny retorted.

"Twelve times," Colt said. "I know because I came with him every time except the last. I was here more than he was, because he spent most of his leave with his father."

"He wrote me—"

"Cards—on birthdays and holidays. I know. I made sure of it."

Jenny's stomach churned. "He loved me, Colt."

His thumb caressed her jaw, but his hold on her hair tightened, forcing her to look up at him. "I know. And you loved him. But be honest, Jenny. If you hadn't been tied to this ranch, hadn't been tied down raising four brothers, would you have kept on loving a man who was never there for you?"

Jenny's eyes misted, and her nose stung with the threat of tears she refused to shed. "You can leave anytime, Colt. Go sniff some jet fuel. Get out!''

''I'm not going to leave you, Jenny. I'm not going to walk away, no matter how hard you push me. Between us, we're going to figure out what to do. There's got to be a solution that'll work for both of us. All we have to do is find it.''

''I don't need you! I—''

He kissed her hard, cutting off speech. Then his mouth softened, and his lips moved over hers, searching for some response.

Jenny's heart skipped a beat before blood surged to her center. She clutched at Colt's bare shoulders, unsure whether she wanted to pull him close or push him away. When she hesitated, his tongue slid into her mouth for a taste, and she was undone. All thought flew out of her head, replaced by sensation.

This is what was always missing with Huck. The need to merge body and soul with another human being. The need to make two halves into one whole. The need—

The kiss ended as abruptly as it had begun. Colt looked dazed. And as distraught as she felt herself. He let her go and took a quick step back. He didn't seem to know what to do with his hands, and he finally stuck his thumbs in his back pockets. "I think maybe we'd better set some ground rules. I want—"

"Holy cow! Holy cow, Jenny! Look what I found!"

Jenny tore her troubled gaze from Colt's face and looked toward the barn. Randy was mounted on his chestnut gelding, but he was pointing at a large animal that was partially hidden from view in the corral behind the barn. "What is it?" Jenny called back to him.

"My wedding gift to you," Colt answered for Randy.

"You got me an animal for a wedding gift?" she said, her brows lowering in confusion as she headed for the corral.

Colt kept pace with her. "Not just any animal," he said. "A Santa Gertrudis bull from the King Ranch."

Jenny halted in her tracks and turned to stare. "Are you kidding? You're *not* kidding," she said as she got a good look at Colt's face. She couldn't catch her breath.

The Santa Gertrudis breed, three-eighths Indian Brahman and five-eighths British Shorthorn, had been developed in the early twentieth century on the King Ranch, which still produced some of the finest Santa Gertrudis cattle to be found anywhere in the world. A bull like the one he described would cost a fortune—and could save the Double D.

Jenny turned and raced for the corral. Randy was off his horse and leaning over the corral, ogling the deep, cherry-red-colored bull when she reached him. "Ohmigod!" she breathed. "It's Rob Roy."

"None other," Colt confirmed with a grin as he put a booted foot up on the corral and leaned over to admire the bull. "Do you like him?"

Jenny couldn't breathe.

Rob Roy had been named grand champion Santa Gertrudis bull at the most recent stock show in Fort Worth. All by himself, this bull could put the Double D in the black.

Randy whooped and said, "Holy cow!"

"Do you like him?" Colt asked softly. "I mean, I thought about getting you something a little more romantic, like a diamond—"

Jenny clutched Colt around the neck and gave him a quick kiss on the mouth. Just as quickly, she let him go and stepped back. It was too tempting to cling to him. "It's a *perfect* gift. No woman could ever have a more perfect gift."

Then she remembered she was planning to call off the wedding.

"I guess there won't be any more talk about

selling the Double D,'' Randy said as he mounted his gelding. ''Wait'll I tell everybody about this!''

He kicked his horse into a lope, shrieking like a Comanche on a raid and kicking up a cloud of dust that Jenny waved away.

Jenny turned back to Colt and said, ''How could you have teased Randy like that, saying you thought I should sell the Double D, when you'd already bought Rob Roy?''

''I wasn't teasing,'' he said.

''But with Rob Roy—''

''One bull isn't going to solve all your problems, Jenny. In fact, he's only going to make more work for you. I suppose with the income he'll bring in you could hire a man to help you out, but—''

''I'll still be alone, because you're not going to be around,'' Jenny finished for him.

''I made my choice a long time ago, Jenny.''

Jenny couldn't keep the bitterness from her voice. ''I know, Colt. You and Huck both. Like I said, I can take care of myself.'' She opened her mouth to call off the wedding, but what came out was, ''Thanks for the bull. It's the nicest gift anybody's ever given me.''

Jenny turned and headed toward the house. She tried to walk, but she was feeling too much, hurting too much, and she started to run. She waited for the sound of Colt's footsteps coming after her.

But she never heard them.

Randy's heart lurched when he caught sight of Faith through the open kitchen window of her house. "Hi, Faith."

"Hi, Randy. Let me finish here at the sink, and I'll let you in."

Randy shifted from foot to foot on the back porch. Faith's dad was foreman for a neighboring ranch, and Randy noticed their single-story white clapboard house sported a fresh coat of white paint. Pink and purple petunias grew in profusion along the back porch. He had a moment to think how much Jenny would have appreciated the paint and the petunias before Faith unhooked the screen door and held it open for him.

He stared at her, stricken mute, unable to move.

Faith smiled shyly and said, "Won't you come in?"

"Uh. Okay."

The instant he stepped inside, he was assailed with a sense of order and the smell of Pine Sol. It was a far cry from his house, which suffered from too much work and too few people to do it.

"I'm glad you decided to come," Faith said.

"I said I would."

"I know but... I'm glad," she repeated, lowering her lids and hiding her eyes from him.

He recognized it for the defensive gesture it was, and couldn't help resenting it. He wasn't going to hurt her. If she'd just give him half a chance, he'd prove it.

He looked around the kitchen, not surprised to see it was pristine. The Butler girls had always come to school in starched and ironed dresses and with their hair in arrow-straight pigtails. At least, they had until Hope took the bit in her teeth and began to defy her parents. After that, it was only Faith who came to school perfectly dressed.

He took advantage of the fact Faith's eyes were averted to take a long look at her. Her left hand was hidden behind her back, so the image she presented was one of perfection. Her long-sleeved pink oxford-cloth shirt had a crisply starched collar and was belted into jeans that had a stiff crease. Her boots were so shiny he could have seen his reflection in them. Her straight black hair was tucked behind her ears.

He thought of the quick dousing he'd given himself in the barn. He'd rinsed off the worst of the sweat, but he wasn't precisely clean. His shirt wasn't ironed because Jenny had long ago given him the responsibility for doing it, and he'd decided he didn't mind the wrinkles. His boots were too scuffed to hold a shine, if he'd been inclined to give them one, which he wasn't.

Randy suddenly felt self-conscious. He should have taken a little more time to make himself presentable. He looked at the large kitchen table full of wedding paraphernalia and realized things were set up so they'd be sitting next to each other.

And me smelling like a workhorse.

"I…uh…I'm not sure how long I can stay," he said, wondering how he could make a graceful exit before she got a good whiff of him.

"Great! You're here!" Hope said, breezing into the kitchen. "I was afraid you wouldn't come, and I'd get stuck with Faith wrapping all that birdseed in net and tying it with ribbons."

Randy was relieved to see Hope wasn't dressed any better than he was. Her skintight jeans were torn at the knees, and she wore a Western shirt with the sleeves ripped out, strings still dangling, the tails tied in a knot that revealed a great deal of her midriff. Her tangled hair hung over her shoulders in disarray.

He almost smiled at the contrast between the sisters. Looking at them, you might easily get the wrong idea about which was the imperfect twin.

"You're not going to abandon us!" Faith said anxiously to her sister.

"I can help for a little while," Hope said. "But I've got other plans for later on." Hope plopped down into a chair on the opposite side of the rectangular oak table. "Let's get going. The sooner we start, the sooner this'll be done."

"You can sit here, Randy," Faith said, gesturing with her right hand to one of the two seats beside each other across from Hope.

He hesitated, then slid into the chair she'd indicated, because he wanted to sit next to her. After all, it was why he'd come. "What do you want me to do?" he asked.

"You can hold the pieces of net while I measure out the birdseed. Then I'll hold the net while you tie the bow. How does that sound?" Faith asked.

"All right, I guess," Randy replied. It dawned on him that she was going to need two hands. And that she was going to be using that hook on the end of her left arm as one of them. He felt a little jittery at the thought, and steeled himself not to shudder or do anything that would make her uncomfortable.

He glanced up and caught Hope watching him through narrowed eyes. And realized she was there not to help her sister with the wedding favors, but to protect Faith from him. He wanted to reassure Hope, but at the moment he wasn't certain how he was going to react when Faith hauled out that hook and started using it so close to his own hands.

Then he saw Faith's right hand was trembling and realized she was as scared as he was. A lump the size of Texas constricted his throat, and his chest felt like four football linemen had piled onto it.

He reached out and picked up a piece of net and placed it on the table in front of her. "Ready for—" He cleared his throat and said, "Ready for some seed."

He watched her pick up a two-pound plastic bag of birdseed at the top with her real hand, then grasp the bottom with the hook and aim the open corner onto the net. Too much poured out.

"Oh," she said, setting the bag down abruptly. Her eyes darted nervously in his direction, then focused on the mess she'd made.

He felt his heart pounding hard in his chest. If he blew this, he was pretty sure he wasn't going to get a second chance. "It's all right," he said, reaching quickly for another piece of net. "I'll divide this in two." He suited word to deed and poured half the birdseed onto the second piece of net. "Now what?"

"Get a piece of that pink ribbon over there."

The narrow silk ribbon had already been cut into lengths. While he grabbed the ribbon, she gathered the net around the seed with one hand, and held it closed at the top with the hook.

As nonchalantly as if he tied ribbons into bows every day, he surrounded the net below her hook with the ribbon and tied a creditable bow. "How's that?" he said when he was done.

She released the hook from the net and slid it away as she surveyed his work, but he noticed she didn't retreat with it under the table. "Pretty terrible," she announced at last.

He shot her an astonished look and saw she was smiling at him. His heart did a flip-flop. He looked back at the lopsided bow and said in an unsteady voice, "I'll do better on the next one."

"Hey, there! Anybody home?"

Randy looked over his shoulder at the screen door and said, "Hi, Jake."

"Hi, Jake," Faith said.

"I'll see to Jake," Hope said. "You two just keep on with what you're doing."

"I've got that delivery of hay your father ordered," Jake said when Hope pushed open the screen door. "Ask him where he wants me to put it."

"I'll show you," Hope said. "Follow me."

Hope was glad Randy hadn't turned out to be a jerk. Otherwise she wouldn't have been able to leave Faith behind with him. She'd been waiting a long time for the chance to get Jake Whitelaw alone.

This was it.

His shirt was dirty, the sleeves rolled up to reveal strong, sinewy forearms. His Stetson was sweaty around the brim, and shaggy black hair was crushed at his nape. His cheeks were hollow, and he had a sharp nose and wide-set, ice-blue eyes. He was half a foot taller than she was, lean at the hip, but with broad, powerful shoulders. He made her body come alive just looking at him.

"How are you, Jake?" she said, walking with her shoulders back so her breasts jutted and her hips swayed.

He eyed her sideways. "Just dandy," he muttered.

"Daddy wants that hay in the barn," she said, hop-skipping to keep up with his long strides.

"Why didn't you just say so? You don't need to come with me, little girl. I know where it goes."

Little girl. Hope ground her teeth. She'd show him she was no *little girl!* "There's some stuff needs to be moved first," she hedged. "Machinery that's too heavy for me to pick up by myself."

"Why didn't your daddy move it?"

"I told him I could do it. That is, before I realized how heavy it was," she fibbed.

Jake didn't look suspicious, but it wasn't going to take long once they got inside the barn for him to realize she'd lied. The space where the hay was supposed to be stacked had been cleared out that morning. She opened the door and went inside first, then waited for him to enter before she closed the door behind him.

Sunlight streamed through the cracks between the planks of the wooden barn, leaving golden lines on the empty, straw-littered dirt floor.

He turned to confront her. "What the hell is going on, little girl?"

She was backed up against the door to keep Jake from leaving. She put her hand over the light switch when he reached for it, afraid of what she'd see in his eyes in the stark light of the naked overhead bulb. He didn't force the issue, merely stepped back and stood facing her, his legs widespread, his hands on his hips.

"What happens now?" he said. "You want

sex? Take off your jeans and panties and lie down over there on that pile of straw on the floor.''

Hope's eyes went wide when he started to unbuckle his belt. ''Stop! Wait.'' She was shocked by his brutally frank speech, by the rough sound of his voice, by his plain intention of taking what she seemed to be offering without any pretense of romance. This wasn't how she'd imagined things happening between them.

He had his shirt unbuttoned and was ripping it out of his jeans when he paused and looked her right in the eye. ''You chickening out, little girl?''

Maybe if he hadn't made it a dare, she would have run, which is what she realized he expected her to do. She stared right back at him and began untying the knot at her midriff.

''I'm not going anywhere.''

She watched his eyes go wide, then narrow. A muscle jerked in his cheek. He no longer seemed interested in taking his clothes off. He was too busy watching her. Waiting, she suspected, to see how far she would go.

Her mouth was bone-dry, but she wanted him to know why she was doing this. ''I...I love you, Jake.''

He snorted. ''Get to it or get out.''

Her cheeks pinkened with mortification, but she refused to run. It wasn't easy undressing in front of him. She kept her eyes lowered, while she fumbled with the knot. He stood watching, waiting like a lone wolf stalking an abandoned calf, certain of the kill.

When the knot came free, her shirt fell open. She let it slide off her shoulders and onto the floor, revealing the pure white demi-cup pushup bra she'd bought with her baby-sitting money, which revealed just about everything but her nipples.

When she lifted her gaze to his face, she was frightened by what she saw. His eyes had a dangerous, feral look, his jaw was clenched tight, and his hands had balled into fists. He looked distant, unapproachable, but she forced herself to walk up to him, to slide her hands around his neck, to lift up on tiptoe to press her lips against his.

A second later she was shoved up hard against the barn door with Jake's hips grinding against her own. His tongue was in her mouth taking what he wanted, and she was so full of sharp, exciting sensations that she couldn't breathe.

Just as suddenly he backed off, leaving her with Jell-O knees that wanted to buckle, a heart that was threatening to explode and her insides tied up tight, hurting and wanting. "Jake," she said. It was a cry of emotional pain. A plea for surcease from her unrequited need.

"I'm twice your age," he said flatly. "You're too damn young for me, Hope."

"You want me," she said boldly.

It would have been hard to deny. His jeans bulged with abundant evidence of his desire. "I'm a grown man. Old enough to know better," he said with a disgusted sigh. He unbuttoned and unzipped his jeans, but only so he could tuck his shirt back in. He buttoned his shirt, buckled his belt and adjusted his clothes, then leaned down and picked up her shirt. "Put this on," he said.

She did as she was told. She hadn't gotten what she'd expected when she'd come in here with Jake. But she'd gotten what she wanted. Proof that he desired her. Proof that if she pushed long enough and hard enough, she might convince him that she was what he needed.

Her hands were shaking too much for her to tie a knot in the shirttails.

"I'll do it," he said, pushing her hands out of the way.

Her stomach quivered as his knuckles brushed against her flesh. She glanced up and saw the feral look was back in his eyes. He yanked the knot tight and stepped back.

"Now get the hell out of here!" he snarled.

Hope yanked open the barn door and ran.

Chapter 8

"Rise and shine, lazybones," Colt said with a laugh as he pulled the covers off Jenny.

She rolled over, then sat up and stared. He'd done it again. Brought her breakfast in bed. The first time he'd arrived unannounced it had provided a few awkward moments, since all she'd been wearing was one of Randy's old T-shirts, the cotton so thin it provided a revealing display of her suddenly peaked nipples.

That incident had led to the first of a dozen silly gifts Colt had given her over the past two weeks.

"If you're really into men's clothes, I thought

you'd appreciate these," he'd said when he presented her with a pair of navy blue men's cotton pajamas.

A set of flower-patterned china cups and saucers had come next. "You need to see something beautiful when you wake up each morning. I've got you," he'd said, making her blush with pleasure, "but I thought you might like these."

One morning she'd stepped outside the kitchen door and discovered the entire back porch was lined with hanging baskets of pink and white impatiens. "I owe you some flowers," he'd said. "For all the times I never brought you any."

What he meant, of course, was for all the times Huck had never brought her any.

While Colt settled the breakfast tray in her lap, Jenny fingered the solitary diamond that hung on a fragile gold chain around her neck. Colt had given her the necklace last night after Randy had gone to bed, when they were alone in the living room.

"I noticed you're still wearing Huck's ring," he'd said. "But I wanted to give you a diamond. I hope this is all right."

After he clasped the necklace around her throat, she'd reached up to touch the dimensions of the stone, to test the fragility of the chain.

An inexplicable feeling of panic had forced her off the couch and across the room to the fireplace. She'd watched the flames lick at the dry wood they'd gathered together that afternoon and fought the urge to cry.

"What's wrong?" he asked, sensing her distress. He didn't follow her. He waited for her to return on her own.

She twisted the diamond ring on her finger, adjusting it, reminding herself of its presence as she had done for ten long years. Huck's ring had been the one visible proof that they were engaged, that he intended to come back to her. Now Colt had laid his claim, slipping a chain—a delicate one to be sure—around her neck, when he had no more intention of staying with her than Huck had.

The hot tears came without warning, filling her eyes and spilling over. Colt crossed to her then, anxious and concerned. He pulled her into his arms, and she felt his lips kissing away the tears as he murmured words of comfort.

"It doesn't mean anything, Jenny. I don't expect you to love me the way you loved Huck," he said. "It's just a gift. Something from me to you. Be happy, Jenny. Please."

That made her cry all the harder, because it would have been very easy to fall in love with

Colt. It was hard not to appreciate a man whose every thought was directed toward making your life easier. But, damn it, she didn't want to fall in love with another man who intended to leave her behind while he went off to fly jets. Especially not someone who was only taking care of her as a duty to his dead friend.

A certain ticking clock reminded Jenny that moments like this had to be seized and enjoyed.

She brushed at Colt's sideburns, which were already growing out, then eased her thumb across the scar on his chin where the stitches had been removed, unable to stop herself from touching him. "I'm crying because I'm happy, Colt. That's all."

He looked deep into her eyes, searching for the truth.

It was the truth. At that moment she was happy. She'd learned a long time ago, as the child of a dying mother, to relish every day for the pleasures it brought her. That lesson was standing her in good stead now.

She saw the lingering doubt in Colt's eyes and did the only thing she thought might convince him she was pleased with the gift—and with him. She kissed him gently on the mouth.

She'd had some inkling in advance of how

powerful her response might be. Yet, she was surprised again. This kiss was different—more devastating—than the ones that had come before, because there was no guilt to dampen pleasure. This kiss was a celebration of joy, of delight in the man who held her in his arms. Passion rose quickly and flared hot.

Tentatively, her hands went seeking, feeling the ropey muscles in Colt's shoulders and sliding down his strong back. His hands weren't idle, and she gasped as his palm closed on her breast. The sensation was exquisite because it was so unexpected. Huck had touched her breasts many times before, but it had never felt like this. Jenny sought for the difference and found it. There was reverence in Colt's touch, along with the hunger.

He'd already eased her shirt off and was reaching for the front clasp of her bra when she suddenly came to her senses and realized what might happen if she took this next step with him.

"Colt, no."

His mouth nuzzled the curve of her breast above her bra, and she nearly swooned before she finally grasped his hand to stop him.

"Not yet," she pleaded. "I'm not ready. Not yet."

She heard his shuddering breath, felt the tautness in his shoulders as he brought himself back from the brink. He kissed her gently on the mouth, his tongue teasing her lips until she relented and let him come inside.

To soothe, to taste, to caress.

It was the kind of kiss they might have shared as teenagers in the back seat of his Mustang, when he knew they couldn't go all the way. Deep and rich and thorough. It was lovemaking without the sex.

And she appreciated him all the more for it.

She heard a moan from deep in his throat, a grating sound of both satisfaction and the need for more, before he finally broke the kiss. When she met Colt's eyes, she saw that the fire had been banked, but it wouldn't take much to fan it back into flames. He was leaving the choice up to her. She knew she had to back away, because it was clear he wouldn't—or couldn't.

For a moment last night Jenny had thought about trusting Colt with her secret. Fear had held her back. Once he knew, he would leave for sure. She wanted to hold on to him for as long as she could.

"Good night, Colt," she said as she backed away.

He'd reached down and picked up her shirt, and she'd flushed as she realized she'd forgotten completely about it. He' given her a lopsided smile and said, ''Good night, Jenny. I—'' He'd cut himself off, swallowed hard and said, ''I'll see you in the morning.''

And here he was with breakfast on a tray, fresh from the shower, with eyes that crinkled at the corners with laughter...and her heart on his plate.

''You're going to spoil me, Colt,'' she said as she held the tray steady and scooted back against the headboard.

''You deserve a little coddling.'' He settled on the edge of the bed by her knees and grabbed a slice of cinnamon raisin toast slathered in butter.

Jenny picked up a flowered china cup, blew on the steaming coffee, then sipped carefully, grateful for the caffeine. She wasn't quite sure how to act after what had happened between them last night and decided to let Colt set the tone.

Colt was trying to act nonchalant, when that was the last thing he was feeling. He'd been buying Jenny little gifts ever since he'd realized how few of them she'd gotten in her life. He'd given her the diamond last night as a symbol of his love and commitment and as a first step toward asking for that same love and commitment from her.

The wary look in Jenny's eyes reminded him not to push too hard or too fast. But he couldn't shake the feeling that time was running out. His leave was more than half over, and their wedding day was rapidly approaching. Then he happened to glance at Jenny's left hand.

"Where's Huck's ring?"

"I took it off," she said, not meeting his gaze.

He watched her reach with her thumb to rub the empty spot where the ring used to be. His chest ached with hope and with fear. Maybe there was a chance for the two of them after all. He opened his mouth to speak, but she spoke first.

"Don't forget Randy's graduation ceremony is tonight," she said. "I promised him we'd go out to dinner first."

"I won't be late."

"Randy asked if he could bring a date to dinner," she said with a smile.

"Anybody I know?" Colt asked.

"Faith Butler."

Colt's jaw dropped. "*Faith* Butler? Not Hope?"

"Faith," Jenny repeated with a grin. "I couldn't believe it myself. Seems they've been seeing a lot of each other lately."

"Good for Randy. You've done a fantastic job raising him, Jenny. A great job raising all of them." He took a deep breath and plunged. "But it's time you started thinking of yourself."

"What does that mean?" Jenny asked, her eyes cautious.

"Just what I said. Why don't you sell this place and come see the world with me?"

"Colt, you promised—"

He grabbed the tray from her lap and threw it onto the dresser hard enough to make the china cup and saucer rattle, then turned to confront her. "I can't leave you here alone, Jenny. I'd worry too much about you."

"Then stay," she said simply.

He shoved both hands through his short hair, leaving it standing on end. "I'm considering that option."

Her eyes went wide. "You are? What's stopping you?"

He wanted to tell her the truth. That he didn't think he could stand waking up every morning to a wife who was in love with another man. He'd grow to hate her and himself. It was easier to go away—to stay away.

He was afraid to read too much into the fact she'd taken off Huck's ring. It might simply be that it evoked too many painful memories for her to wear it.

And that kiss last night?

Mere gratitude for the gift he'd given her. It was getting harder and harder to conceal his true feelings, but he wasn't about to let Jenny know he loved her when he had no hope of having that love returned.

"I'd like to stay Jenny," he said quietly. "But you're Huck's girl. You always have been, and you always will be."

"Huck is dead," she said, her voice cracking.

"I know," he said sadly. "I can't fight a ghost."

Jenny's brow creased. "Why would you need to?"

If she couldn't figure it out, he wasn't going to explain it to her. So he changed the subject. "I figured we'd start scraping down the barn today so we can give it a new coat of paint."

"I've got a few personal errands to run in town," she said, slipping off the bed and crossing to the dresser to run a brush through her hair. "I'll be back by six to shower and change for dinner."

"You're going to be gone all day?" he asked, startled.

She gave him a smile in the mirror as phony as a three-dollar bill. "I've put off a lot of things that can't wait any longer."

"What aren't you telling me?" he said, frowning. "Is there some complication at the bank? Some problem I don't know about?"

She laughed, a brittle sound that sent a chill up his spine. "It's nothing like that." She set down the hairbrush and turned to face him. "If I'd known you were going to get so upset, I wouldn't have told you about it."

"And then what?" he said, crossing to her, putting his hands on her shoulders from behind and looking at their two faces in the mirror. "You just disappear for the day? You don't think that might have given me a few gray hairs?"

"You're making too much of this," she said, shaking off his hands and sliding past him toward the bathroom, where she could shut herself in—and him out.

He caught her arm and whirled her around. "You don't think I'm entitled to an explanation?"

"I don't have to explain myself to you or anyone else," she said sharply.

"I'm your husband."

"Not yet you aren't!" She jerked her arm free. "And maybe not ever, if this is the kind of inquisition I can expect when I want to go somewhere without you tagging along."

"Tagging along—" He was too furious to finish.

She poked a finger in his chest to back him off. "I've survived a very long time without you, Colt. Don't you get it? I don't need you. I don't need any man. Especially one who only wants to marry me out of a sense of guilt."

"A sense of—" he spluttered. "Where is this coming from?"

"You know very well you're only marrying me because you feel obligated as Huck's friend to make sure the widow's taken care of."

"That's not true!" He grabbed her by the arms and shook her. "I love you, damn it! I always have."

Her eyes went wide, and her jaw dropped. She was speechless, leaving a great deal of silence in which to absorb what he'd said.

Colt felt like he was going to throw up. He let her go, and she took a quick step back. "Jenny, I—"

"I don't understand. You were Huck's friend! Or you pretended to be."

"That's unfair, and you know it. Let's sit down and discuss this. Please, Jenny."

"I have an appointm—" She bit her lip. "I've

got errands to run. This discussion will have to wait.''

She was backing away toward the bathroom, but he wasn't going to let her escape so easily. ''Wait until when?'' he demanded.

''Until later.''

He reached out and caught her chin with his hand, forcing her to look at him. ''When, Jenny?''

''Later. Tonight,'' she added when his grip tightened. ''Let me go, Colt.''

He let her go, and an instant later she was gone.

Colt was still scraping down the barn when Randy approached him after school. Colt was hot and tired and irritable, because he knew he had to decide whether to stay in the Air Force or stay here with Jenny, and an entire day of scraping paint hadn't done much to resolve his dilemma.

It was hard to imagine his life without flying jets. It was impossible to imagine it without Jenny. He wanted both. But it was becoming very clear that he couldn't have both.

''Where's Jenny?'' Randy asked.

''She's still in town running errands.''

''Oh.''

Colt slapped at a fly that had landed on his

nose, but it buzzed away unharmed. "What does that mean, 'Oh'?"

"Nothing," Randy said quickly. "You want some help?"

Colt had three-quarters of the barn scraped free of old paint. Maybe with Randy's help he could finish today. "Sure. Why not? There's another scraper on the tool rack in the barn."

Randy slipped his book bag off his shoulder and dropped it on the ground. "I'll be right back," he said.

Colt swatted at the fly again, which was now buzzing his ear. He'd already done all the work that needed to be done on a ladder, so he and Randy worked side by side scraping the lower half of the barn.

"When did you know what you wanted to do with your life?" Randy asked.

Colt shot him a sideways look. "From the time I was a kid. Why?"

"I thought I knew what I wanted, but lately I've been less certain of what I should do."

"I see," Colt said, neither encouraging nor discouraging further discussion of the subject.

"I planned to study business because I figured that's where the money is," Randy said, keeping his eyes focused on the work he was doing. "But earning money doesn't appeal as much to me now as something else does.''

''What's changed your mind?'' Colt asked.

''I met someone.''

Colt smiled. ''A woman has a way of making you think twice about a lot of things.''

Randy stopped scraping and stared at him. ''How'd you know it was a girl?''

''Lucky guess.''

''Anyway,'' Randy continued, ''ever since I started seeing this girl, Faith Butler, I've been thinking maybe I'd like to study something else entirely.''

Colt resisted the urge to ask what and said, ''Mmm-hmm.''

''Funny thing is, I don't even know what kind of courses I'd need to take to learn about it.''

Colt wanted to know what ''it'' was, but there was an unwritten code, going all the way back to the days when people came west to escape their checkered pasts, that said a man didn't ask for information that wasn't volunteered. Instead he said, ''The university could probably tell you what you need to study.''

''I suppose. I guess I'd better find out whether Texas Tech teaches anything about orthotics. Maybe I'll need to go somewhere else.''

"I give up," Colt said. "What's orthotics?"

Randy grinned. "Making mechanical limbs for people who need them. Faith says there's a new silicone hand that looks a lot more real than a latex one, but nothing works as well as an old-fashioned hook. I want to invent a mechanical hand that works like a real one—you know, like in the *Terminator* movies."

Colt eyed him speculatively. "What does Faith have to say about all this?"

"We haven't discussed it." Randy began to scrape vigorously on the barn wall. Colt figured that meant he didn't want to discuss the subject with him, either, so he let it drop.

A moment later Randy's hands dropped to his sides, his chin fell to his chest and he heaved a great sigh. "How do you know when you're in love?"

Colt stopped scraping and turned to face the teenager. His first instinct was to tell Randy he was too young to fall in love, that he had a lot of living to do before he settled on one woman, and the best thing to do was ignore the feeling and it would go away. But Randy was four years older than he'd been when he'd fallen for Jenny. And that love had lasted a lifetime.

"Have you asked your sister that question?" he hedged.

Randy's face was suddenly suffused with blood, which could have been the heat, but was more likely embarrassment. "I never needed to before now. And now...I couldn't talk to her now about being in love. I mean, not with Huck dying like that, and you guys getting married in some kind of business arrangement."

"Is that what Jenny told you?" Colt said, his stomach clenching. "That our marriage is a business arrangement?"

"Well, it is, isn't it? I mean, you guys aren't in love or anything. And you're planning to leave and go back to flying jets, so what else could it be? Not that I blame Jenny for marrying you. I mean, how else can she get the money to keep the ranch?"

Colt spoke through his teeth because his jaw was clamped so tight. "Let's get one thing straight, Randy. Our marriage may have some financial benefits for your sister, but it's going to be real in every way." Colt barely kept himself from shouting that he loved Jenny. That would require an explanation that he wanted to make to Jenny first.

Randy's flush heightened. "I'm not criticizing

you and Jenny. I just...I always thought people got married because they loved each other and wanted to spend their lives together. I know how hard it was for Jenny all those years with Huck gone. I hate to think of her alone when you're gone, too.

"I'd offer to come back to the ranch after I finish college," Randy said, "but I know that wouldn't really solve the problem. I think I've found the woman I'm going to marry someday, and having me and my wife living here at the Double D would just point out to Jenny how alone she is. I mean, I think I love Faith."

Which brought them back to Randy's original question. "I don't know how to tell you whether this girl is the right one for you," Colt said. "I can only tell you my own experience. When you love someone, your every thought begins and ends with her. What is she feeling? Is she happy? What can you do to make her life easier? And you want her physically. Fiercely, completely. That's part of it. Mostly, love is always considering her needs before your own. Is that how you feel?"

Colt could almost see the tension easing from Randy's shoulders. "Yeah," he said. "That's *exactly* how I feel."

Colt gave him a cuff on the shoulder. ''Sounds like you're in love, pal.''

''Thanks for listening, Colt.''

Colt stood back and surveyed the work they'd done and realized the job was finished. ''Why don't you go on in and get cleaned up? There's going to be a lot of demand for that shower if we're all going to get gussied up in time for your graduation ceremony tonight. I'll put away the tools.'' He reached for Randy's scraper, and the boy handed it to him, then picked up his book bag and trotted toward the house.

Colt stared after Randy, realizing that in talking to the boy he'd found his own answers. His days as a jet pilot were numbered. But to his surprise, he didn't feel resigned or sad or desperate. Because when it came to a choice between having Jenny or living life without her—there really was no choice. If he truly loved Jenny, it meant putting her needs before his own. It meant staying here to be a husband to her instead of running off to fly jets.

And it meant finding a way to handle the pain, if she could never love him back.

Chapter 9

"You look so grown-up," Jenny said as she straightened Randy's tie. She reached up to brush back the lock of golden hair that always fell onto his forehead, and he ducked away.

"Give me a break, Jenny," he said, thrusting his hand into his hair, leaving it mussed. "It's just graduation."

"Just graduation," Jenny repeated past the painful lump in her throat. The tears came without warning.

"Aw, Jenny." Randy's arms closed awkwardly around her, and she laid her head against his shoulder.

"I can't believe you're all grown-up," she said, her voice cracking. She made herself step back, quickly wiped away the tears and once against straightened his tie, while he shifted impatiently from foot to foot.

"Can I leave now? I need to pick up Faith."

"We'll meet you at Buck's Steakhouse. Drive carefully."

He rolled his eyes and said sarcastically, "Yes, Mother." He stopped abruptly, the screen door half open, and turned to face her. "Jenny, I'm sorry. It just slipped out."

"Never mind. Go. You're going to be late."

He disappeared, the screen door slamming behind him.

Jenny had been a mother to her brothers, but she'd warned them against labeling her that way. Because they knew it bothered her, they addressed her as "Mother" whenever they were angry or upset, knowing it would get a rise out of her.

Right now, she felt very much like a mother hen whose nest had just been emptied of its last chick. A huge hole gaped inside her that once had been filled up with the responsibility for her brothers. She didn't feel free. She felt empty. This didn't feel like the beginning of a new life. It felt like the end.

''Hey. Give me a break.''

Jenny turned to find Colt wearing a white button-down shirt, khaki slacks and a conservative regimental-striped tie. He leaned against the doorway to the kitchen, a navy suit coat slung over his shoulder, his hip cocked.

''I suppose you witnessed that scene,'' she said.

''I did.''

''I'm going to miss him.''

''I know.''

A tear slipped down her cheek, and she quickly rubbed it away. ''I don't understand where all these tears are coming from,'' she said with a shaky laugh.

''Don't you?'' Colt asked, crossing toward her. He laid his suit coat across one of the ladder-back chairs at the kitchen table and opened his arms. ''Come here, Jenny.''

She didn't resist his offer of comfort. She took the few steps that put her within his embrace, and his arms closed around her. ''I've been waiting and wishing for this day for so long, but now that it's here, I just feel sad,'' she admitted.

She felt his hand smooth across her hair. Felt his lips at her temple and on her closed eyes.

''I feel like my life is over,'' she whispered.

"I promise you, Jenny, it's just beginning. Have you been thinking about what I said to you this morning?"

Jenny had thought of little else during the day besides Colt's confession. *I love you. I always have.* "I remember."

"I've decided to resign from the Air Force, Jenny. I want to stay here and marry you and raise babies with you. If that's want you want, too."

Jenny felt her heart squeeze with joy and with pain. "Oh, Colt."

Tell him now, Jenny. If he really loves you, it won't matter.

She leaned back and looked up into his face, surprised at what she found. He was afraid, she realized. Of what? Suddenly Jenny knew. Afraid that she could never love him. That she would always—only—love Huck.

"I told you I've been thinking a lot today, and I have," she said. "About me and Huck. About me and you."

Colt cleared his throat, but he didn't speak. Which was a good thing, because if he'd interrupted her, she might not have been able to say what she knew had to be said.

"There was a time when I loved Huck body and soul. I wanted to make a life with him. I wanted to have his babies. I wanted to grow old with him." Jenny sighed and looked away. "I'm not sure when the loving stopped."

Colt inhaled a sharp breath of air.

She forced herself to look at him. "It wasn't until you said you loved me this morning that I made myself take a brutally honest look at my relationship with Huck. I realized that all these years I haven't been in love with Huck. I've been in love with a dream of what life could be like with him—if he ever settled down."

She lowered her gaze to Colt's throat and watched his Adam's apple bob as he swallowed hard. Her voice was barely audible as she admitted, "The last couple of times Huck came home, we didn't even make love."

"Jenny, I—"

She put her fingertips over his lips. "I'm not finished." She looked at him and said, "I never suspected how you felt. How you feel," she corrected when she felt his mouth open to protest. "I do know I've always been grateful for your friendship. You were there so many times when Huck wasn't."

She felt his lips flatten under her hand and removed it. "I'll admit I'm tempted by what you seem to be offering. But I'm afraid of making the same mistake twice. Maybe we can never be more than friends. You've caught me at a vulnerable time and—"

"Can I get a word in here?"

She gave a jerky nod.

"All I'm asking is that you give us a chance, Jenny. Can you do that?"

"Colt, there are things you don't know. Things—"

He shook his head to cut her off. "The past is the past. We start fresh from here."

Tell him, Jenny.

Jenny opened her mouth, but the words wouldn't come out. It could wait. Maybe there would be no need to tell him anything. Maybe they would mutually decide they didn't belong together any more than she and Huck had. If the buds of feeling she had for Colt began to blossom, that would be soon enough to confess her secret.

"What do you say, Jenny? Will you let me court you?"

"Court me?" she said, her lips curving. "Is that really necessary? I've already promised to marry you."

He smiled for the first time since their discussion had begun. "It's the time-honored way a cowboy wins his lady's love. How about it?"

Jenny gave him a shy look from beneath lowered lashes. "If you insist."

"I do. Are you ready to face the world as a couple?"

"As ready as I'll ever be," Jenny said with a determined smile. "Let's go."

"Do you realize this is our first date?" Colt said as he opened the passenger door to the classic red Ford Mustang convertible he'd been storing at his parents' ranch while he was overseas.

Jenny smiled up at him as she slid into the black leather bucket seat. "This is certainly the right car for it. How about putting the top down?"

"You wouldn't mind?"

"I'd love it," Jenny said. And she did. The night was warm, and the sky was filled with a million stars. She found herself laughing as her hair whipped around her face, making it impossible to see. "I should have brought a scarf," she said.

"Look in the glove compartment," Colt said.

She opened the glove compartment and found a small turquoise silk scarf. "This is mine!"

He shot her a sheepish grin. "I found it in the car after Huck borrowed it."

"I remember when I lost this," she said as she tied back her hair at her nape. "Huck said it must have blown off. But I was sure I'd taken it off when we—'' Jenny stopped herself.

''Yeah. That's what I figured, too,'' Colt said. He shot her a quick look. ''You have no idea how much agony I suffered thinking about the two of you in the back seat of this car.''

Jenny was grateful for the darkness that prevented Colt from seeing her blush. ''Maybe I can make it up to you,'' she said.

Colt turned to stare at her. ''Are you saying what I think you're saying?'' His eyes looked hungry, and she felt both frightened and exhilarated at the prospect of joining Colt in the back seat of his Mustang.

A blaring horn brought them both to their senses.

''Watch out!'' she cried.

Colt yanked the wheel to avoid the car coming from the opposite direction, overcompensated and went off the road. He hit the brakes, and the Mustang skidded to a halt on the dirt and gravel shoulder.

''Are you all right?'' Colt asked.

Jenny was trembling, the result of too much adrenaline. ''That was close,'' she said with a small laugh.

''Yeah. Too close. We could've been killed.

And I would've missed getting to kiss you in the back seat of this car." Colt opened his door, trotted around the front of the car, then opened her door. "Out," he ordered.

"Colt, it's the middle of nowhere. What are you doing?"

"We're taking a little trip down memory lane." Once she was out of the seat, he pushed it forward, making a space for her to slip into the back seat. "Get in."

Jenny slid into the back seat and scooted over to make room for Colt, who stepped in behind her. Before she had a chance to think, Colt slid one arm around her shoulder and pulled her close. With his eyes on hers, with their lips only an inch apart, he slowly tugged the scarf from her hair and sieved his fingers into her hair.

"I love you, Jenny. I want to hold you and kiss you and make love to you until I can't see straight."

"Oh, Colt."

Huck had never said such things, even though Jenny had always wished he would. Maybe it was because they'd become sweethearts at such a young age. Maybe it was because Huck hadn't known how much she needed to hear them said.

She couldn't honestly tell Colt she loved him, or even that she was ready yet to make love to him. But she returned the favor of asking out loud for what she wanted.

"I want to kiss you, too," she said. She put her hand at his nape and urged his mouth down to hers, feeling the desire shoot through her as his mouth captured hers.

"I want to touch you," he murmured against her lips.

She suddenly felt shy, like an innocent who'd never been touched. She reached for his hand and brought it to her breast. She moaned in her throat as his hand closed around her breast and his forefinger and thumb rolled her nipple. "Ohmigod," she gasped.

How could she feel so much? How could she need so much? There was something more she wanted. "I want to touch you," she murmured.

Colt made a guttural sound in his throat as his hand left her breast and reached for her hand, guiding it toward his mouth. He kissed her palm, then pressed it against his cheek.

His skin felt soft and smooth after his shave and smelled of piney woods. She found the scar on his chin with her fingertips first, then with her lips. Her hand slid down Colt's throat to his chest, where she felt his heart thudding under her hand.

He held his breath as her hand moved lower, past his belt until she reached the hardness and heat between his legs. He stilled as she tentatively touched, tracing the shape of him, learning the feel of him. He groaned, then grabbed her wrist to stop her exploration.

"I love the way you kiss and touch," he said. "But the first time we make love, I want enough privacy to know we're not going to be disturbed for a good long while. We're already ten minutes late for supper at Buck's Steakhouse."

Jenny managed a crooked smile. "At least I know I have a great deal to look forward to."

Colt laughed. "Come on. Let me help you out of here."

"Wait."

Colt paused halfway out of the back seat. "What's the matter?"

She grinned. "You're going to have to help me find my scarf."

Colt laughed, kissed her quickly on the mouth, then pulled the scarf from his jeans pocket and gave it back to her.

It took them only five minutes after they were on the road to reach Buck's Steakhouse. To

Jenny's surprise, Colt curved his arm possessively around her waist as he led her inside. She knew he didn't give a damn what people thought. He never had. But she'd lived here for more than fifteen years as Huck's girl. She couldn't help feeling a little trepidation as they stepped inside the restaurant.

She hadn't overestimated the effect their appearance arm-in-arm would have on their friends and neighbors. Curious eyes focused on them as she and Colt followed the waitress to their table. Jenny shivered. It felt like a caterpillar was crawling on her skin.

"Ignore them," Colt whispered in her ear. "They'll get used to it."

Jenny wasn't so sure. They might get used to seeing her with Colt, but people in small Texas towns had very long memories. When she and Colt were old and gray, her name would still be linked with Huck's when it came up in conversation.

Assuming you live that long.

It had been dishonest not to tell Colt all the facts before he began his courtship. But it was entirely likely that once he knew the truth, he'd hightail it in the other direction. Jenny wanted to be wooed. She wanted to fall in love with Colt, perhaps even make love with him someday. Was that so wrong?

"You're beautiful, Jenny," Colt murmured. "I'm the envy of every man here."

She flushed with pleasure and turned to look at him. The admiration was plain in his eyes, along with something else.

Love.

That was how she justified keeping her secret. Colt already loved her. He had nothing to lose by trying to win her love. She was the one risking everything. She was the one planning to fall in love with a man who might very well leave her in the end—as her father had left her mother— not because he didn't care, but because he cared too much.

She was glad Randy and Faith were sitting at the table, because otherwise she might have been tempted to confess everything. She was surprised to see that Hope had come along.

"Hello, girls," Jenny said. "You're both looking very pretty tonight."

"Thank you, Miss Wright," they replied in unison.

The twins did look remarkably pretty, Jenny thought, but for identical twins, they also looked remarkably different. Hope wore a sophisticated strapless black sheath that was cut low enough to reveal a great deal of cleavage. Faith was dressed in a simple, V-necked powder blue dress with capped sleeves.

Hope's hair was swept up in an elegant French twist, and she wore earrings that dangled, drawing male attention to her slender throat and bare shoulders. Faith wore her straight black hair tucked behind her ears, which held tiny diamond studs.

Faith looked like the fresh-faced teenager she was, with only a hint of pink lipstick to emphasize her natural beauty. Her dark eyes glowed from within.

Hope's face was expertly made up, but she looked like a picture in a book, not a real person, and beyond the thick mascara on her lashes, Jenny saw a hint of desperation in the girl's dark eyes.

"Hope didn't have any other plans, so Faith asked if she could come along," Randy said. "I said it'd be fine. It's okay, isn't it?"

"Sure. I'm glad you could both join us," Jenny said as Colt seated her. She knew Randy well enough to sense he was annoyed at Hope's presence, but she was proud of him for being gracious. "Looks like there's plenty of room at the table," she said.

"Jake asked if he could join us," Colt said. "So I asked Buck to make sure we had a big table."

Jenny eyed Colt speculatively, but he didn't explain why Jake had invited himself along for a celebration to which he could have only a tenuous connection.

Then Jenny looked across the table at Hope, all dressed up with no date at her side, and remembered how Hope had cornered Jake on her back porch during Huck's wake. Hope had flirted openly, but Jake hadn't seemed interested. Had Hope known Jake would be coming tonight? Was that why she'd invited herself along?

Jenny prayed the young woman hadn't developed a crush on Jake. Since his divorce five years ago, he'd been hell on women. Hope's youth might provide some protection from Jake's crude behavior, but if she pushed, Jake was likely to shove right back.

Jenny had an unsettling thought. What if Jake had arranged for Hope to be here so he could meet with her?

Once Jenny had ordered iced tea, she hid behind the menu and leaned over to ask Colt, "Did Jake say why he wanted to join us?"

Colt shrugged. "He always has a steak at

Buck's on Friday night. When he realized we were coming, he asked if he could join us. Do you mind?''

"Of course not," Jenny said. "I always liked Jake." She'd liked him a lot better before he'd been married to Lucy Palance, a girl he'd met when they were in college. Their ten-year marriage hadn't seemed to bring much happiness to either of them. She'd often seen Jake with women over the past five years, but they weren't the kind of female a hard-working rancher married.

So Jenny was amazed when Jake showed up with a schoolteacher on his arm. Miss Amanda Carter was not only a proper lady, she was also fun-loving and pretty. She was twenty-nine and still unmarried, though she'd been pursued by all the most eligible bachelors in town. She wore a tailored cream-colored silk suit that accented her female curves. Amanda was exactly the sort of woman Jenny would have chosen as a second wife for Jake. She just wasn't the sort of woman she'd expected to find at Jake's side. Was Jake turning over a new leaf?

Jenny glanced at Hope and saw from the girl's stunned expression that she might very well have known Jake was coming tonight but hadn't expected him to show up with a date. The blood leached from her face until her eyes were like two burned spots on a sheet of parchment.

Judging from Faith's equally stricken expression, she was aware of her sister's distress. Faith had seated herself so her good hand was next to Randy, so it was necessary to reach out to Hope with her prosthesis. Jenny watched in surprise as Hope tightly gripped the metal hook for comfort, as though it were a flesh-and-blood hand.

Hope's eyes never left Jake's face. She seemed to be waiting for something. *For Jake to acknowledge her,* Jenny realized.

Jake avoided speaking directly to Hope, or even looking at her, by saying to Amanda, "You know the Butler twins."

"I do," Amanda said with a smile. "You both look very pretty tonight."

"Thank you, Miss Carter," Faith replied.

Hope said nothing. Her gaze dropped to her lap, and color—an entire rose garden of color—suddenly grew on her pale cheeks. Her jaw was clamped, and she was blinking furiously.

Jenny gave Jake a surreptitious glance to see whether he was affected by Hope's despair and caught him stealing a look at Hope from the corner of his eye. It dawned on her that Jake was very much aware of Hope, that his indifference was a calculated act. He apparently cared for Hope a great deal more than he wanted her to know. And just as apparently had decided she was too young for him.

What was it about the Whitelaw men that made them fall in love with unavailable women? Jenny wondered. She only had Colt to judge by, but if Jake was crazy enough to go through such an elaborate charade to discourage Hope, he wasn't going to be happy with a substitute bride, even one as appropriate as Miss Amanda Carter.

Jake ordered a beer for himself and Amanda, then asked if she wanted to dance to the live country and western band that played at Buck's on Friday and Saturday nights. A moment later Jake pulled Amanda into his arms and began two-stepping around the wooden dance floor. Jake was a good dancer, and Jenny was forced to admit the couple looked very much like they belonged together.

A glance at Hope revealed tight lips and narrowed eyes.

Hope had obviously gotten the message Jake had sent by bringing along Miss Carter tonight. It wasn't the gentlest setdown Jenny had ever seen a man give a woman. But it was certainly effective.

She felt sorry for Hope. And angry at Jake. This was Hope's graduation night, one of the most important nights in her life. What Jake had done was cruel, even if he'd believed it was necessary.

Colt leaned over to speak in her ear. "What's got you frowning?"

"Your brother is an idiot," she whispered back.

"I've always thought so," Colt agreed with a grin. "What has Jake done this time?"

"Coming here with Amanda was—"

Before she could finish, the music stopped and Jake and Amanda headed back toward the table. Jake seated Amanda next to Hope, then sat across from her.

"Thanks, Jake," Amanda said. "That was fun."

"You're a good dancer, Amanda," Jake replied.

Jenny watched as Jake stole another glance at Hope. The teenager's chin had dropped to her chest, and she was twisting her paper napkin into a knot. It was small comfort to see the flash of pain in Jake's eyes.

As soon as Amanda was settled and had taken a sip of her beer, she turned to the twins and asked, "Have you girls decided yet where you're going to college?"

Jenny had expected Faith to answer, but to her amazement, it was Hope who spoke. She lifted her head until her chin jutted and her shoulders were squared. Her eyes gleamed with unshed tears, but her voice belied her agitation as she replied, "Faith and I have both been accepted at Baylor, Miss Carter."

"Have you decided on a major yet?" Amanda inquired.

Hope's chin lifted another notch. "Animal husbandry."

Jake choked on his beer.

"I want to learn how to put the right mare with the right stud," Hope said, staring right at Jake. "That's so important when you want to end up with good stock, don't you agree, Mr. Whitelaw?"

Jake's eyes narrowed. "Absolutely."

Jenny figured any second now things were going to get ugly. She opened her mouth to intervene, but Jake spoke first.

"That's why I proposed to Miss Carter tonight."

Hope inhaled sharply.

"I didn't know you two had been seeing each other," Jenny said to Amanda.

"I've had my eye on Jake for a long time. He's been a hard man to pin down," Amanda said with a smile. "But he was worth the wait," she said, leaning over to kiss Jake on the mouth.

"Congratulations," Colt said, grinning and slapping Jake on the back. He stood up enough to lean over and kiss Amanda on the cheek. "I can always use another sister. I wish you both the very best."

Jenny turned to see how Hope was handling this latest announcement and discovered her chair was empty. The shredded napkin lay on the empty plate where she had been.

Jenny's gaze shot to Randy, who shrugged helplessly. To Jenny's surprise, it was Faith who saved the day.

"Hope hasn't been feeling well today," Faith said as she stood. "I think we'll wait and eat at the senior picnic later tonight. Will you excuse us, please?"

"Be careful on the—"

"I know," Randy said, cutting Jenny off as he rose to go with Faith. "I'll drive slow. See you at the ceremony, sis. Bye, Colt. Bye, Miss Carter. Congratulations, Jake."

Once the teenagers were gone, the empty seats at the table loomed large. Jenny searched for something to say, but could think of nothing. Jake's face looked pale, and Jenny noticed he had let go of Amanda's hand.

"You're not the only one with news, Jake," Colt said with a smile to his older brother. "You can wish me happy, too. I've decided to resign from the Air Force and stay at the Double D with Jenny."

Jake's lips curled in a bleak smile. "Well, little brother, looks like we're both going to settle down and live happily ever after."

Jenny shivered as a chill of foreboding ran down her spine.

Chapter 10

"Why are you so fidgety?" Faith whispered.

Randy shot a glance at Faith, who was sitting next to him on the front seat of Old Nellie, then at Hope, who was sitting to Faith's right, and then back to the winding dirt road. "Guess I'm just excited about graduating."

After what had happened at supper, he should've known Faith wouldn't go to the senior picnic without Hope. Randy was beginning to wonder if he'd ever get Faith alone.

Everyone had brought along jeans and T-shirts to change into at the rest rooms at school, because the picnic consisted of a midnight hot dog and marshmallow roast around a bonfire at the Whitelaw ranch. The Whitelaw Brats had started the tradition, and long after their youngest had graduated, Zach and Rebecca Whitelaw continued to make the site at Camp LittleHawk available for the party.

Drinking alcohol was forbidden, and couples were discouraged from wandering off into the dark. Randy figured one couple wouldn't be missed in all the excitement, and he'd made special plans for himself and Faith—if he could manage to separate her from her sister.

This year Jenny had volunteered to be one of the chaperons, along with Colt and his brother Jake. Randy supposed that meant Miss Carter would be present, too.

Too bad for Hope.

Faith had told Randy about Hope's crush on Jake. He felt sorry for her after what had happened tonight, Jake getting engaged and all, and he understood Faith didn't want to leave her twin alone at a time like this. But he was determined to have some time alone with her.

"We're here," he announced as he pulled Old Nellie in line with two dozen other vehicles.

"I've got a blanket in the bed of the pickup we can sit on," he said to Faith.

"I'll get it," Hope volunteered, hopping out of the truck.

Within minutes, Randy was sitting next to Faith on a blanket beside the fire—with Hope perched on Faith's left side. He racked his brain to think of a way to distract Hope. Once he found it, he had to wait almost an hour before he found a moment when Jenny was busy enough that he and Faith could escape the party without their absence being immediately detected.

"Say, Hope," he said at last. "Why don't you see if Jake wants to roast some marshmallows? He's been standing over there all by himself with his arms crossed, just staring into the fire, ever since Miss Carter left to take care of her mother."

He watched Hope hesitate, then rise. "All right," she said. "I will."

Randy waited barely long enough to see the back of Hope before he turned to Faith and said, "Would you like to take a walk with me?"

She laid her right hand in his and said, "Sure."

He helped her to her feet and edged out of the light of the fire and into the shadows beyond. They weren't the only ones who'd decided to "take a walk." They passed several couples standing in the dark kissing. Most lingered just outside the light from the fire. For what he had in mind, Randy wanted more distance.

"Where are we going?" Faith asked as he led her farther into the moonlit darkness.

"Just a little farther," he said.

"It's awfully dark out here."

Randy stopped and looked up. "There's got to be a zillion or so stars up there, and the moon's pretty full. Trust me, Faith," he said, squeezing her hand.

She squeezed his hand back and followed without more argument. He saw the concern on her face when a glow appeared in the distance. They slid down an incline and into a gully, where he had previously set out a Coleman lantern, a blanket, and a picnic basket.

"We're here," he announced.

"What's all this?" Faith asked, turning to look at him.

Her eyes were wide and wary, and Randy knew he was about to find out whether she really did trust him. "I wanted us to have our own party," he said. "Do you mind?"

Her smile was slow in coming, but when it finally arrived, the muscles in his stomach unclenched. "I think it's a wonderful idea," she said. "Won't your sister wonder what's happened to us?"

He settled onto a ring-patterned quilt that had been made by his mother and pulled Faith down beside him. "We're no farther away than a shout, if anybody really wants to find us. I just thought...I wanted some time alone with you tonight."

"Why?"

He was gripping her right hand tightly, trying to get up the courage to say what he was feeling. "You know I like you an awful lot," he managed.

"I like you, too, Randy."

"I want you to be my girl," he blurted. He could feel the heat in his face where the blood had rushed. He was tempted to look away, but he made himself face her while he waited for her answer.

"You know we're going to different colleges in the fall," Faith said tentatively. "I'm headed for Baylor in Waco, and you'll be at Texas Tech in Lubbock. They're hours and hours apart."

"We could each drive halfway on the weekends," he said.

"We've never even kissed," Faith said with a gentle smile, "and you want me to drive halfway across Texas—"

Randy leaned over and touched her lips with his. The shock was electric. He broke the kiss and stared, stunned, into her eyes. She looked equally shaken.

Faith's right hand came up to touch her lips as she searched his face. "I've never been kissed before. Is it always like that?"

"It's never been like that for me," he said.

"It was good?"

"Better than good. Terrific," he replied. "You want to try it again?"

"Oh, yes," she whispered.

He moved slower this time, pressing his lips more firmly against hers, but feeling the same delicious, unbelievable shock to his senses. His heart catapulted in his chest, and his body turned rock-hard. His mouth slanted over hers, seeking more, and his tongue went searching.

She was breathing as hard as he was, and he felt her body quiver as the kiss grew into something greater than the thing it was. Their bodies remained separate, but their souls merged.

He wanted to hold her in his arms, to touch her. He reached out to encircle her waist and drew her close so he could feel her soft breasts against his chest. He was aware of her right arm around him, holding him, but she kept her left arm down and her body on that side angled away.

"Put your arms around me, sweetheart," he whispered.

"But—"

"Please, Faith." She had to trust him not to hurt her. He only hoped he was worthy of that trust.

Slowly, hesitantly, her arm with the prosthesis attached encircled his waist. He could feel the plastic against his back, the nudge of the metal hook at its end against his flesh. She looked up at him, searching for repugnance, for revulsion or disgust.

Randy kept his expression neutral, knowing how important it was that he accept this part of her that was no part of her. "It's okay," he said. "I can handle it."

She gave a shaky laugh. "I'm not sure I can."

"It's no big deal. Just a bunch of plastic and metal you need because you don't have a hand."

She stared at him wonderingly. "You don't mind?"

He separated their bodies, though it was the last thing he wanted to do, and slid his hands down her arms. He made himself take her hook in his left hand, while his right hand held hers. He didn't wince, though her fingernails dug into him, because he didn't want her to think he minded holding that hook.

"You've never really told me how this works," he said, staring at the hook that lay in his open palm.

"It's myoelectric."

In response to his confused look, she explained. "Impulses from the brain are received in receptors in the elbow of the device."

"So you *think* this hook open and closed?"

"That's about it," she said with a smile.

"Neat," he said. "Now, will you put your arms around me, please, and give me another kiss."

She grinned. "With pleasure."

Her enthusiasm was such, that very shortly they were lying side by side on the quilt, their bodies aligned, their mouths merged. Randy was having a hard time breathing, let alone thinking, but he knew they had to stop. Faith trusted him. He had to be worthy of that trust.

He broke the kiss and pressed his face against her neck. "We have to stop, Faith."

Her hand tangled in the hair at his nape, and he shivered at the exquisite sensations her touch provoked. She kissed his temple and whispered, "If you want, I'll be your girl."

"Oh, God, Faith." That provoked another deep kiss, to express his gratitude and his love. When her tongue traced the seam of his lips, he opened his mouth and let her in. And felt her become a part of him. Four years wasn't so long to wait. *Four years.* "I can't wait, Faith," he groaned against her neck.

"I want you, too," she confessed breathlessly.

He'd meant he couldn't wait four years to marry her, but as he looked into Faith's lambent eyes, he realized she'd mistaken his meaning. Well, he'd wanted her trust. She'd given it to him in spades. He brushed her hair back from her face with a trembling hand. "I meant—"

"There you are!" an accusing voice cried.

Randy sat bolt upright, bringing Faith with him. They found themselves staring into four disapproving faces.

Hope was wearing jeans, a cut-off T-shirt and cowboy boots, but as she marched the twenty or so feet that separated her from Jake Whitelaw, she felt naked, as though he could see through all the trappings to the vulnerable female inside.

Jake's eyes never left hers, but his grim look

warned her away. She ignored it and walked up to him, carrying the unbent hanger she was using to roast marshmallows. "How about a roasted marshmallow?" she asked.

He hesitated, then said, "Sure. Why not?"

He followed her to a table that had been set up with bags of marshmallows and waited while she stuck a couple on the end of the wire hanger. "How do you like yours?" she asked as she crossed with him back to the fire.

"Hot on the outside, soft and sweet on the inside."

"That's me," she said softly. "Hot and soft and sweet." She looked at him and saw the glowing embers flare.

"I warned you before to stay away," he said. "I don't play games with little girls."

She held the hanger over the fire, making sure the marshmallows stayed well out of the flames. "I'm not playing, Jake. And I'm not a little girl. I know exactly what I want. I want you."

"I'm engaged to be married."

"You don't love her. You love me. You want to touch me, to kiss me, to put yourself inside me."

He stood behind her, close enough that she could feel the heat of him, but he didn't touch her. She felt his moist breath against her ear. "I thought you'd learned your lesson in the barn."

Hope felt the heat on her face and was grateful she could blame it on the fire. "It seemed to me that you liked what you saw," she said brazenly.

"Too damn much," he muttered.

She angled her head to meet his gaze, and the heat in his eyes melted her bones. She stiffened her knees to keep them from buckling. "Don't marry her, Jake. Marry me."

He swore under his breath, but he never took his eyes off hers.

"I'll make you a good wife. I can—"

"Shut up. Shut the hell up," he said in a guttural voice.

"Hey there, Hope!" Colt yelled from the other side of the fire. "Your marshmallows are on fire."

Hope jerked around and discovered the two marshmallows had been swallowed in flames. She yanked them out of the fire and blew hard to put them out, but it was too late. They were both charred beyond recognition.

"Let that be a warning," Jake murmured in her ear. "You keep playing with fire, little girl, you're going to get burned. Go away, Hope. Get as far from me as you can."

He moved away and left her standing alone. It was then Hope noticed that Faith and Randy were missing.

Colt told himself he must have misconstrued the look that passed between Hope Butler and his brother Jake before her marshmallows caught fire. He considered whether he ought to confront Jake but decided it wasn't necessary. His brother knew better than to get involved with a girl half his age, especially when he was engaged to another woman.

But he had to admit that an evening campfire in the middle of the prairie had a way of encouraging romance. Colt had fond memories of a night he and Huck and Jenny had roasted marshmallows with friends and family around a similar campfire. Mac Macready, who'd later married his eldest sister, Jewel, had sat around the campfire vying for Jewel's attentions with Gavin Talbot, who'd ended up marrying his sister Rolleen.

"What's put that smile on your face?" Jenny asked.

"I was remembering a time when we were fourteen and we did this."

"The night Mac Macready warned off Gavin Talbot from Jewel?" Jenny inquired.

"You remember that, too?"

She laughed. "The way sparks were flying between Mac and Jewel, we didn't need a fire to roast marshmallows."

"They're an old married couple now with three kids. Gavin and Rolleen have four between them. Where has the time gone? I can't wait till we've got a brood of our own."

Jenny's face blanched.

"Jenny? What's wrong?" Colt asked.

"I never realized you wanted a big family."

"I guess I never thought about it before, because I never wanted to marry anyone but you. I assumed you'd still want kids. Are you saying you don't?"

"I've already raised one family, Colt. I'd like a little time for myself. I'll understand if that changes your mind about marrying me."

Colt felt like he'd been kicked in the stomach. But Jenny and kids went together like peanut butter and jelly. She'd always loved kids. Apparently, raising four boys by herself had taken its toll. "I suppose I can live without having kids," he said slowly.

"Don't do me any favors," Jenny snapped.

He caught her arm before she could escape. "Hold it right there! I've told you it's okay."

"You don't mean it," she said. "I saw the look in your eyes, Colt. You're shocked and disappointed."

"So what if I am? It's not the end of the world. I'll get over it."

"Will you?"

"When it comes to a choice between you and kids," he said, "there's no question which I'd choose. I've waited too long for you, Jenny. I love you too much to give you up for any reason."

"You say that now," she said. "What about later? What about a year from now or five years from now? What if you change your mind?"

"All I can do is tell you how I feel right now," Colt said. "Nothing could make me leave you, Jenny."

She looked stricken. She opened her mouth to speak, but they were interrupted by Hope Butler.

"Miss Wright, my sister is missing and so is your brother Randy."

"They've probably gone for a walk," Colt said.

"I've looked around, but I can't find them," Hope said. "I'm worried."

Colt exchanged a glance with Jenny. They both knew why the couple had probably disappeared. If it was up to him, Colt would have waited for them to return. He was in a position to know Randy's feelings about Faith, and knowing Jenny, he was sure she'd raised her brother to respect a woman's feelings. Randy wouldn't be doing anything Faith didn't want.

But the fear in Hope's eyes was real and couldn't be ignored.

"What's up?" Jake asked as he joined them.

Colt watched as Jake exchanged an inquiring look with Hope.

"Faith and Randy are missing," Hope said.

"I'll go take a look for them," Jake said.

"I'm coming with you," Hope said.

Jake halted in his tracks.

It was plain Jake didn't want her along, and equally clear Hope wasn't going to be left behind. Colt remembered the look he'd seen pass between the two of them at the campfire. "Why don't we all go?" he said. "It shouldn't take us long to find them."

Jake shot him a look of appreciation, then headed into the shadows with Hope a step behind him.

"She's in love with him," Jenny murmured as they followed after them.

Colt frowned. "I hope you're wrong."

"I don't believe I am."

"She's only eighteen."

"I fell in love with Huck when I was fourteen," she reminded him.

"Poor Hope," Colt said, shaking his head.

"Poor Jake," Jenny countered.

"What do you mean?"

"Have you seen the way he looks at her?"

Colt remembered the look he'd seen Jake and Hope exchange. "He can't be thinking of doing anything about it," he said half to himself.

"Oh, he won't do anything about it," Jenny said. "The idiot."

"What are you saying? That he should go after her? He just got engaged!"

"He's a fool to ignore his feelings. He should admit he loves her, and let her love him back."

"I suppose you think I should have told you I loved you, even when it was hopeless."

Jenny stopped and turned to face him. "Maybe if you'd said something fifteen years ago we would've been together when there was still a chance—" She cut herself off and hurried to catch up to Jake and Hope.

Colt's mind was reeling. Jenny had always—only—loved Huck. Hadn't she? As soon as he caught up to her he demanded, "Are you saying you had feelings for *me* fifteen years ago?"

"It doesn't matter now," she said. "We can't look back, Colt. We can't focus on what might have been. We have to live in the here and now. I shouldn't have said anything."

Colt should have felt ebullient at Jenny's revelation. It took him a moment to figure out what was bothering him.

Maybe if you'd said something fifteen years ago we would have been together when there was still a chance— A chance for what? Colt wondered. For true love? For a family? What was it she'd been about to confess when Hope Butler had interrupted them.

In the far-off glow of a lantern, Colt spied Randy and Faith lying on a quilt. Jake and Hope reached them first.

"There you are!" Hope said in an accusing voice. "What are you doing to my sister?"

"I'm fine, Hope," Faith said, quickly rising to her feet and self-consciously rearranging her blouse.

Hope turned on Randy. "What's the big idea sneaking off into the dark with my sister?"

"Hope, that's enough," Faith said. "I came with Randy willingly. We were just talking."

Hope snorted. "Talking. Right. That's why your lips are all puffy and—"

"That's enough," Jake said.

"Can't you see—"

"Leave them alone," Jake said. "Your sister's entitled to make her own choices."

"But—"

"Randy, why don't you take Faith back to the fire," Jenny said. "Colt and I will gather up these things for you."

"Thanks, sis," Randy said. "Come on, Faith."

"I'll walk you back," Hope said, reaching a hand toward her sister.

"I'm going with Randy," Faith said, meeting her sister's gaze, but not moving toward her.

Colt saw the shock and pain on Hope's face as Faith took the hand Randy held out to her and began walking back to the fire, leaving Hope behind.

Colt would have stepped into the breach, but Jake beat him to it.

"I'll walk you back," he said to Hope.

"I don't need an escort," she retorted, turning and marching back toward the fire.

"I'll make sure she gets back okay," Jake said as he left Colt and Jenny alone.

Instead of picking up the blanket, Jenny sat down on it. "Join me?"

"We're supposed to be chaperoning kids."

"They'll manage without us for a few

minutes," she said, patting the blanket beside her. "Join me."

Colt wasn't going to turn down the chance to be alone with Jenny under a moonlit sky. He sat down cross-legged on the blanket. "Now what?" he said.

"If I have to ask, you aren't the man I think you are," she said teasingly.

Colt leaned over and kissed her on the mouth. The sound of satisfaction in her throat made him ache. He reached out to palm her breast and heard a moan of pleasure that sent his blood thrumming through his veins. He lowered Jenny onto the blanket until they were fitted together from breast to belly. "We missed doing this as kids, didn't we?" he said.

"Uh-huh."

"I'll make it all up to you, Jenny," he promised.

"I only wish you could," she murmured against his neck.

"What does that mean?"

"Only that some moments are lost forever, Colt. That's all."

The sadness in her voice made him want to weep. "Just promise you'll let me try, Jenny."

She leaned over and gave him the softest of kisses. "All right, Colt," she said as she met his gaze in the moonlight. "I promise to let you try."

Chapter 11

"You look good enough to eat," Colt said.

Jenny blushed as she stepped farther into the living room. "Thank you, Colt."

He held out his arms, and she walked into his embrace, letting her body settle against his. "This feels good," she said.

"No argument from me," he said. "I can hardly wait till you're my wife. How's that wedding gown coming along?"

"It's not finished yet."

Their wedding was one week away, but Jenny hadn't finished making her wedding dress. There was a good reason for the delay. She still wasn't sure there was going to be a wedding, for the simple reason she hadn't yet told Colt her secret.

He'd become so dear to her that she couldn't bear the thought of losing him. The temptation was overwhelming not to tell him at all. But how could she take vows "to love and honor and cherish" in the midst of such a deception?

Trust him, Jenny. He loves you. It won't matter.

Colt's arms tightened around her. "Is it my imagination, or are you losing weight?"

Jenny stiffened. "It's this dress," she said.

He held her out at arm's length and critically surveyed the short black satin sheath held up by narrow rhinestone straps. It was cut low enough in front to reveal her modest cleavage and short enough to reveal her long, slender legs.

He whistled, long and low. "You're one gorgeous lady, Miss Wright. But once you're mine, I think we're going to put a few pounds back on those beautiful bones."

She didn't dare meet his gaze, afraid he would find something in her eyes that would give her away. Worry had caused her to lose her appetite. But explaining even that much would require her to reveal the source of her anxiety—the secret she was keeping from him. "We'd better get going.

Your mother and father will be wondering where we are.''

"I'm not sure I want to share you with anybody else just yet.''

"Randy will—''

"Randy left fifteen minutes ago to pick up Faith.''

"Your parents—''

"My parents won't mind if we're a little late to our own engagement party.''

"Colt, I don't think—''

"Don't think,'' he murmured as he pulled her back into his arms. "Just let me hold you. I can't believe this is real. For so many years I dreamed of moments like this, and now I want to enjoy every one of them.''

She hid her face against his neck and clutched at his shoulders. "I love you, Colt.''

She heard his sharp intake of air before he separated them so he could look into her eyes. "I've been waiting a long time to hear you say that.''

"There's just one thing—''

His mouth captured hers in a kiss of claiming, preventing the words that might have torn them apart.

A frisson of pleasure shot through her. How could Colt make her feel so much, so fast? It had never been like this with Huck. Never. Her nipples peaked with the brush of his hand across the satin. He kissed her throat, then suckled, causing her insides to draw up tight. She moaned, a sound of desire and despair.

Her heart beat against her ribs like a butterfly caught in a jar, as he reached for the zipper at the back of her dress. It slid down easily, and the straps fell off her shoulders along with the top of the sheath. Beneath it she wore a black merry widow. The avid look in his eyes made her body quiver with anticipation. He reached behind her to unhook the bra, and she panicked.

"Colt, no!"

His hands paused, but his eyes quickly sought hers for an explanation. "What's wrong?"

"I..." Her hands gripped his arms, as though to shove him away. *Tell him. Tell him. Tell him.*

"This isn't the right time," she said breathlessly. She saw the disappointment in his eyes, but, thank God, no suspicion. "We're supposed to be at your parents' home in twenty minutes."

His lips curled in a lopsided grin. "I'm sure I'd enjoy making love to you however little time we took." He held up a hand to stay her protest. "But I'm willing to wait, if that's what you what."

"It's what I want."

He lifted the straps back onto her shoulders and reached around her to zip up the dress. All the while, his hips were pressed against hers, so she could feel his arousal. She ached for him, yearned for him. And feared his discovery of the truth.

"It's all right, Jenny," he murmured in her ear. "I understand why you're afraid."

"You do?" she said, her voice catching in her throat.

He nodded solemnly as he brushed her hair back behind her shoulders. "You're afraid it won't be the same with me—" He swallowed hard and corrected himself. "As *good* with me, as it was with Huck. Just remember that I love you. If you want me to do something differently, all you have to do is ask."

She wanted to tell him he was wrong, that he made her feel so much more than Huck ever had. But she bit back the words. It wasn't Huck's fault he hadn't made her feel more. It wasn't Huck's fault she hadn't been in love with him. She hadn't known what a difference love would make. Until Colt had come along and shown her.

Jenny leaned forward and kissed Colt gently on the lips, feeling the need that arose whenever she touched him. "I love the way you touch me, Colt.

I love the way you kiss me. I want to make love to you. But I need a little more time.''

"We're getting married in a week," he reminded her. "Do you want to wait until our wedding night? Is that what you're telling me?"

She couldn't wait that long. Colt had to know the truth before they stood in front of a preacher and said vows that bound them for a lifetime. *A lifetime. Who are you kidding, Jenny?* She couldn't mislead Colt any longer. It seemed time had run out.

Jenny swallowed past the lump in her throat. "Tonight," she said. "After the party."

"I'm going to hold you to that promise," Colt said, leaning down to kiss her tenderly on the mouth.

As she stepped out onto the back porch, Jenny stopped abruptly. Parked at the door was a brand-new forest-green Jeep with a gigantic yellow bow on the hood. She turned to Colt, who was grinning.

"Do you like it?"

"Oh, Colt. It's too much." *Especially when you may not want anything to do with me after tonight.*

"I'd hand the world to you on a platter, if I could."

"I don't know what to say."

"Say you like it."

Jenny smiled. "I like it." She stepped off the back porch and walked completely around the Jeep, peering inside.

Colt pulled the ribbon away from the vehicle, then reached into his trouser pocket to retrieve the key. "You want to drive?"

"Oh, yes, please."

Jenny didn't say much on the trip to Hawk's Pride because her heart was lodged in her throat. This was all a dream, and she was afraid to wake up. Colt was everything Huck had never been— generous, thoughtful, helpful—and he made her body hum whenever he touched her.

But he wasn't perfect. He had one fatal flaw. He couldn't bear to be around sick people. She'd gotten the measles when she was sixteen, and Colt hadn't come to visit her once until she was well again.

When she'd questioned him later, he'd admitted, "Something happens inside me when I see somebody I know who's sick in bed." He had put a hand to his belly. "My insides sort of squeeze up tight, and I can't breathe."

She'd laughed at him and asked, "What do you do when you get a cold?"

"Oh, I don't have any problems when *I'm* sick. Only when somebody else gets ill."

"What do you do when one of your brothers or sisters gets sick?" she asked.

"I stay away until they're well."

"You can't mean that," she said.

"I most certainly do."

"You don't even bring them magazines or something to drink?"

Colt shook his head.

"That's awful!"

"I didn't say I was proud of the way I act," he said. "And believe me, I've tried to get over it. I visited Avery's bedroom when he got the mumps, but it was a disaster. I was with him maybe a minute when my hands started trembling, and I broke out in a sweat. I barely got out of there before I lost my lunch!"

"Why do you suppose that happens?" she asked.

"I think I'm afraid," he confessed in a low voice.

"That you'll get sick, too?"

"That someone I care about will die."

"People don't die of a cold, Colt, and not very often anymore from measles or mumps," she chided.

He grimaced. "I know that! I didn't say what I feel makes sense. It's just what I feel. I can't help it. So don't give me a hard time about it. Okay?"

In all the years she'd known Colt, she hadn't once seen him visit anyone in the hospital. When her mother was sick, he only came by when he was sure he wasn't going to catch a glimpse of her in bed. Another time, when he discovered Tyler and James had chicken pox, though he'd already had the disease himself, instead of coming inside, he offered to help with the chores in the barn.

Jenny wished she had told Colt the truth from the beginning. It was going to be much harder to give him up now than it would have been before he'd come to mean so much to her.

"For a lady on her way to a party, you don't look very happy," Colt observed.

Jenny made herself smile. She was determined to enjoy their engagement party, especially since it might be their last night together. "I was thinking how strange life is. If Huck hadn't been killed...I would have missed so much."

"I feel the same way. I miss him a lot, but if he were here, I wouldn't have you."

Jenny reached a hand across the seat to Colt,

and he gripped it tightly. "I'm glad we found each other," she said.

"Me, too."

Jenny brought the Jeep to a stop at the back door to the Whitelaws's ranch house. The white-washed adobe house, with its barrel-tile roof, had been built in a square around a gigantic moss-laden live oak, and the party had spilled into the grassy central courtyard.

Jenny felt Colt's arm slide possessively around her waist as he escorted her into the fray.

"Hey, there, Slim," he said, shaking hands with an old high school friend. "Buck, Frank," he said, shaking more hands.

"Congratulations, Colt," Buck said. He dipped his head, touched the brim of his Stetson and said to Jenny, "We all wish you the best, Miss Wright."

"Thanks, Buck," she said.

There was something lovely about being sur-rounded by friends who'd known you since the days when you'd all played ring-around-the-rosie together. At the same time, it was unsettling to see the speculation in their eyes as they tried to gauge whether she and Colt might have been lov-ers when she was still Huck's girl.

A huge beef was being barbecued on a spit, and

there was a keg of beer, along with iced tea and soft drinks. A group of women, Amanda Carter among them, were setting up a buffet table with side dishes everyone had brought. Jenny's brother Tyler was pounding on one leg of the sawhorse table with a hammer, while Colt's brother Rabb held it up.

She looked for Jake and found him standing in a circle of ranchers and their foremen, including Zach Whitelaw, her brother Sam, Wiley Butler— and his daughter, Hope. She located Randy and Faith talking with a bunch of teenagers beneath an arbor of bougainvillea.

She looked at Colt and realized he was making a similar survey to locate his siblings and his myriad aunts, uncles and cousins. "You've sure got a big family," Jenny murmured.

"Yeah," Colt said. "And a close one. It was great growing up as one of the Whitelaw Brats."

Jenny turned her eyes away. If Colt married her, he wasn't going to be adding any branches to this awesome family tree. He'd said he didn't mind, that she was enough for him. But seeing all these Whitelaws with their children and grandchildren made her realize how much Colt would be giving up if he married her.

It would be easier to push him away now than

to endure the regret in his eyes for however much time they had together.

Stop it, Jenny. Stop looking for reasons to break up with Colt. Oh, you can come up with a few. He'd be happier flying jets than living with you. He'd be happier marrying someone who could give him kids. He'd be happier if he didn't have to hang around and maybe watch you die. But isn't the choice really up to him? Are you going to give him a chance to choose you?

That was the crux of the matter. Jenny wasn't sure she had the strength to survive Colt's rejection. It was easier to avoid that possibility by rejecting him first. She could drive him away. He wouldn't stay where he wasn't wanted.

But one of the lessons the past two precarious years had taught her was to reach out for happiness. Loving Colt made her happy. Making love with Colt would bring her joy. After that… Life was uncertain. No one got any guarantees.

Jenny turned to Colt and let him see the need she felt, the yearning to be held and loved. "How soon do you think we can leave without our absence being noticed?"

Colt's eyes lit with a fire that warmed her insides. "My father wants to say a few words and make a toast. After that, I think we could slip away."

"Why don't you see if he wants to do that now?" Jenny said.

"Come with me," he said. "We'll ask."

Colt's parents were surprised that he wanted them to make their speeches so early in the evening, but they were more than willing to accommodate their youngest child.

"May I have your attention, please," Zach said, arranging Jenny and Colt between himself and Colt's mother Rebecca. "Before we carve up that beef, I'd like to say a few words to my son and future daughter-in-law."

The noise died down, but it didn't get completely quiet. Babies still cried and children still played. But the adults gathered around them, drinks in hand, ready to offer toasts to their future happiness.

"First I want to thank Jenny for loving my son. And my son for being smart enough to settle down and marry her."

There was general laughter, shouts of "Here! Here!" and clinking beer glasses.

"I want to tell my son how proud I am of him. How much we feel blessed for having been given the chance to make him a part of our family. I only hope he and Jenny find as much joy in raising their Whitelaw Brats, as we did in raising ours.''

There was more laughter, more clinking glasses.

Jenny felt her face turn to stone. She was afraid to look at Colt, afraid to look at anyone. She prayed that Colt would let the statement pass, that he wouldn't feel the need to tell his parents, ''My future wife doesn't want children.''

From the corner of her eye, Jenny saw that Colt's face was frozen in a smile. A muscle in his jaw jerked, and she realized his teeth must be clenched.

Then it was Rebecca's turn to speak. Colt's mother put her arm around Jenny and said, ''We know you and Colt could live on love alone, but we've decided a little bread wouldn't hurt. We hope you'll let us pay off the mortgage on the Double D as a wedding present.''

There was a gasp and then applause.

Jenny's heart was stuck in her throat. There was no way she could speak. She could barely breathe, she was so overwhelmed with joy and with pain. This good family had raised a wonderful son, and all she had offered him—all of them—was deceit.

"I'm sorry," she blurted. "I can't accept your gift. Because I can't marry your son."

Colt didn't know when he'd been so angry with anyone in his life. "Don't you dare run away from me," he snarled, grabbing Jenny's arm as she reached for the door to the Jeep. "What the hell's going on, Jenny?"

She was panting, and her eyes look frightened. "You heard me. I can't marry you."

"What is it you're so scared of?" he demanded.

She looked like a deer caught in a set of headlights. "This—the two of us—would never work."

Colt realized they'd acquired an audience. Not surprising, considering the bombshell Jenny had dropped. He was still reeling himself. "Get in," he said. "We're going home."

"You are home, Colt."

"Get in the damned car, Jenny." When she didn't move, he swept her up in his arms, carried her around the hood of the Jeep and deposited her in the passenger's seat. "Don't get any smart ideas," he warned.

He half expected her to leap out of the Jeep and run. She was good at running from trouble, his Jenny. But the running was going to stop. Here. Tonight.

Colt started the engine and spun the wheels, kicking up dirt and stones as he backed out of the driveway. "Buckle up," he said. "It's liable to be a bumpy ride."

He didn't say another word until he cut the Jeep's engine at Jenny's back door. "Come inside. We're going to talk."

"I have nothing more to say," Jenny said as she shoved open her door and hurried up the back steps. "Go home, Colt. Leave me alone. I don't want to see you again."

"That isn't going to cut it, Jenny. I told you I wasn't going to leave you. And I meant it."

Jenny reached the porch first and whirled on him. "What if I don't love you?"

Colt froze with his boot on the bottom step. "What?"

Jenny turned her back on him and thrust both hands through her hair. "I lied when I said I loved you."

"I don't believe you," Colt said, his voice soft but furious. "Turn around and look at me. Say it to my face, goddamn you!"

Jenny dropped her hands to her sides. She turned slowly until she was facing him. Her eyes brimmed with tears, and her mouth was curled down at the corners. "I thought I could go through with this. To save the ranch. But I can't."

Colt hissed in a breath. It sounded like the truth. "Oh, God, Jenny."

"Go home, Colt."

"I can't," he said, the words torn from his throat. "You're home for me, Jenny. I still want you. I still need you."

"I won't marry you, Colt. That would be a living hell for both of us."

"You made a promise to me earlier this evening. I expect you to keep it," he said implacably.

He saw her confusion, the moment when she realized what he meant. Her nostrils flared, and her lips thinned. "It wouldn't be lovemaking, Colt. It would be sex."

"Sex is fine with me," he said, moving up the steps toward her.

Jenny took a step back. "Don't come any closer."

"I intend to get a hell of a lot closer before the night is over," he said, backing her up against the frame of the house. He shoved his knee between her legs and pinned her body against the wall with his hips. His hands thrust into her hair, angling her head back at a painful angle. "You're mine,

Jenny. You've always been mine. You just didn't know it."

"Colt, I—"

His mouth covered hers, angry and afraid, searching for answers that always seemed a step beyond his reach. A spark of electricity leaped between them, shocking his senses. His body hungered as much as his soul, and he felt a sense of desperation that was impossible to deny. There was nothing gentle about his kisses. He forced her lips open for his intrusion, biting them, sucking on them, demanding a response.

Her body betrayed her. And he knew he had her soul.

He lifted his head and stared down into her panicked eyes. "You lied, Jenny. I don't know why. But before we're through, I'm going to find out the truth."

"You can't handle the truth," she cried. "Why do you think I've been lying!"

"We can discuss this later," he said as he thrust his hips against hers. "After we've made love."

"Colt, you can't—"

"Watch me." He picked her up and carried her into the house.

Colt snapped on the tiny lamp that sat on

Jenny's chest of drawers, then threw her onto the four-poster. He began stripping himself while she watched in stunned disbelief. He took off his shirt, then yanked off his boots and socks. He pulled down jeans and Jockey shorts together and stood before her completely naked.

He heard her gasp, saw her eyes go wide.

"That's something else Huck and I *didn't* have in common," he said. "Move over, Jenny. Make some room for me."

She scuttled across the bed and landed on the floor in the shadows on the opposite side. He stalked around the foot of the bed and dragged her to her feet. "Need a little help getting undressed?"

Before she could protest, he had her zipper down and the black sheath stripped off her shoulders. His arms imprisoned her as he unsnapped the black merry widow. He felt her tense as he pulled it free and threw it onto the floor. Her eyes slid closed as he looked at her naked breasts for the first time. He leaned over and kissed the tips, one at a time, and heard her harsh, indrawn breath.

Then he slipped one nipple into his mouth and suckled.

She cried out and her hands reached for him,

grabbing handfuls of his hair to hold him where he was. "Oh, Colt. It feels...it feels..."

She didn't finish the sentence. But she didn't have to. He could see the ecstacy on her face.

He shoved the sheath the rest of the way down, only to discover she was wearing a garter belt and black nylons. "This is the kind of gift a woman plans for her lover, Jenny."

She didn't deny it.

"I thank you," he said as he looked his fill.

He took off her black silk panties but left the nylons and garter belt, since they weren't in his way. He pulled her close, reveling in the feel of the soft fabric and her even softer flesh against his own. He kissed her eyes, her nose, her cheeks, her lips. He caressed her arms, her back, her stomach. Any part of her he could find. But he came back often to her breasts, because she seemed to have so much sensation there.

To his surprise and pleasure, she touched him in return. Her hands marveling, seeking, scratching, squeezing, making his body pulse and tighten and yearn.

It had been too long since he'd had a woman. He was afraid if she kept touching him, he would spill himself too soon. So he laid her on the bed and caught her hands and pinned them against the pillows and made himself go slow.

"Colt, I can't wait," she begged.

"Another kiss here," he said, his lips against her belly. "And here," he said, moving his mouth lower.

Her body writhed beneath his caresses and then became taut. "Please," she gasped.

He took his time. And he brought her joy.

She was like no other woman he had ever known. Softer. Sleeker. More responsive.

He kept his weight on his arms as he spread her legs with his knees and positioned himself between her thighs. "I'll be as gentle as I can, Jenny. Let me know if I hurt you."

He was so big. And she was so small. Suddenly he was afraid. He looked into her eyes and saw that she was not.

Then she reached for him, pulling him toward her, and he pushed slowly into the warmth and wetness of her. She angled her hips, gasping as he sank to the hilt.

"You fit," she said, surprise evident in her voice.

He couldn't help smiling. "Did you think I wouldn't?"

"I wondered," she said, her hands brushing the hair from his forehead. "But I'm glad you do."

"Me, too," he said with a smile.

He took his time, moving slowly, kissing her face and her throat, his hands moving over her, feeling, touching her perfect body—except for one spot on her breast. He felt her stiffen as his fingers traced the blemish. A dimple in her flesh. And some kind of scar.

His body didn't allow him time to consider what he'd found. It demanded culmination. He lifted her legs and wrapped them around his waist and drove them both toward satisfaction. He waited for her. And it wasn't easy. But he was many times rewarded, because her climax came so close in time with his own, that both of them were lifted higher. He threw his head back and gritted his teeth against the almost unbearable pleasure, as he spilled his seed in her womb.

Afterward, he pulled her close, kissing her again.

"I love you, Jenny. I love you," he said between panting breaths.

"And I love you, Colt," she admitted in a quiet voice.

He didn't have the strength to ask all the questions that were tumbling around in his head. So long as she loved him, they could work everything out. He still had no idea what had made her so frightened. But he felt certain that whatever it was, they could handle it together.

As he held her close, his fingertips grazed the blemish on the side of her breast, almost beneath her arm. He lifted his head to look, but he could barely make out the dimpled flaw in the shadowy light. "What is that?" he asked.

"A scar," she said.

"I didn't know you were hurt. How did it happen?"

"I wasn't hurt. I have cancer. Had cancer. May still have cancer," she said breathlessly.

Colt sat up and stared down at her. He swallowed hard. Sweat beaded on his brow. His body began to tremble. He bolted from the bed and ran for the bathroom, his hand over his mouth. He barely made it in time.

Chapter 12

It took Colt a moment to realize where he was when he woke up. Not in Sam's bedroom at the Double D, but in his own at Hawk's Pride. He felt the sweat break out on his forehead at the mere thought of *Jenny* and *cancer* together in the same sentence.

Oh, God. What had he done?

Memory returned like a hideous nightmare, and he saw himself, eyes wide with horror, stomach churning, and then his ungainly race for the bathroom. He recalled the foul taste of vomit, and the hot wash of shame.

Colt groaned in agony and pressed the heels of his hands against his grainy eyelids.

He'd failed her. She'd shared her trouble with him, trusted him, given him a chance to prove his love. And he'd failed her...and himself.

Oh, God. Why cancer? Of all the maladies in the world, why give my Jenny cancer?

Then he remembered more. Jenny had come into the bathroom, dampened a cloth and gently wiped the sweat from his brow and the spittle from his mouth. He'd kept his eyes closed, afraid of what he'd see in her eyes if he looked at her. Then her touch was gone.

"Go home, Colt," she'd said in a flat voice. "Go home."

When he'd come out of the bathroom, he'd found his clothes laid out on the bed and Jenny nowhere in sight. He'd had an urgent need to see her. To make excuses for himself. To explain what had happened.

But he didn't need to explain. Jenny understood his irrational fear of illness better than anyone.

Sick people sometimes die.

No. Not my Jenny. Not so young. Not when she's barely had a chance to live!

Colt struggled to remember her exact words. *I have cancer. I had cancer. May still have cancer.*

The terror of what she'd said had kept him from asking for more information. He speculated with what little knowledge he had.

The dimpled scar meant she'd had some sort of surgery. A lump removed? And then what? Radiation? Chemotherapy? How had that been possible without anyone noticing the effects of such treatment? The vomiting. The hair loss.

Of course. It had been easy to conceal her illness when she was so very much alone. She'd only have to hide it from him and from Huck for a few days at most while they were home on leave. For the past two years she'd been alone on the Double D except for Randy, who was probably in on the secret. It was likely Randy knew everything and had been sworn to silence. He had to talk with Randy. Randy would be able to tell him the details he hadn't gotten from Jenny.

Colt leaped out of bed and dragged on some clothes. He shoved his feet into a pair of boots, grabbed his battered Stetson and left the house as quietly as he'd returned late the previous evening.

As he approached the Double D ranch house, Colt felt the bile rise in his throat. He swallowed it down. His skin felt clammy as he quietly shut the door of his Mustang and moved up onto the back porch. The back door was unlocked. Even in these dangerous days, Westerners left their doors open as a gesture of range hospitality. Strangers were welcome.

A man who betrayed his woman's faith and her trust likely was not. So he entered as silently as he could and made his way down the hall to Randy's bedroom. Colt knocked once, then opened the door and stepped inside, closing it behind him.

Randy was still sound asleep, the covers thrown off, so Colt could see the boy wore only a pair of cotton pajama bottoms. Colt sat on the edge of the bed, gave Randy's shoulder a shove and whispered, "Wake up."

Randy rolled over, scraping at the sand in his eyes and yawning. "Oh. Hi, Colt." He shoved himself upright and scratched at his belly. "Sorry I was so late getting in last night. I saw Jenny's door was closed and your bed was empty and I figured... Well, I didn't want to bother the two of you, so I just—"

"This visit isn't about how late you came in last night," Colt interrupted. "It's about—" His throat constricted, making speech difficult, but he forced the words out. "About Jenny's cancer."

Colt saw the flicker of pain on Randy's face

before it was replaced by guilt. "She finally told you, huh?"

"Yeah," Colt said, releasing a gust of air.

Randy looked anxiously over Colt's shoulder toward the door. "Is she coming here to tell me about it?"

Colt was confused. "You mean she hasn't said anything to you before now?"

Randy swallowed hard and shook his head. "I—" His voice broke, and he cleared his throat. "I figured it out for myself. There were days she'd be sick. And she lost weight. And once I heard her crying. Then I found a bill from the doctor, and I knew."

"You never confronted her and asked for the truth?" Colt asked, incredulous.

Randy shook his head. "If she'd wanted me to know, she'd have told me."

"Did you at least share what you knew with your brothers?"

Randy's chin dropped to his chest, and he shook his head.

"It never occurred to you to write to Huck. Or to me? To tell someone who could give her some help?" Colt said, his rage as palpable as his voice was quiet.

Colt saw a tear drop onto the sheet.

''I was scared,'' Randy said in a voice hoarse with tears he was trying not to shed. ''I kept hoping it would go away. Jenny's always been so strong. I figured if she really needed help, she'd ask for it. But she never did.''

Colt pulled the tearful boy into his arms, and felt Randy's arms close tightly around him. How awful it must have been for him to know. How terrified he must have been of losing his sister. Colt offered comfort and received it in return. In a little while he asked, ''When did you first notice Jenny was ill?''

''Two years ago,'' Randy answered.

Two years, Colt thought. And she hadn't yet succumbed to the disease. But she looked so frail. And she'd lost weight even since he'd come home. Didn't she have to see the doctor sometime?

Then he remembered the day she'd spent in town, the day she hadn't invited him along. *She must have seen a doctor then.* Maybe he could find out who it was and ask— No. A doctor wouldn't tell him Jenny's secrets. And he shouldn't be asking. If he wanted to know anything, he should get it from her.

He patted Randy's back and said, ''Don't

worry, boy. I know now, and I'm going to take care of her.''

Randy sat back and scrubbed at his eyes with his hands. ''You don't know what a relief it is to hear you say that.''

Colt tousled Randy's hair. ''Go back to sleep.'' He rose and headed down the hall toward Jenny's room, stiffening his buckling knees and determinedly swallowing down the nausea that rose as he approached her door. He felt the sweat bead on his forehead and fought back a wave of dizziness as he reached out to knock on her door.

''Jenny, it's Colt. Let me in.''

There was no response. He wouldn't have blamed her if she never wanted to see him again. But he wasn't going to leave this time—or ever again. Even if he spent the rest of his life hanging over the toilet bowl every morning, he was here to stay.

He knocked again. ''At least say something,'' he said. ''Let me know you're all right.''

Silence.

''I'm coming in,'' Colt said. ''We need to talk.'' He turned the doorknob, but it was locked.

He laid his cheek against the smooth wood. She'd locked him out, and herself inside. ''Please, Jenny. Give me another chance.''

He waited, his ear pressed against the door, for any sign that she might relent. And then he heard her reply.

"Good-bye, Colt."

He's gone.

Jenny stared, dry-eyed, at a water mark in the ceiling where the rain had leaked before Colt fixed the roof. There was no repairing such a stain. It could be painted over, but in her experience, it had a way of seeping back through. It was better just to tear down the ruined part and get rid of it.

Better to send Colt away, than to let him try to make amends. She would never—could never—forget his reaction last night. Or forgive it. It was hard enough facing her illness, without seeing her own terror reflected back in his eyes.

What did you expect? a voice asked. *That he would be miraculously cured? That his abhorrence of illness would magically disappear because you were the one who was sick? Did you think he'd pull you into his arms and tell you everything would be all right, that he was there for you, always and forever, "in sickness and in health"?*

Foolish woman. Did your father stay to help

your mother? Whom have you ever been able to rely on besides yourself?

Jenny felt cold and empty inside, as though a block of ice had frozen around her, insulating her from the world, from its pain and its joys. She wanted to spend the day in bed with the covers pulled up over her head. But there were animals to be fed, chores to be done and a life—however brief—to be lived.

She left the bed and walked across the room to stare at her naked body in the mirror. The slight defect in her breast didn't even show from the front. She had to turn sideways and lift her arm to see it. There was only a slight indentation in her skin and a thin scar where the cancerous tissue had been removed.

She turned away and headed for the shower. She made the spray as hot as she could stand it and stood there as long as she dared, wishing the warmth would seep into her bones and melt the ice that held her feelings frozen inside. If only she could cry, she might feel better. But all she could muster was an awful sense of desolation.

She dressed in the most comfortable jeans she owned and her favorite shirt. She made herself smile into the mirror as she dried her hair, hoping that would make her feel better. Her grin had the look of a corpse in rictus.

That did make her smile. The curl of her lips was fleeting, a single instant of relief from the oppressive sorrow she felt. But it gave her hope that she could survive this second, even more devastating loss of a loved one.

She smelled coffee as she headed toward the kitchen. She was grateful there would be something hot and strong to drink, but she wasn't looking forward to seeing Randy. The two of them were going to have some hard times together—considering it was no longer possible to save the Double D.

She stopped dead on the threshold to the kitchen. Colt stood with his back to the sink, his hips resting against the counter, his hands gripping it on either side.

"What are you doing here?" she said cuttingly.

"I thought you might need some coffee," Colt replied.

She watched him swallowing furiously. Any second, he was going to have to bolt for the bathroom.

"Oh, for heaven's sake! Eat a cracker," she snapped.

"Will that help?" he said, his face tinged with green.

"It works for pregnant women with nausea. It ought to work for you." She crossed to the cabinet and pulled out a box of soda crackers, ripped open the bag and stuck a cracker in front of his mouth. "Open up." He opened his mouth, and she stuck it inside.

He bit off a bite, chewed carefully and swallowed. He took another small bite, and another, until the cracker was gone. "Thank you," he said at last.

His color still wasn't too good, and sweat dotted his forehead, but at least he didn't look in imminent danger of puking. "Sit down," she ordered. "Have you tried drinking any of that coffee you made?"

"Not yet," he admitted.

"Something carbonated might be better for your stomach." She crossed to the ancient refrigerator, pulled out a can of ginger ale and popped the top. "Drink this."

He looked wary. "My stomach—"

"Drink it," she ordered, shoving the can into his hand.

He took a sip, then looked down at her. "Satisfied?"

"I'll be satisfied when you're gone from this house."

"I'm not leaving," he said.

"I make you sick, Colt. Physically ill. You look worse than a calf with the slobbers."

He grimaced. "That bad? Then you shouldn't be shoving me out the door. Sick as you make me out to be, I'm likely to ruin the upholstery in my Mustang. Now *that* would make me truly ill."

Jenny felt a rising hope shoving its way upward from inside, trying to get out. But there was no way it could get past the ice that was frozen around her heart.

"Why are you here, Colt?"

"I need some answers, Jenny. I want to know about your cancer."

She was shocked to hear him say the word aloud. She watched to see if he was going to be sick, saw him swallow hard and reach for another saltine.

He's trying, Jenny. Give him a chance.

She'd given him a chance. And he'd broken her heart. It had taken all night to put the pieces back together. Why should she let herself be hurt again?

"All I want to do is talk," he said, anticipating

her refusal. "Have a cup of coffee and talk with me, Jenny. You owe me that much."

She stiffened. "I don't owe you anything. Not after last night."

She watched all the blood leave his face. She pulled a kitchen chair out from the table, grabbed him by the arm and shoved him into it. "Put your head down before you faint," she said, shoving his head between his knees.

Too late, she realized she should never have touched him. His hair felt soft beneath her fingertips, and the warmth of the skin at his nape heated her skin. Melting the ice. Thawing her heart.

She jerked her hand away and backed up. She turned and crossed to the percolator and poured herself a cup of coffee. He started to lift his head, and she snapped, "Keep your head down!"

She placed a handful of saltines and the can of ginger ale on the table in front of him, then retrieved her cup of coffee—a mug, not one of the delicate china cups he'd given her—and sat down on the opposite side of the table from him. "All right. Take your time and come up slow."

He looked pale, but at least he was no longer white as a ghost.

"Ask your questions. Then get out."

"Why didn't you tell Huck? Or me? Why did you keep it a secret?"

"I was afraid if I told Huck it would be the excuse he needed never to come back," she said. "And we both know how you feel about sick people."

"You didn't give us a chance."

"You were both thousands of miles away. In Germany, I think. Or was it somewhere in Southeast Asia? Huck had a dozen chances to quit flying and come home and marry me. He never took one. Why should I think my being sick would make a difference?"

She saw the pain and regret on Colt's face, but he didn't contradict her.

"How far along was the cancer before you discovered it?" he asked.

"Because of my family history, my gynecologist suggested I get a baseline mammogram when I turned thirty, a healthy mammogram for comparison purposes, to make it easier to identify anything abnormal if it showed up in the future. Since my mother got breast cancer when she was thirty-four, I figured it might be a good idea.

"Except, that first mammogram revealed a tiny spot, not much bigger than a pencil tip, but there, just the same.'' She shivered and took a sip of hot coffee to warm the cold inside.

''It was a shattering moment,'' she admitted, meeting Colt's gaze with difficulty. ''There was something hard and foreign inside me, attacking me, trying to kill me.''

She watched Colt swallow hard and reach for a saltine.

''I couldn't even feel a lump,'' she continued inexorably, mercilessly detailing the facts he'd demanded. ''But it was there. Without the mammogram, I might not have known until it was too late.''

''So you had surgery to remove the cancer?'' Colt asked.

''My doctor performed a lumpectomy.''

She saw Colt cringe and remembered how she'd felt the first time she imagined a knife slicing through the soft flesh of her breast. ''My doctor told me she thought she'd gotten all the cancerous tissue. But there was no way to know whether the disease would come back. I had radiation.''

''How?'' he asked, his brow furrowing. ''I mean, without anyone but Randy finding out.''

''Randy knows?'' she said, her eyes darting toward the doorway that led to his room. She started to rise, to go to her brother, to assuage his fear.

Colt grasped her wrist from across the table and held her in place. "Randy's fine. I want to hear the rest of it."

She sank back into her chair, staring at his hand until he released her. Her eyes locked with his. "The rest of it. You mean the fury and resentment I felt? The fear of losing a part of me to the surgeon's knife? And of all things, a breast—the part of a woman that most symbolizes her femininity, the one truly sensual gift she can give to her husband and lover, the means of nursing her children.

"I ranted at fate. I was quite melodramatic. I frightened the horses in the barn. Better them than Randy or any of my brothers."

"You should have told them."

"Don't tell me what I should have done! Do you think I don't know they would have dropped everything to come running? Do you think I don't know how much they care? But I love them just as much as they love me. What could they do, really, to change anything? The cancer is either going to kill me, or it's not. Nothing they do or say is going to change that.

"In the meantime, their lives would have been

turned upside down. They would have been miserable worrying about me. It was better my way.''

''How do you think they're going to feel when they find out the truth?'' Colt asked.

''If the lumpectomy had worked, they would never have needed to know.''

She saw Colt go still. Saw the growing awareness in his eyes of what she'd just revealed.

''It's back?'' he asked, his voice grating like a rusty gate.

She threaded her hands together in front of her, gripping them so hard her knuckles turned white. ''I had a follow-up mammogram the day I went into town by myself. The doctor called last week. She wants me to come in for a needle biopsy. She's afraid she made a mistake not doing more radical surgery the first time.''

Jenny saw Colt was swallowing furiously. He closed his eyes and gritted his teeth so hard she saw a muscle jerk in his cheek as he fought off the nausea. When he opened his eyes, the terror was barely hidden behind a facade of composure. ''Is that why you never finished the wedding dress?'' he asked.

She nodded.

''When is the biopsy scheduled?'' he asked.

''I was going to spend the day in town tomorrow 'running errands,' for the wedding,'' she confessed. ''I have to be at the doctor's office at eight-thirty. I planned to have the surgery, recuperate at her office, and be home in the afternoon.''

''I'll go with you,'' he said.

''You don't need—''

''How the hell do you know what I need?'' he said in a voice filled with barely controlled rage. ''I need to live my life with you. I need to go to sleep with you in my arms and wake up with you in the morning. If all we're going to have is a few months or years together, I want every minute I can get.''

''I have *cancer*,'' she said, emphasizing the word.

''And it makes me sick—literally—to know that,'' he retorted. ''I'm as angry and frightened as you are, Jenny. Maybe more so, because I've wanted you all my life, and now, when I thought we'd have a lifetime together, you tell me you may already be dying. I don't know how to cope with the anger I feel. Or the fear.''

They stared at each other for a long moment, both aware of the crossroad they had reached. Jenny could go on alone, or she could ask Colt to join her.

"You could hold on to me," Jenny said at last, reaching a hand across the table.

Colt grasped her hand like a lifeline. Their fingers entwined, but soon that wasn't enough for either of them. As though led by some unseen hand, they both rose and moved around the table toward each other. Colt's arms closed around Jenny, and she knew she was where she belonged.

"Give me another chance, Jenny," Colt whispered.

The ice cracked around her heart, leaving the pulsing organ exposed and vulnerable, capable of feeling...everything. "Oh, Colt."

"Don't deny me, sweetheart. Let me love you. Let me be a part of your life for however long we have left together on this earth."

What woman could refuse an offer like that? "All right, Colt. For as long as we have together, I'm yours."

Chapter 13

The hardest thing Colt had ever done was sit in the doctor's office, surrounded by sick people, and wait for Jenny while she underwent a needle biopsy on her breast. Jenny had explained Colt's problem to her doctor, who had prescribed something to control his nausea.

But no pill could relieve his dread that Jenny might die from cancer. The disease was arbitrary; it killed with equal disregard for age or gender, race or creed. And Jenny was right; there was nothing he could do about it.

Except live life with her to the fullest every day.

The instant they left the doctor's office after the outpatient surgery was completed he said, "Marry me, Jenny. On Saturday, as we planned."

"We won't have the results from the biopsy by then," she countered as he helped her into his Mustang.

"I don't care."

"There's no time to finish my wedding gown."

"I dropped it off with my mother this morning. She's taking care of it," he said as he settled into the driver's seat. "Any more excuses?"

She eyed him solemnly. "I don't think it's fair to you. I may not have very long to live."

"I'll take whatever time I can get."

"You seem determined to do this."

"I am."

"What will people say?"

He shot her a triumphant grin. "I know I've won when that's the only argument you can come up with. You know I don't give a damn what other people say. If it feels right to you and me, that's all that matters. Will you marry me on Saturday?"

She chewed on her lip for a moment, then seemed to make up her mind. He held his breath until she said, "All right. Okay. You win. I'll marry you on Saturday."

He hit the brakes and swerved the convertible to the side of the road, skidding to a stop on the shoulder.

"What's wrong?" Jenny cried.

"Nothing's wrong," he said. "I simply felt an irresistible urge to kiss you silly, that's all."

Impossibly, unpredictably, she laughed. "You're crazy, Colt!"

"Crazy in love with you," he said, leaning over to touch his lips to hers.

She moaned, and he deepened the kiss, slipping his tongue inside her mouth and tasting her. His heart beat wildly in his chest, with joy and with fear. She was so very precious. How would he bear it— Colt forced himself to focus on the delicious sensations caused by her tongue sliding between his lips, touching the roof of his mouth, then withdrawing to be followed by his tongue, tasting her.

He would find a way to make her understand that, even if more radical surgery became necessary, it wouldn't matter to him. The only thing that mattered was keeping her alive. He broke the kiss at last, but pressed his cheek against hers. "I love you, Jenny."

"And I love you," she whispered.

"We'd better get going," he said, forcing himself back to his own side of the car. "We've got lots of company waiting at home."

"Oh, Colt. What have you done?"

"What you should have done two years ago. I called your brothers, had them meet me at Hawk's Pride, and told them about the cancer."

"You had no right!" Jenny said, her hands clenching into fists.

"I have every right," he retorted. "I love you. That means I'll do everything within my power to make your life easier and happier. Even if it means making your brothers' lives a little unhappier."

"What did they say?" she asked anxiously. "How are they taking the news?"

"How do you think they took it? They were angry and hurt." He rubbed his jaw and said, "Sam took a swing at me. He thought I'd known all along and had kept it from them."

"I'm sorry. Sam always was a little hotheaded."

"Once I explained, he apologized. But now that they know, they want to be there for you, Jenny. It was all I could do to keep them from coming to the doctor's office this morning. They compromised by agreeing to see you after the surgery at the Double D."

"How can I face them?" she said.

"Just remember they love you."

When they arrived at the house, they found all four of her brothers putting a coat of fresh, white paint on the house. But they weren't the only ones at work. All of Colt's brothers and sisters had joined in to make various improvements on the property.

The shutters on all of the windows, as well as the front door, had been painted a deep green that matched Jenny's new Jeep. Flowers and shrubs had been planted around the front porch, and an entire lawn had been laid in thick patches of green.

"Ohmigod, Colt! Look what they're doing," Jenny said.

"It's a wedding gift, Jenny. From my family and from yours. They're helping to make our house a home."

Colt saw the sheen of tears in Jenny's eyes and felt his own throat swell with emotion. "You don't mind, do you? James and Tyler suggested it, and I said it sounded like a good idea. When Mom and Dad and Jake heard what your brothers planned to do, they wanted to be a part of it. And when my brothers and sisters—"

She cut him off with a kiss. "I love them for

it,'' she said simply. "All of them." She let herself out of the car before he could get the door
for her and headed around to the front of the
house to survey their work.

Colt had to walk fast to keep up with her.
"Jenny, are you sure you're up to this?"

She smiled at him over her shoulder. "I want
to thank them, Colt. I want to tell them all how
wonderful I think everything looks."

And she did, even going so far as to drop onto
her knees and tuck a little extra earth around the
red geraniums his mother was planting beside the
front steps.

Jenny had guts, all right. And stamina. He kept
a wary eye on her, wanting to make sure she
didn't do too much. The surgery had been done
with a local anesthetic, and Jenny swore she was
okay. But Colt had seen enough of Jenny to know
that if someone she loved asked her to pick up a
house, she would give it try.

When the painting was finished, Jenny watched
over the cleanup, and more than one brother said,
"Yes, Mother," as she issued instructions on how
it should be done. As the afternoon wore on, her
too-bright eyes and her too-fast speech told him
she had reached the limits of her endurance.

He announced it was quitting time, and everyone should gather on the back porch for a glass of iced tea and fresh-baked, hot-from-the-oven chocolate chip cookies his sister Cherry had made. Jenny sat in one of the two wooden rockers on the back porch—a gift from his parents—while his mother occupied the other. His father stood behind his mother, in much the same protective way Colt stood behind Jenny. Some of his siblings sat in chairs that had been brought outside from the kitchen.

Sam and Tyler leaned on the porch rail, while Randy sat cross-legged at Jenny's feet, with Faith by his side. His brother Jake leaned against the house, his eyes focused on Faith's sister Hope, who was sitting with Colt's sister Frannie on the wooden swing Jake had hung by ropes from the porch rafters that afternoon.

There was a lot of laughter and joking, everyone careful to keep the mood light. No one had spoken the ''C'' word all afternoon. No one had mentioned the desperate disease that had brought them together.

''I can't thank you all enough,'' Jenny said for the umpteenth time. ''This was a wonderful surprise.''

''You should have told us sooner,'' Sam said curtly.

Jenny stopped rocking. It got so quiet Colt could hear the single fly buzzing around the last chocolate chip cookie on the plate. He put a hand on Jenny's shoulder and squeezed.

I'm here, love. You're not alone.

She smiled gratefully at him over her shoulder, then met Sam's embittered gaze. "I thought I could spare you this pain," she said. "I was wrong. Please forgive me."

"We can't get back the two years you stole from us," Sam said.

Jenny arched a brow. "I've been right here, Sam."

"But I didn't know— I would have come—" Sam lifted his hat, forked his fingers through his hair, then resettled the Stetson low on his brow. "What are we supposed to do now?"

"What you've always done," Jenny said. "Be there when I need you."

Once the subject had been opened, it seemed there were others who needed to speak.

"When will you get the results of the biopsy?" Tyler asked.

"On Monday."

"What about the wedding? Is that on or off?" James asked.

Jenny reached up and laid her hand over Colt's,

which still rested on her shoulder. She smiled and said, "The wedding is on."

"On Saturday? Before you know the results?" Sam asked, staring hard at Colt.

"On Saturday," Colt confirmed.

"Which reminds me, I have a wedding dress to finish," Colt's mother said, rising from her rocker.

"I've got some errands to run," Jake said. "Can I give anybody a lift anywhere?"

"I need a ride into town," Hope said, jumping up from the swing.

"If you're driving Hope into town, can you take me and Faith, too?" Randy said, rising and then helping Faith to stand.

"Why not?" Jake said. "Anybody else? I've got one of the vans."

Everyone else had their own transportation. In a matter of minutes, the porch was empty except for Colt and Jenny. "Come sit with me on the swing," he said, taking her hand and helping her out of the rocker.

As Colt sat down on the hanging swing and lifted Jenny into his lap, she slid her arms around his neck and laid her head in the crook of his shoulder. He could feel her warm breath against his throat.

He set the swing in motion with the toe of his boot, and they sat without speaking and watched the sunset. The sky was streaked with bright yellows and rosy pinks, and the sun looked like an orange ball as it began its descent beyond the horizon.

"All we need to make this picture-perfect is a dog at your feet," Jenny murmured.

"That can be arranged," Colt said as his lips curved in a smile.

A jet broke the sound barrier, and Colt looked up, knowing he wouldn't be able to see it, but searching the sky anyway.

"Will you miss it very much?" Jenny said quietly.

"Flying? Sure. I'd be lying if I said I wouldn't. But life is about choices, Jenny. Being with you is the right choice for me."

"What if—"

"You want to play that game? All right. What if I get bucked off my horse tomorrow and break my neck? What if we get abducted by aliens? What if—"

Jenny giggled. "Abducted by aliens?"

"What if the cancer does come back?" he said seriously. "It won't change anything. I plan to treasure every moment I have with you—however many there are.''

He felt her kiss his throat, then his chin, then the side of his mouth. He turned his head and blindly found her mouth with his. He felt her moist breath against his flesh as she whispered, ''I have the irresistible urge to kiss you silly. Will you please take me to bed?''

Living life to the fullest, Colt mused as he lifted Jenny and carried her into the house, definitely had its compensations.

As Randy helped Faith into the back seat of the van, Hope jumped into the front with Jake. Randy shot a glance at Faith to see whether she thought he ought to try to do something to get Hope to sit in back with them. She gave a slight shake of her head, and he slid into the back seat with her.

As they headed toward town, the silence in the front seat was palpable.

''How about some music?'' Hope said finally, turning on the radio.

Jake glanced at her, then aimed his eyes back at the road without speaking.

Randy was grateful for the noise, because it meant he could talk to Faith in the back seat without being overheard. ''Does Hope really have something to do in town? Or is she just trying to get Jake alone?''

"Do you really have an errand?'' Faith countered. "Or do you just want to get me alone?''

Randy grinned and slid his hand along her jeans from her knee upward along her inner thigh until she reached over to clamp a hand over his to stop him. "I definitely want to get you alone,'' he said. "But I actually have an errand in town. I promised I'd pick up some white ribbon for Jenny. Now, answer my question.''

Faith removed his hand and set it on his own thigh, then laid her hand on the inside of his thigh close enough to his zipper to cause serious repercussions. She shot him a mischievous sideways look from beneath lowered lashes. "My suggestion is that you mind your own business. I plan to keep you so well occupied that you won't have time to worry about what's going on between Hope and Jake.''

Randy made a strangled sound in his throat as Faith's hand brushed tantalizingly across his erection and disappeared back onto her own side of the seat. "That sounds fair,'' he said.

For the rest of the ride into town, Randy wasn't aware of anything except Faith's teasing touches, her impish glances, the intimate promises she was making that he hoped she planned to keep. He responded with caresses of his own and heated glances and a whispered question. "When?"

He saw her cheeks pinken, and knew she'd heard him. "We can slip away during your sister's wedding reception. My parents won't miss me for a few hours during all the celebration."

"Will you let me see your other hand? I mean, without the prosthesis?"

Her mouth flattened into an unhappy line. "You may not like what you see. Is it really necessary?"

He took her hand in his, caressing the normal fingers. His mind had conjured up an image of deformity beneath her prosthesis that he was sure couldn't be worse than the real thing. "You take it off at night, when you go to bed, don't you?" he asked.

She nodded.

"If we're going to spend our lives together, I figure I better get used to how you look without it."

"Maybe you won't want to be with me anymore after you see me without it."

He was surprised that Faith was able to state her fear so clearly and succinctly. If he could accept the hook and the plastic arm, he didn't think

real flesh and bone—no matter how malformed—
could make him reject her. But he knew words
alone weren't likely to assuage her fear. "You'll
just have to take that chance," he said at last.
"Unless you want to break up right now."

He watched myriad emotions—doubt, fear,
hope—flicker across her face as she evaluated the
risk, and balanced the possible reward. *Like Colt
did with Jenny,* he realized. *Balancing the risk of
losing her against the joy of loving her.* As Faith
must balance the risk of trusting him against the
joy of being fully loved.

"All right," she said at last. "I'll let you see
my hand. But only if you promise—"

He squeezed her trembling hand to cut her off
and said, "It'll be all right, Faith. Believe me. It
won't make a difference."

He only hoped he was right.

Jake was angry. Hope recognized the signs.
The vertical lines on either side of his mouth became more pronounced because his jaw was
clamped, and his eyes narrowed to slits. There
was an overall look of tautness to his body—
shoulders, hands, hips—that suggested a tiger
ready to leap.

She knew she shouldn't have invited herself

along. She knew Jake didn't want her around. She also knew he didn't want her around because he was tempted by her presence, like a beast in rut responding to the relentless call of nature.

Hope let her gaze roam over Jake and saw his nostrils flare as her eyes touched what her hands could not. She wondered whether she ought to push him into something irrevocable. Like taking her virginity.

He would marry her then. She was sure of it. But would he love her? She didn't want him without his love. She knew that much. But she was running out of time. Why, oh, why, had he gotten engaged to Miss Carter? She wouldn't feel this desperation if he hadn't forced her hand. She knew in her bones that they belonged together, and she didn't intend to lose him to another woman.

When they arrived in town, Hope was surprised that Jake volunteered to drop off Randy and Faith first after setting a time to pick them up again. She offered a reassuring smile in response to Faith's anxious look as she and Jake drove away.

"You haven't asked where I want to be let off," she said when Jake had driven half the length of the main street in town without stopping.

He shot her a look filled with scorn. "Don't insult my intelligence. You haven't got any errands to run. But I do. So sit there like a good little girl and be still."

It was the *little girl* that did it. It was a flash point with her and always would be, because it diminished who she was, which was more than the sum of her age. She began to unbutton her blouse right there, driving down Main Street.

Jake glanced in her direction and nearly had an accident. "What do you think you're doing?"

"Taking my clothes off?"

"Do you want to get me arrested?"

"I'm not a minor, Jake. We're two consenting adults."

"I'm engaged. I'm promised to another woman."

"Not once word of this gets around," she said, glancing at the passersby who gawked in through the window as she pulled her shirt off her shoulders, leaving her wearing only a peach-colored bra.

Jake swore under his breath and gunned the engine, heading for the old, abandoned railroad depot on the outskirts of town. He braked to a halt in front of the depot and turned to glare at her.

She saw the flicker of heat as he glimpsed the fullness of her breasts above her bra.

"What the hell do you think you're doing?"

"I'm not a little girl, Jake. I don't know what I have to do to prove it to you."

"I'm not going to marry you, Hope. You're not what I want. I want someone who can share my memories of the world, someone who's lived a little."

"I can catch up," she said desperately.

He shook his head. "No, little girl. You can't."

Hope felt her chin quivering and gritted her teeth to try to keep it still. "So you're going to marry Miss Carter?"

"Yes, I'm going to marry her. Put your blouse back on, Hope."

She grabbed her shirt and tried to get it on, but the long sleeves were inside out, and her hands were shaking too badly to straighten it.

She heard Jake swear before he scooted across the bench seat, pulled the shirt from her hands and began to pull the sleeves right-side out. He held the shirt for her while she slipped her arms into it. Her cheek brushed against his as she was straightening. She turned her head and discovered his mouth only a breath from her own. Their eyes caught and held.

She wasn't sure who moved first, but an instant later their mouths were meshed, and his tongue was inside searching, teasing, tasting. He was rough and reckless, his hands cupping her breasts as a guttural groan was wrenched from his very marrow. His mouth ravaged hers as his hands demanded a response.

She couldn't catch up. He was moving too fast.

And then he was gone. Out the opposite door. She scrambled after him, pausing in the driver's seat when she spied him leaning against the van, his palms flat against the metal, his head down, his chest heaving.

He stood and faced her. "That was my fault," he said. "I..." His eyes were full of pain and regret. "You're formidable, Hope. I'll grant you that. Somewhere out there is a very lucky young man."

"I want *you*," she cried.

"I belong to someone else."

"You're only marrying Miss Carter because you don't think you can have me. But you can," Hope insisted. "There's nothing stopping us from being together except your own stubborn bias against my age."

"Your youth," he corrected.

She snorted. "Eighteen years isn't that much. Lots of men marry younger women."

"You need to go to college. You need to find out what you want to do with your life. Maybe you'll decide you want more out of life than simply being some rancher's wife. If I were to marry you now, the day might come when you decided marriage to me wasn't fulfilling enough, that you needed to go find yourself."

"Is that what happened with your first wife?" Hope asked, her eyes wide.

"I've seen it happen," Jake said without answering her question directly. "You're too young to know what you'd be giving up, Hope. Go to school. Get an education. Find out what you want to do with your life."

"If I do that, if I go to college, will you wait for me?"

She saw the struggle before he answered, "In four years I'll be forty. I—"

"Wait for me," she said, stepping out of the van. "Don't marry Miss Carter. Promise you'll wait for me."

"I can't promise anything, Hope. There's another person in this equation you're not considering. I've proposed to another woman, and she's said yes. Unless Amanda breaks the engagement, I'm honor-bound to marry her.''

"Even if you don't love her?"

"Who says I don't?"

The shock of his words held Hope speechless. "How could you love her and want me like you do?"

He shoved a frustrated hand through his hair. "I respect and admire her. And she loves me. We can have a good life together."

"You *don't* love her," Hope said accusingly.

"I don't know what I feel anymore," he retorted. "You've got me so damned confused—"

"Wait for me," Hope said. "There are such things as long engagements."

"That wouldn't be fair to Amanda," Jake said stubbornly.

"It is if you don't love her. Don't you think she'll notice? Don't you think she'll miss being loved?"

Jake stared at the ground, then back at her. "I'll go this far," he said. "I won't press her to get married. But I'm not going to walk away if she sets a date."

"Thank you, Jake. At least that gives me a chance."

Jake shook his head. "I'll say this much. Life with you would never be boring."

Hope laughed. "I hope I get a chance to prove that to you someday."

Chapter 14

"Stand still, Jenny, or I'll never get all these buttons done up," Rebecca said.

Jenny looked at herself in the oval standing mirror in the corner of her bedroom, hardly able to believe that she was the beautiful woman reflected there. She looked like Cinderella, ready for the ball, except her dress was white, instead of pink. She'd pieced the dress together herself, but Colt's mother had finished it, adding lace and ribbons and seed pearls like one of Cinderella's mice.

The satin gown had a wide boat neck, open

almost to her shoulders, with long sleeves that tapered to the wrist. The bodice was fitted to the waist with a wide skirt belling out below. A narrow train decorated with tiny seed pearls began where the last cloth buttons ended in back and trailed several feet behind her.

Jenny reached up to adjust the net veil, held in place by a circlet of fresh white daisies, and brushed at a stray wisp of hair at her temple that had escaped the knot of golden curls at her crown. "Are you done yet?" she asked.

"Not yet," Rebecca said.

"Whatever made you decide to put thirty-two buttons down the back instead of using a zipper?"

Rebecca smiled. "I was thinking of my son."

Jenny's brows lowered in confusion. "I don't understand. A zipper would make it easier for him to get me out of this dress in a hurry."

Rebecca's smile became a grin. "I know. But think how much his anticipation will have built by the time he gets the last button undone."

"If his patience lasts that long," Jenny said with a laugh.

Rebecca joined her laughter. "There. All done." She put her hands on Jenny's shoulders and looked at their side-by-side faces reflected in the mirror. "My son loves you, Jenny. I'm only beginning to understand how much. I wish you both all the joy that love can bring. I'm sorry your mother isn't here to see you today. I know she'd be very proud of all you've accomplished.''

Jenny felt the sting in her nose and the tickle at the back of her throat. "Thank you, Mrs. Whitelaw.''

"I wish you'd call me Rebecca. Or Mom, if you wouldn't mind.''

Jenny turned and hugged Colt's mother. "I've missed having a mom. It'll be good to have one again.''

Rebecca levered Jenny to arm's length and looked her over. "You're beautiful, Jenny, inside and out. I wish you much happiness with my son.''

Jenny looked at Colt's mother through misted eyes. "Thank you, Mom.''

Rebecca grabbed a Kleenex from the box on the dresser and dabbed at the edges of her eyes. "We'd better get moving if you don't want to be late to your own wedding.'' She reached down to pick up the dragging train, brought it around and layered it carefully over Jenny's arm. "There. Are you all set?''

"Ready as I'll ever be," Jenny said.

"Are you sure there's nothing else you need?" Rebecca asked.

"Let's see. Something old—my mother's pearl necklace. Something new—this beautiful gown. Something borrowed—the Whitelaw family Bible you gave me to carry. Something blue—my wedding bouquet of bachelor's buttons. I have everything I need."

"Except a groom," Rebecca said with a laugh. "I'll see you at the church."

Once Rebecca was gone, Jenny didn't linger long in her bedroom. She knew her four brothers were waiting in the living room to escort her to church. As she came down the hall she heard Randy say, "Holy cow!"

The moment she stepped into the living room, her brothers, who'd been lounging on the furniture, all stood up. Sam spoke first.

"I'll be damned. You're gorgeous, Jenny."

Jenny smiled. "Thank you, Sam."

"Stunning," Tyler said.

"The prettiest bride I've ever seen," James added.

"Holy cow!" Randy repeated.

Jenny laughed. "I'd love to stand here and listen to more of your compliments, but I think it's time we left for church."

The four brothers exchanged looks before Randy stepped forward. ''We got together and decided to give you something special as a wedding gift.''

Randy looked into the inside pocket of the navy blue suit jacket he was wearing but didn't find what he was looking for. He looked in the other side of the coat and pulled out some papers. He stepped forward and handed them to Jenny. ''For you.''

''What's this?'' she asked.

''A honeymoon,'' Sam said.

''At the Grand Canyon,'' James added.

''We figured you deserved a *monumentally* good time,'' Randy said with a grin.

''We'll take care of the ranch while you're gone,'' Tyler said, cutting off the objection on the tip of her tongue.

Jenny was astonished. ''I don't know what to say.''

'''Thank you' might be nice,'' Sam said.

Tears filled Jenny's eyes, and she tried to sniff them back.

''Don't you like it?'' Randy asked, confused by her tears.

''I'm overwhelmed,'' Jenny said. ''Thank you all.'' She held her arms wide, and her brothers moved to hug her all at once. She gave them each a kiss wherever she could reach.

Randy wiped the kiss from his cheek and said, "We don't have time for any more of this mushy stuff right now. We're gonna be late if we don't get outta here."

"Right, brat," Sam said, tousling Randy's hair. "So get moving."

Jenny laughed, banishing her tears, and followed her brothers out of the house.

Her wedding day had dawned sunny, but the ceremony was scheduled for eleven-thirty to avoid the heat of the day. The reception was being held in the courtyard at Hawk's Pride, beneath the cool shade of the moss-draped live oak.

Jenny's stomach was full of butterflies, which she suspected was normal for a bride on her wedding day, but she had put her fears on hold. Today was about joy and love.

Once they arrived at church, she waited by herself in a small room off the vestibule, while her brothers helped to seat guests. In a departure from the norm, Jenny had neither bridesmaids nor a maid of honor. She didn't have any close girl-friends, and she didn't know any of Colt's sisters well enough yet to feel comfortable asking them to stand in such a role. She had asked her four brothers to stand up with her instead.

"If you're going to be unconventional, I don't see why I can't do the same thing," Colt had said.

"Meaning what?" Jenny asked.

"How about a Best Lady instead of a Best Man?"

"Who did you have in mind?"

"My sister Jewel," Colt said. "She was like a second mother to me, and we've always been close. If you don't mind, I think she could hang on to the rings as well as one of my brothers. And Frannie will kill me if Jewel gets to dress up and she doesn't. So I guess I'd better include her.

"Actually, it might balance things better if I use all my sisters for 'groomsmen,'" Colt mused. "That way, with Rolleen and Cherry, we'll have an even number of girls and guys coming down the aisle. What do you think?"

"It sounds like a wonderful idea!" Jenny said.

"Who's going to give away the bride?" Colt asked.

"I don't know. I forgot all about that."

"It's usually a parent or an older relative," Colt said.

"I don't have any of those. Any suggestions?"

"As long as we're being unorthodox, how

about my parents? They've adopted eight of us kids. I don't see why you can't adopt them.''

Jenny smiled. ''Done.''

''Then it's all settled,'' Colt said.

''What will people think?'' Jenny wondered.

''This is our wedding,'' Colt said. ''We can do as we damn well please.''

Colt was wishing they'd eloped. He was standing in his father's bedroom, dressed in a black dinner jacket, studded white dress shirt, cummerbund and black trousers, fidgeting nervously as his father tried for the third time to tie his bow tie. His brothers watched the comedy of errors from vantage points around the room.

''Hold still,'' Zach said as he adjusted the black silk, ''and give me a fighting chance to get this straight.''

''It's too tight,'' Colt said, slipping his finger between the bow tie and his throat.

''That's the marital noose you feel tightening around your neck,'' Jake said.

''Just because your marriage didn't work out—'' Rabb began.

''The bride's got cancer,'' Jake said.

''*Had* cancer,'' Avery corrected.

''May still have cancer,'' Colt said quietly.

"And if she does, we'll deal with it. I love her. Be happy for me, Jake." He met his brother's remote, ice-blue eyes and felt as though they were miles apart.

Jake shrugged. "It's your funeral."

Avery hissed in a breath.

"Bad choice of words," Jake said repentently. "I don't know what's wrong with me today. I hope you and Jenny have a long and happy life together, Colt. I really do. I'll see you after the ceremony," he said, backing his way out of the room.

It was clear, at least to Colt, that Jake considered marriage on a par with walking through a minefield barefoot. Which made Colt wonder why his brother had gotten himself engaged to Amanda Carter. And whether Jake would follow through and take a second trip down the aisle. Only time would tell.

"I'd better get going," Rabb said. "I promised Mom I'd help greet people at the church."

"Me, too," Avery said as he followed Rabb out the door.

Colt's father stepped back to admire his handiwork. "That ought to do it," he said.

"Any last words of advice?" Colt said.

"Be happy," Zach said.

Colt saw the tears in his father's eyes and felt his throat swell with emotion. "Thanks, Dad."

He took the step that put him within his father's reach and felt his father's arms surround him. As a child, he'd found support and succor, even surcease from pain, within these strong arms. Zach Whitelaw had taken a child that was not his own flesh and blood and made of him a devoted son.

"I love you, Dad," he said.

His father gave him a quick hug, then pushed him away. "We'd better get going. Your mother will kill me if I don't get you to the church on time."

"Sure. Then she'll kiss you all over till you're well again."

"Maybe being late isn't such a bad idea," Zach said with a laugh.

They made the trip to the church in Colt's Mustang convertible with the top down. The wind ruffled Colt's hair and left his bow tie once more askew.

"Let me fix that tie," Zach said.

Colt waved at friends and neighbors as his father arranged his bow tie, then watched his father head for the front of the church. He headed for a door at the rear, where the choir usually assembled, and which was used during weddings for the groom and his "groomsmen."

The room was filled with his sisters, arranging their hair and putting on makeup and getting dressed. Colt grinned as he observed the cacophony and confusion. It felt like old times. Cherry was walking around in a bra and half slip; Jewel's hair was still in hot curlers; Frannie was buttoning up Rolleen's dress, while Rolleen talked on a cell phone.

"Hi," Colt said.

"Finish buttoning Rolleen for me," Frannie said. "While I pin some flowers in my hair."

Colt crossed to Rolleen and began buttoning up her dress. "Who's that on the phone?" he asked.

"Gavin's grandmother," she whispered back. "The baby's teething and has a little fever."

"When you finish with Rolleen, can you do me?" Cherry said, pulling her dress on over her head.

Colt crossed to the sister who'd been most like him in temperament, the other rebel in the family. Cherry had come to the Whitelaw family as a mutinous fourteen-year-old juvenile delinquent and ended up—in Colt's humble opinion—as a damned good wife and mother. "How're the twins—both sets—and what's-his-name?'' he asked.

''The girls are in the high school pep squad, and the boys are into G.I. Joe. What's-his-name hit a home run in his Little League game this morning. Why do you think I'm running so late?''

''Tell Brett I said congratulations,'' Colt said.

''You can tell him yourself at the reception. He'll be there, along with forty-three dozen other screaming Whitelaw brats.''

Colt groaned. ''Surely you jest!''

''I'm not off by much,'' Cherry warned.

''Colt, will you come hold this mirror so I can see the back of my hair?'' Jewel said.

''Duty calls,'' Colt said as he buttoned the last button on Cherry's dress. ''Hey there, Jewel,'' he said as he took the mirror from his eldest sister and held it up for her. ''How's it going?''

''There's a lump in my hair,'' she said. ''Right...'' She reached up, trying to locate it backward in the mirror.

''There?'' he said, poking at a cowlick at the back of her head.

''That's it. Stubborn little cuss.'' She took the mirror from his hand and threw it onto the table in front of her. ''Why do I bother? Plain brown eyes, plain brown hair, plain old face. You'd think I'd get used to it."

Colt tipped her chin up and surveyed her face, which still bore remnants of the faint, crisscrossing scars she'd acquired in the car accident that had originally left her orphaned. "You look pretty good to me," he announced.

She brushed his hand away and wrinkled her nose. "You have to say that. You're my brother."

The organ began to play and Jewel looked at her wristwatch. "Oh, Lord. Five minutes. Is everybody ready?"

Colt looked around. The chaos had ceased. Before him stood his four sisters looking remarkably lovely in pale rose full-length gowns. Every dress was cut in a different style that had been especially designed by Rolleen to make the most of each sister's assets.

"You all look...wonderful," Colt said, his voice catching in his throat.

"You look pretty wonderful yourself," Jewel said, crossing to link her arm with his. "Come on, Colt. It's time we made our appearance in church."

They walked out to stand in front of the altar and wait for Jenny to appear. Her brothers had already taken their places on the opposite side of the altar. Colt found his parents sitting in the front pew, waiting for the appropriate moment to give away the bride, and smiled at them. His mother dabbed at her eyes with his father's hanky and smiled back.

Their choice of attendants might have been unusual, but Jenny had selected Lohengrin's ''Wedding March'' as the processional. At the sound of the familiar opening chords, the congregation stood, and Colt searched the back of the church, waiting for his first look at the bride.

Jenny walked down the aisle alone, as she had lived most of her life. Colt felt his throat constrict as he caught sight of her. She looked ethereal. He could see her face through her veil, and her joyous smile made his heart swell with love.

His parents met her and said the words that gave her into his care. He reached out and took her hand, then turned with her to face the preacher.

''Dearly Beloved,'' the minister began. ''We are gathered here...''

The vows were familiar, but they seemed to have a great deal more meaning, Colt discovered, when you were the one taking them.

''Do you, Jennifer Elizabeth Wright, take this man to be your lawful wedded husband, to have and to hold…to love and to cherish…all the days of your life?''

''I do,'' Jenny said.

Then it was his turn.

''Do you, Colt David Whitelaw, take this woman to be your lawful wedded wife, to love and to honor…in sickness and in health…as long as you both shall live?''

Colt's throat was so swollen with emotion, he couldn't speak. He nodded, but the minister was waiting for the words. He felt Jenny squeeze his hand. ''I do,'' he rasped.

Putting the simple gold band on Jenny's third finger somehow linked them together. When she placed a gold band on his finger in return, it felt as though the two of them had been made into one.

Then the minister was saying, ''By the power vested in me, I now pronounce you husband and wife. You may kiss the bride.''

Colt's hands were trembling as he lifted the veil and looked into his wife's shining eyes. He lowered his head slowly, touched her lips gently, then gathered Jenny in his arms and gave her a kiss that expressed all the tumultuous emotions he felt inside.

The congregation began to applaud.

Colt lifted his head, grinned sheepishly, then slipped Jenny's arm through his and, to the swell of organ music, marched with his bride back down the aisle.

The newlyweds were spending one night at the Double D before they left for their honeymoon at the Grand Canyon the following morning, so Randy was supposed to spend the night in Colt's room at Hawk's Pride to give his sister and her new husband some privacy.

It had been difficult for Randy to keep his mind on the wedding ceremony, when he knew he had a test of moral courage coming up in a matter of hours. Once the wedding reception was in full swing, he planned to sneak into Colt's bedroom with Faith—and see what she'd been hiding beneath her prosthesis.

He hadn't seen Faith before the ceremony began, and in all the excitement afterward, they'd ended up going to Hawk's Pride in separate cars. He searched for her in the courtyard and spied her near the punch bowl. He hurried in her direction, but stopped ten feet away and gawked.

She wasn't wearing the prosthetic device.

She had on a pair of white cotton gloves that ended at the wrist, exposing her arms. The left glove had something inside it to fill out the fingers, but apparently the gloved hand wasn't functional, because Faith didn't use it when she helped herself to a cup of punch. Her left arm, including the wrist, which was usually covered by the prosthetic device, looked perfectly normal.

It was the rest of her hand—or rather lack of it—he needed to see.

But suddenly he was in no hurry to see it. He stayed by Faith's side all afternoon. He laughed with her as Jenny cut the wedding cake and stuffed a big piece into Colt's laughing mouth. He shared a shy glance with her as Colt retrieved the garter from Jenny's leg, and he cheered with her as Colt's brother Rabb caught it. He stood by her side as Hope leaped high and grabbed Jenny's bridal bouquet.

He even took her with him when he helped decorate Colt's Mustang convertible. The guys ended up spraying as much shaving cream on each other as on the car, and made water balloons and threw them, too, before finally tying a bunch of old cowboy boots to the back bumper and declaring they were done.

Shadows were growing on the lawn before Randy finally acknowledged that putting off this reckoning wasn't going to make it any easier. He took Faith's right hand in his and said, "Will you come with me?"

"Where are we going?"

"Colt's room."

He saw the flash of fear in her dark eyes before she gripped his hand and said, "All right."

The house was built in a square, and it should've been easy to find Colt's room, since he'd been there once before, but he went down the wrong hallway, and they ended up going down three more hallways, full of wandering wedding guests, before he found the one he wanted.

He knocked on the door, in case anyone was in the room, then looked both ways to make sure no one was watching, and stepped inside. Once he and Faith were both inside, he closed the door and locked it. When he turned back around, Faith was sitting at the foot of the bed staring back at him. He crossed and sat down beside her...on her left side.

"I've never seen you wear gloves before," Randy said, unsure how to begin.

"I've had this special glove for quite some time. My doctor designed it especially for me. I just never had a reason to wear it." She held out her hands for him to see. "I look pretty normal," she conceded. "But it's more aesthetically pleasing than functional. In an emergency I can use the heel of my hand." She waggled her left hand to show the flexibility allowed by the bit of palm she had. "But I miss the versatility I get with a hook."

She was chattering, Randy realized, because she was frightened. And he was listening, because he was afraid to speak. They made a fine pair, he thought wryly.

"Take off the glove," he said. "Or would you rather I do it?"

"I'll do it," she said quickly.

He had situated himself on her left side purposely, to make sure there'd be no hiding anything—neither her hand, nor his reaction. He steeled himself for what he would see, tensing his muscles, gritting his teeth to hold back any sound of disgust or dismay that might come out.

She kept her eyes lowered. The glove was attached around her wrist with a Velcro strap, and there was a tearing sound as she pulled it free. She laid the glove on the bed beside her and dropped her left hand into her lap.

Randy kept his own eyes lowered as he examined what she'd revealed. The skin was pale, because it never saw the sun. There was a bit of a wrist and five tiny nubbins that had never grown into fingers. He reached over and slid his hand under hers, feeling her tremble as he did so.

"It's okay, Faith. Your hand just stopped growing. That's all."

She laid her head on his shoulder and closed her eyes. A tear dropped off her lash and onto his palm where he cradled her hand. He leaned over and licked up the tear. And kissed her hand.

He felt her right hand on his head, and then her kiss on his hair.

"I love you, Randy," she said.

He sat up, then lifted her left hand and drew it toward his cheek. "I love you, too, Faith."

He knew the courage it had taken for her to trust him. He willed her to believe in him and felt his heart thump hard in his chest when she lifted her left hand and caressed his cheek. He covered her hand with his own, then leaned over to kiss her lips.

A hard knock on the door broke them apart.

"Who is it?" Randy called, jumping to his feet.

"Who do you think?" Hope said. "Have you got my sister in there?"

"I'm here," Faith answered, crossing to open the door for her sister. "What's wrong?" she asked.

Randy watched as Hope looked down at her sister's uncovered hand, then up at his face. A smile curved her lips. "Why, nothing's wrong," she said with a grin. "Nothing at all."

At that moment Sam came walking past the door, noticed Randy and Faith and said, "Jenny and Colt are getting ready to leave the reception. You might want to come and see them off."

"Just let me get my glove," Faith said, turning back to the bed. "And I'll be ready to go."

"I'll see you two out back," Hope said, heading for the courtyard.

Randy and Faith weren't far behind her.

Randy had stuck at least a dozen pieces of net filled with birdseed into his coat pockets, so he'd have plenty of birdseed to shower on Jenny and Colt.

"Untie those ribbons," Faith instructed. "And pour the birdseed into your hand, so it'll be ready to throw."

"Oh."

"Will you untie mine, too?"

"Sure," Randy said, realizing that she was essentially one-handed without her hook. "I'm gonna invent something, Faith."

"What?"

"A hand—like in the *Terminator* movies—that you can really use."

"Oh, Randy. I hope you do."

Randy heard cries of "Here they come! Get ready!"

He turned to find his sister, Colt's arm wrapped tightly around her waist, her eyes bright, her smile wide, making her way through the crowd.

The reception was half over before Jenny realized the significance of the wedding gift her brothers had given her. She searched frantically for Colt and found him drinking champagne and laughing with his brothers. She dragged him away to the arbor, chasing away at least a dozen shrieking children to have even a modicum of privacy.

"My brothers gave me a wedding gift," she said. "A honeymoon trip to the Grand Canyon."

"I know all about it," he said, alternately tickling his sister's, Cherry's five-year-old twin boys, Chip and Charlie. "We leave tomorrow morning, 7:00 a.m. flight out of Amarillo."

"The doctor's office doesn't open till eight."

"So what?" Colt said, hefting Rolleen's ten-year-old son Kenny up over his shoulder and letting him drop until he was dangling by his heels. Kenny howled with glee.

"Don't you see? We won't have the test results before we leave," Jenny said.

"We're going to have a honeymoon whether you have cancer or not," Colt replied. "The news will wait till we get back." He leaned over and kissed her on the nose, struggling to stay upright with Chip and Charlie each entwined around one of his legs like vines around an oak. "Anything else bothering you?" he asked.

She lifted a brow and said, "Well, if we're going to get up so early in the morning, isn't about time we took our leave?"

Colt's eyes went wide, and then he smiled. "Mrs. Whitelaw, that's the best suggestion I've heard all day," he said, prying the twins off his legs.

"Thank you. I love getting compliments from my husband."

Colt's gaze locked hers. "Husband. That has a nice sound." He slipped his arm around her waist and headed for the car. "Let's go, wife."

Jenny went with Colt to tell his parents they were leaving, and the word spread quickly.

"Hurry up if you want to get a last look at the bride and groom before they take off!"

"Does everybody have some birdseed?"

Jenny ducked and laughed as birdseed caught

in her hair and her eyelashes and slid down the front of her dress.

Colt laughed and ducked right along with her. "Hurry up, wife, or we're going to turn into two bird feeders!"

Colt didn't even open the door to the convertible, just dropped her in over the top, then came running around and jumped in behind the wheel.

As they drove away, Jenny reached across the seat and took Colt's hand. He smiled at her, and she smiled back. This was the beginning of a new life. A new love. And happily ever after.

Epilogue

Benign. Jenny had never heard a sweeter word. She still had three more years before she'd feel satisfied that the cancer was truly gone. But she'd been given a respite, a time in which to live life to the fullest. And a husband who was determined to help her do it.

Jenny snuggled closer to Colt, spooning her body against his. She heard him make a sound of pleasure in his throat and whispered, "Are you awake?"

"I am now."

She pulled his arms tighter around her, and he

cupped her breasts and held her close. It was always like this after they made love, holding each other, reaffirming their joy with each other.

"I visited my doctor today," Jenny said.

She felt Colt stiffen. "Oh?" he murmured cautiously.

"I wanted to ask her what she thought about me getting pregnant."

"I see," Colt said. "And what did she say?"

Jenny turned over in Colt's arms, so she could see his face. "She said it was up to me."

"There's no risk to you?" Colt asked.

"I didn't say that. But I think what we have to gain is worth what risk there is. I want us to have children, Colt. Is that too much to ask?"

"I already feel like I've dodged a bullet," Colt confessed. "I want kids, but not at the risk of losing you."

Jenny pressed her face against Colt's throat and felt his arms close around her. "If we have a boy, we can name him Huck."

She heard him chuckle. "Huckleberry White-law. Now there's a name to give a kid nightmares."

Jenny smiled. "Growing up in a houseful of boys, I always wanted a little girl."

"We could name her Becky," Colt said.

Jenny laughed. "And the next boy Tom."

"Three kids," Colt said. "That's a houseful."

"Not like the eight your parents raised," she pointed out.

"Three's plenty for me," he said, lifting his head and finding her mouth with his.

They kissed slowly, letting the passion rise, feeling the hope and ignoring the fear. They would find a way to be happy, living each day and loving each night. For all the rest of their lives.

* * * * *

Look for Joan Johnston's new novel,
Breathless Seduction, *coming in*
September 2007, only from M&B™.